David Grant

Metrical tales and other poems

David Grant

Metrical tales and other poems

ISBN/EAN: 9783337174279

Printed in Europe, USA, Canada, Australia, Japan

Cover: Foto ©Andreas Hilbeck / pixelio.de

More available books at **www.hansebooks.com**

Metrical Tales

AND

Other Poems,

BY

DAVID GRANT,

ASSOCIATE OF COLLEGE OF PRECEPTORS, ENG., AND FELLOW
OF EDUCATIONAL INSTITUTE, SCOTLAND.

EDITED BY MRS. LEITH-ADAMS.

First Series Complete.
1880.

SHEFFIELD:
W. C. LENG AND CO., PRINTERS, "TELEGRAPH" OFFICE, HIGH-ST.

Preface.

FROM the first I have taken a great interest in this Book of Poems, and looked forward to its appearance under the happiest auspices. Now, when its publication is an accomplished fact, the Author is suffering from an illness that we would fain hope may be temporary, but which, from its very nature, totally incapacitates him from saying a word on his own behalf.

I therefore venture to do for him what he cannot do for himself, namely—plead for a kindly reception from the public for the work upon which he has expended so much time and thought.

BERTHA LEITH-ADAMS.

18, CLARENDON GARDENS,
LONDON, W.

September 1880.

Contents.

CONTENTS. ix.

VARIETIES—CONTINUED— PAGE.
A Choice 260
A True Friend 260
To Thomas Mahonie, Esq. 261
To J. D. 261
On the Death of the Rev. Dr. Corbet 262
Love and Death 264
Obermeier The Brave 264
In Memoriam 267
Our Mother 267
On the Death of Earl Russell 269

ODDS AND ENDS—
The Leagured City 272
After Sedan 273
Random Thoughts on Woman's Rights 276
An Old Fable... 280
Death in the Slums 281
Catastrophe at Tay Bridge 284
The Death of the Beautiful Child 285
The Speech of Galgacus 288
Time will Answer All 291

To My Book.

———

CHILD of my brain midst troubles born,
    It grieves me now to feel
How weak thou art to baffle scorn,
    To bide the critic's steel,
    To battle for a standing place
      Amidst the millions of thy race !

Yet go, my child ! I send thee forth ;
    The path of Fortune try ;
Go ! live supported by thy worth,
    Or by thy follies die.
'Tis not with wholly hopeless heart
    I bid thee on thy way depart.

Truth, love, and joy are all of God ;
    So far thou art divine,
And sure at last will be thy road
    So far as these are thine.
Nor breathes there one would more than I
    Delight to see thine errors die.

Sheffield, June 14th, 1880.

To the Public.

(Imitated from Horace's Ode to Mæcenas.)

DEAR Public, sprung from kindred sires,
Sweet patron whom my soul desires,
Some burn to name the winning horse,
And net their thousands on the course.
Some guide the car with skilful hand,
Where gaping crowds admiring stand,
Well pleased to draw the vulgar gaze,
And win perchance a Jehu's praise.
This man is radient with delight,
If fickle crowds their votes unite
To raise him to the Council board,
Where Fate may yet the chance afford
The higher dignity to bear
Of Alderman or e'en Lord Mayor.
That man, unmoved by civic state,
Will yet behold, with mind elate,
His barns filled with goodly grain,
His flocks and herds on hill and plain,
Nor him would Rothschild's wealth allure
To quit his friends and home secure,
His rural plenty, peace and ease,
And plough for fields the stormy seas.
The merchant, with his gains content,
On future ease and pleasure bent,
Erects a villa near the town,
Pulls ancient walls and buildings down,
Lays out his grounds and gardens fair
With flowers that scent the summer air,

And strives, regardless of expense,
To please the eyes and charm each sense;
But lo! he suffers loss of cash;
The Diddle Bank has gone to smash;
The money's lodged with Grub & Co.,
Returns an interest so low
That he must spend with prudent care,
And stint he knows not how to bear,
But trims anew his tattered sails,
And trusts his bark to fortune's gales.
Vain pleasure's clients, not a few,
Will spend the hours to business due
Reclined beneath the leafy shade
By beeches, near the fountain made,
Or in resorts of worse repute
Consume the odorous cheroot,
And frequent drain the brimming glass
Before the hour of mid-day pass.
War, which the mother hates and fears,
Or deprecates with sighs and tears,
The martial tramp, the rattling drum,
The cannon's roar are dear to some.
The hunter feels a special pride
To scour the country far and wide,
Nor fears to risk the total wreck
Of sturdy limbs or precious neck,
If but his panting steed have breath
To bear him first at Reynard's death,
Or far amidst the bogs and brakes
Of Caledonia—" Land of Cakes,"
He welcomes toils the most severe,
To bag the grouse or stalk the deer.
Far different my delights from these,
Me learnèd leisure most can please.

Let me but stray through leafy groves,
Where feathered songsters chant their loves,
Or sit where silver waters flow
Beneath the summer sunset's glow,
And, sep'rate from the vulgar throng,
Entwine my fancies into song ;
And should the Muse inspire my strain,
The public hear, and not disdain
To turn on me its kind regards,
And rank me with my country's bards,
My soul, uplifted to the skies,
Sublime o'er meaner joys, would rise !

Metrical Tales.

Introduction to Tales.

IN my hours of idle leisure,
　　Many, many years ago,
　I gathered tales and legends
　　As I wandered to and fro ;
And according to my fancy,
　　In convenient place and time,
I wove them for my pleasure
　　Into easy forms of rhyme—
Forms so facile, critic's censure,
　　Not his praise, may be my meed,
But I wove them for my loving,
　　Not my learned, friends to read.

The Tales of the Storm Bound.

PRELUDE.

ONE evening in Calais, when tempests were loud,
  And snows on the township were spread like a cloud,
  Some voyagers, who travelled for trade or caprice,
Were held weather-bound in the "Hotel Meurice."
Time hung on their hands with a terrible weight,
Till at last they agreed that each should narrate
Such tale or adventure, in prose or in verse,
As seemed to him worthy to hear or rehearse—
Should sing a song *solus*, or join in a glee,
Whatever seemed fittest to make the hour flee.
The plan was an old one, yet all were agreed
'Twas not the less likely for that to succeed.
And if it made time fleet, what matter the plan,
Though old as the earliest wanderings of man?
My Muse, on the watch, caught the tales at the time,
And offers them now to her patrons in rhyme

THE SWABIAN'S TALE.

REGINALD AND GUNHILD.

THE burly Baron Ludiwick
    Held castles on the Rhine,
With menials low, and spearmen stout,
    And maiden daughters nine;
By far the fairest of them all
    The peerless Caroline.

Her face was like the rosy morn,
    With vernal glories set;

Her large and lustrous azure eyes
    Enchanted all they met;
And none on whom she deigned to smile
    Her smile could e'er forget.

The Baron's daughters all were fair,
    Except the eldest born,
Gunhild, whom little grace of form
    Or feature did adorn;
Whom all her sisters did despise,
    Her very father scorn.

The burly Baron held his own
    From lawless neighbours' wrong,
The foremost still in war or chase,
    For he was brave and strong;
And dearly did he prize the sweets
    Of wassail, jest, and song.

One night he feasted in his hall
    In more than wonted state;
A hundred lackeys watch his nod,
    And rival knights await
To heap the choicest fruits of earth
    Upon his golden plate.

They fill his ample goblet up
    With frequent draughts of wine
The noblest hills or vales produce
    On all the lordly Rhine,
Till o'er his broad and rugged face
    There spread a smile benign.

"Enough, enough, my merry men,
    The banquet's pleasures cloy;
Go, bid our choicest minstrel come,
    And bring the chorded toy

With which he pours into the soul
Alternate grief or joy."

The minstrel stood before the throng
Of lords and ladies bright,
A comely youth of noble mien,
And goodly girth and height;
And well he played the minstrel's part
Before them all that night.

Now pouring forth a warlike strain,
To kindle martial fire ;
Now melting into dulcet notes,
To waken soft desire,
He played with lords' and ladies' hearts,
As each had been a lyre.

"Now, by my sooth!" the Baron said,
"It is a wondrous thing
How thou canst stir the human soul
With that same simple string;
Strange youth, that power of thine is worth
The ransom of a king.

"Nor shalt thou now at our award
Have reason to repine;
Ask what thou wilt of all we own,
We swear it shall be thine!"
"Then give me," cries the minstrel bold,
"Your daughter Caroline!"

"Sir Bard, thou art a daring rogue,
Who dost desire to wed
The daughter of a baron bold,
Who holds so high a head:
But thou my *daughter* shalt espouse—
Yea, by my sooth, I've said."

The priest was called at early morn,
  The bridegroom was not slow,
The bride with tottering steps advanced,
  Close veiled from top to toe.
Such were the Baron's stern commands,
  And none might answer "No."

Now, when the priest made one of twain,
  The bridegroom bore his bride
Where pawed a gallant charger near,
  A palfrey by his side;
And fifty gallant spearmen stood
  Prepared to mount and ride.

"Why tremblest thou, my chosen one,
  My peerless Caroline?
Palfrey and steeds, and spearmen stout,
  Alike are yours and mine;
Ne'er sigh to leave your father's halls,
  Nor yet the lordly Rhine.

"I bear you to as fair a home,
  Amidst a trusty band,
For I am lord of wide estates
  In pleasant Swabian land.
I only donned the harper's garb
  To win your heart and hand."

The trembling bride said ne'er a word,
  But closer drew her veil;
Yet mounted on her palfrey fair,
  She did not flag nor fail,
As on they rode, and further on.
  O'er sunny slope and vale.

Until on Swabian soil they reached
  A castle old and grand,

Where first the noble Count made halt
　His gay and gallant band,
And gaily welcomed to her bower
　"The lady of the land."

"Right well you have obeyed your sire,
　My peerless Caroline.
You've worn your veil at his behest,
　Be now unveiled at mine."
Yet ne'er a word the lady spake—
　The cause ye may divine.

He raised the veil from off her face—
　No Caroline was there!
'Twas poor Gunhild, who gazed on him
　With face of pale despair,
But yet with éyes which moved his heart,
　So full of love they were.

"Now, on my word, a scurvy trick!"
　The angry bridegroom cried,
"Not played on you by my consent,"
　The trembling bride replied,
"I only yielded to a will
　None living e'er defied.

"I feared my father's savage wrath,
　But you are kind and meek,
And never, never once were known
　To trample on the weak."
She ceased, for burning blushes glowed
　Like roses on her cheek.

The bridegroom gazed upon his bride,
　And tender thoughts did rise
As he beheld her troubled breast
　Which heaved with stifled sighs,

And met again the soul of love,
  Which pleaded in her eyes.

"I loved your sister Caroline,
  I fear she loved me not,
For many a scornful look from her
  The fancied minstrel got;
While you deserve my grateful thoughts
  Despite this scurvy plot.

"And since I find that thou therein
  Didst play no willing part,
And since I know how fair in soul,
  If not in form, thou art,
I'll strive to banish other loves,
  And take thee to my heart."

"May heaven reward thee," cried Gunhild,
  "With blessings evermore.
I do not *love* thee, Reginald—
  I worship and adore!"
And love and hope around her flung
  A charm unknown before.

Oh, woman's love! oh, woman's love!
  Thou art a wondrous thing;
Thou twin'st thyself around the heart
  With many a subtile string;
Yea, till thou dost become the stay
  Where thou dost seem to cling.

A tress may wing, a glance direct
  The flight of Cupid's dart;
A charming face doth seldom fail
  To fire the stripling's heart;
But mental charms to wedded life
  Its lasting sweets impart.

And dearer still, as time rolled on,
  To Reginald became
The wife to whom he gave at first
  But friendship cold and tame,
And even blushed that men should think
  He bade her bear his name.

Her pure, unselfish, gentle soul
  Bestowed a nameless grace
On all the actions of her life,
  And beautified her face,
Till friendship in her husband's breast
  To boundless love gave place.

May never pure and patient love
  Inspire a less regard,
Nor less of woman's soothing care
  Be given the faithful bard
Who strikes the lyre for love and fame—
  The minstrel's true reward.

THE LADY'S SONG.

HE told me not of treasured wealth,
  Nor of a noble name,
From sires who wrote their titles high
  Upon the roll of fame;
He promised not that I should walk
  In robes of silken sheen,
Nor deck my hair with jewels rare
  As grace an Eastern Queen.

He did not plight his faith and troth
  With vows to Heaven above,
But few and simple were the words
  That told me of his love;

And by the glistening drops that gemmed
His eyes of deepest blue,
And by the sighs which heaved his breast,
I knew his words were true.

I read his love in every look;
It spoke in every tone
The feelings he so well described—
I knew them by my own;
For I had thought, had dreamed of him,
Had deemed him nigh divine;
And how, when he declared his love,
Could I dissemble mine?

THE HEIDELBERGER'S TALE.

WILHELMINA VANDECKER.

IF e'er you were at Heidelberg,
  Which stands upon the Neckar,
You may have known mine ancient friend,
  The excellent Vandecker.
You may have met his only child,
  The lovely Wilhelmina,
Declared the belle of Heidelberg,
  By every one who'd seen her.
If e'er you knew mine ancient friend,
  You never knew a better ;
If e'er you saw his charming child,
  You never can forget her.
Her ringlets, softer than the down
  That floats from August thistles,
Should have been papered every night
  With scented love-epistles.
Her eyes were brighter than the stars
  That sparkle in December,

And liker to the blue of heaven
  Than any I remember.
The bloom upon her peachy cheek,
  No painter's skill could catch it,
Nor any colours mixt by man
  Be shaded forth to match it;
And when I let my fancy stray
  O'er classic forms and nations,
I see her graceful figure rise
  O'er all their fair creations.
'Tis possible there might be some
  Who could have wished her thinner,
For Wilhelmina's appetite
  Was rather sharp at dinner.
But out of all your model forms—
  And I have gazed on many—
The Graces Rubens' pencil traced
  Delight me most of any;
For they, to all the elegance
  Of noble birth and breeding,
Unite the solid charms which spring
  From good substantial feeding.
Let novel writers, if they will,
  Exalt their belles ethereal,
My belle ideal, I confess,
  Inclines to the material.
And " Mina's " form awoke delight
  In me and all beholders,
And might have been the choicest work
  Of Nature's master moulders.
In all her movements was a grace
  As elegant and airy
As you could fancy floating round
  A well-developed fairy.

Ah ! pity 'twas that Albert Burt
  Should have beheld and loved her ;
And, sadder still, that words of his
  To mutual passion moved her ;
For though he might admire her more
  Than all the world together,
His head was far too like his purse,
  Which scarce outweighed a feather.
Young Burt was but, the truth to tell,
  A wild, beer-swilling student,
And matrimony with such men
  Is very far from prudent.
Love in a cottage may exist
  'Mongst others than romancers,
But with a youth so wild as Burt
  It very seldom answers ;
For Beauty's cheek will lose its bloom,
  Her love be changed to loathing,
Without sufficient sustenance,
  And frequent change of clothing.
Yet vainly did my friend declare,
  That wedded love cost money,
And could not live on becks and smiles,
  Though joined to words of honey.
The pair were deaf to wisdom's voice,
  And listened but to passion ;
Alas ! to look before he leapt
  Was never Albert's fashion.
And wilful Wilhelmina, though
  By wisdom's voice entreated,
Would like a wilful woman prove
  That adage oft repeated,
Which says that when a woman will,
  She will, you may depend on't,

And adds that when a woman won't,
    She won't, and there's an end on't.
The pair were wed, and spent their days
    Like turtle-doves in cooing,
Till poverty stept sternly in,
    And cried, " Be up and doing ! "
Mine ancient friend, Vandecker, died,
    And, as he oft had told them,
With him expired the revenue
    Which did till then uphold them ;
And they were roused from dreams of bliss
    To battle stern reality—
A fight for which nor he nor she
    Possessed one fitting quality ;
For Wilhelmina's kind papa
    Had caused to teach her nothing,
Except to sing and play and dance,
    And talk about her clothing—
A grave mistake, since Fate may force
    The richest, fairest-looking,
To darn and drudge for daily bread
    On very slender cooking.
And every business Albert tried,
    His habits were against it ;
And he would have to leave it off
    As poor as he commenced it.
To trace their failing fortunes down
    Through all their sad declension,
Would be a most ungrateful task,
    And is not my intention.
I loathe to speak the sordid shifts
    They daily had recourse to ;
As Albert's gains grew less and less,
    His morals worse and worse, too.

Now 'lated travellers picked him up
    Reposing in a gutter;
Now boon companions bore him home
    Inglorious on a shutter;
And down from clothes in fashion's cut
    He crawled to tattered fustian,
And died at last of something like
    Spontaneous combustion.
And what of Wilhelmina, once
    So handsome and so dashing ?
Alas ! she keeps a mangle now,
    And takes in Students' washing.

Young ladies who have kind papas,
    Attend to counsels prudent,
And shun, as you would shun a snake,
    A wild, beer-swilling student.
Ah ! never, dears, let worthless rakes
    Your guileless hearts entangle,
Lest you, like " Mina," be condemned,
    To wash and keep a mangle.

THE BON VIVANT'S SONG.

LET northern bards attune their lyres
    To sing a fiery strain, O !
In honour of the potent draughts
    That fire the drinker's brain, O !
But I would woo the gentle Muse,
    And strive in verse to twine, O !
The praises of the purple juice
    Whose parent is the vine, O !

Give Scotia's sons their " Mountain Dew,"
    Give Englishman his ale, O !

Let Paddy drink his dear " Poteen "
Till cash and credit fail, O !
Let me but stray through sunny France,
Or ramble by the Rhine, O !
And gaily drink the purple juice
Whose parent is the vine, O !

A fico for your fiery draughts,
Degrading soul and sense, O !
The pleasures which they bring are bought
At ruinous expense, O !
Give me, instead, the nect'rous cup
Whose flavour is divine, O !
The cup that lifts us to the gods—
The cup of sterling wine, O !
Give me, give me the purple juice,
Whose parent is the vine, O !

THE LITERARY WANDERER'S TALE.

AT the Chapeau Rouge in Paris,
     I met a broken man,
     Of whose remaining sands of life
     The last grains swiftly ran.
His history none there could tell,
     His converse was with few ;
A stranger he, a stranger I ;
     Thus each to each we drew.
One stormy winter eve we sat
     Before the fire alone,
And talked in turn of fairer years
     And hopes for ever gone ;
And as he warmed his wasted hands
     Above the dying fire,

He murmured, " Thus do youthful hopes
    But flicker to expire.
I've hoped and dreamed for half my life,
    I've schemed and wrought amiss,
Or reaped but sorrow from the schemes
    To which I looked for bliss ;
And long to quit this troubled scene
    Of sin, mischance, mistake,
For rest, which but the angel's trump
    Shall have the power to break.
But ere I go, one little task
    To you I would confide,
For friends that loved me long ago
    Are gone, or scattered wide.
Amid my melancholy verse,
    I've twined a cherished name,
And fain would give it ere I go
    A chance to live in fame.''
He drew a paper from his breast,
    And trembled as he spoke,
As thoughts and feelings long asleep
    Were painfully awoke.
" The lines are in *Flamand*," he said,
    " A language little known ;
But you may one day find a way
    To tell them in your own."
I took the paper from his hand,
    But did not care to speak,
For tears had gathered in my eyes,
    And almost wet my cheek ;
And he had risen with restless look
    And wandered to and fro,
Like one that waits a coming train,
    And seems in haste to go.

Nor e'er again did he and I
    Engage in long discourse,
For, during night, the Messenger
    Who rides the pale white horse
Had visited his little room
    And summoned him away;
And when we entered there at noon
    We found but lifeless clay.
For that we made a humble grave
    Within the "Common Ground,"
Unnamed but for the wooden cross
    I placed above the mound.
'Twas little likely eye of friend
    Might e'er espy the same,
But yet I could not bear to leave
    His grave without a name,
Nor would my slender means afford
    A monumental stone
Like those around, where wealth repaired
    With ostentatious moan.
Since then I've had his mournful lines
    Translated from Flamand,
And humbly offer them to you
    In the language of your land.

THE FLEMING'S LINES, intituled in the Manuscript "MARIA MAHIEU; or, LEAVES FROM THE HISTORY OF A POET'S HEART."

MARIA MAHIEU.

1.

MY gentle Maria Mahieu,
    'Twas June the first time I saw you,
        And, gazing bewitched on your face,
    Methought when nature was fairest

No flower, the sweetest and rarest,
　Could equal your beauty and grace.
Your eyes, beneath their dark lashes,
Spoke in their eloquent flashes
　A language my heart understood;
And sweeter were your whispered words
Than all the songs of all the birds
　That ever charmed the wood,
Though few and simple were the same—
" Mon ami, ah ! comment je t'aime."

ii.

Your lips were fresh as the roses,
Whose blushing leafage encloses
　The dew which the honey-bee sips.
Was't strange I saw you enchanted ?
Is't strange that I'm constantly haunted
　By dreams of those eyes and those lips ?
Times are when I grieve to have met you,
Because I can never forget you,
　Nor ever behold you again—
Never meet those eloquent eyes,
Never hear those love-speaking sighs
　With feelings of rapture and pain,
Nor drink those words of liquid flame—
" Mon ami, ah ! comment je t'aime."

iii.

Oft by the stream that meanders,
Near to your village in Flanders,
　Was my youthful passion confessed.
Trembling, its first words I uttered
To you, whose little heart fluttered
　Like a dove's alarmed from its nest.

To these those days seem as olden,
To these those prospects as golden,
 Illumed by the sunshine of hope.
Ah ! little, little knew we then
Of wasting toils, or worldly men.
 We dreamt, if my genius had scope,
Nor fame nor fortune could refuse
To crown the efforts of my Muse.

IV.

"Is not," said we to each other,
" Man to man a friend and brother,
 Who aids the weak, restrains the strong ;
Who helps forward in his labour
Every bravely struggling neighbour,
 And most the trembling sons of song,
Whom he loves to cheer and strengthen,
Till their furtive warblings lengthen,
 To a loud, continuous strain ?"
Alas ! alas ! we little knew
How many sing, and yet how few
 The scantest meed of praise can gain, .
Far less awaken notes so clear
That distant lands and ages hear.

V.

Of the world, that mighty ocean,
With its turmoil and commotion,
 Its tempest-toss'd and stranded ships,
Just as much we knew or noted
As the little child that floated
 His fleet of leaves and tiny chips
On the slumberous stream that wanders
Past your village home in Flanders ;
 And just as skilled were we to guide

With resolute, unswerving hand,
Our fragile bark to friendly land,
　　Through raging winds and rolling tide,
Through worse than elemental strife,
Through this wild, troublous sea of life.

VI.

Ours were dreams which quickly vanished,
"Sunny memories," to be banished,
　　Realities of sternest mien—
Toilsome years to years succeeding,
Cares increasing, hopes receding,
　　Such, only such, my life hath been.
You, in whom my soul delighted,
I was doomed to see united
　　To one whose star more brightly shone:
And I no hind'rance offered—
Merely bow'd my head and suffered,
　　And sadly, wearily lived on;
Lived on, of you and love bereft,
With nothing save my poesies left.

VII.

How I blessed benignant heaven
For the gift of poesy given—
　　My solace in a thousand woes;
Making all my pleasures sweeter,
Making tedious moments fleeter,
　　And blunting fortune's sharpest blows!
And my griefs, when they were sorest,
I sang in the secret forest,
　　To murmuring streams and leafy woods,
To ocean's ripple, ocean's roar,
On sandy beach and rocky shore,
　　In many measures, tones, and moods;

Sang down the passions in my breast,
As fretful babes are sung to rest.

VIII.

You I called nor false nor fickle,
But believed that tears would trickle
    For him you loved in early youth.
Yea, believed your heart was slowly,
Hardly schooled to leave me wholly
    With seeming shadow on your truth;
And with a sombre, sad delight,
Like what a friend might feel to write
    On a friend's memorial stone,
I would please myself with thinking
That the lines which I was linking
    Might tell the world when I was gone
That stern necessity's decree,
Not falsehood, severed you and me.

IX.

For my poesy or my passion
Little cares the world of fashion;
    And you, for whom I sought its praise,
No longer love to hear it now.
Why, therefore, should my withered brow
    Be circled with unnoticed bays?
Yet I sigh to leave a token
Ere the silver chord be broken,
    That I have loved to link your name
With the virtues that are meetest
For the fairest girl, and sweetest,
    That ever kindled passion's flame;
Then I would joyously expire
Amid the last notes of my lyre.

THE PHILOSOPHER'S SONG.

CORRAGIO AMICI !

COME, friends, let us join with each other
　　In cheering life's way with a song;
　Thus brother may comfort a brother,
　　The weak gather strength from the strong.

Dame Fortune may slight or forsake us,
　Each promise of hope prove untrue,
Stern poverty rudely awake us
　To fight our past battles anew.

The love of our dearest devotion
　May value our worship at naught;
Ah, well! there are fish in the ocean
　As fine as the fish that are caught.

Our road may get steeper and rougher,
　And louder and keener the blast,
But the rudest of toils that we suffer
　Must come to an end at the last.

To those who are ever repining
　Life's burdens are hardest to bear;
Look up to the cloud's silver lining,
　And merrily tramp with your share.

We'll mingle the shady and sunny,
　And temper our sorrows with joy;
If life were all sugar and honey,
　How quickly the banquet would cloy!

JOSEPH BROWN.

A TALE OF CANTERBURY.

THERE lived in Canterbury town,—
    What boots the time to state ?—
An honest man named Joseph Brown,
    Esteemed by small and great.

Joe loved his pipe and pint of ale,
    With neighbours two or three,
His merry jest and pleasant tale,
    But yet no toper he.

A stranger to domestic strife
    Or sore affliction's rod,
Joe lived a happy, single life,
    Till he was fifty-odd.

But then his locks got mixed with grey,
    His person rather stout,
And sometimes too, the truth to say,
    He suffered from the gout.

And so one night when goutish pain
    Had kept him long awake,
Cried honest Joe, "I see it plain,
    I've made a great mistake.

" I pass the weary nights alone,
    In undeplored distress;
There's none to cheer me when I groan,
    Nor make my sufferings less.

" While married men have kindly wives,
    To soothe their hours of pain,
We who have chosen single lives,
    Unloved, unsoothed remain.

" I've made a grand mistake, I know,
  But is repair too late —
Are there not men as old as Joe,
  Who've entered wedlock's state ?

" There's Gibbs, who woo'd at sixty-eight,
  And married Mrs. Brooks,
And Harrison who linked his fate
  At sixty with his cook's.

" I know of neighbours half a score
  Who've changed their single life
When they were more than fifty-four,
  By George ! I'll have a wife !"

Joe rose betimes on marriage bent ;
  " I know of maids," cried he,
" And widows by the score in Kent,
  And why not one for me ?

" I'll first step o'er to Nelly Bell,
  And if she say me nay,
Why, then my tale of love I'll tell
  To worthy widow Gray."

" If both reject my proffered hand,
  No cause for idle sorrow ;
There's still a chance with widow Bland;
  I'll call on her to-morrow.

" And after these, there's widow Lowe,
  Who keeps the ' Star and Crown,'
And widow White would not be slow
  To change from White to Brown."

Away went Joe to Nelly Bell,
  A maid of forty-four ;

But strange and wonderful to tell
  He scarce had crossed the door,

Ere trembling seized each massive limb,
  The blood forsook his cheek.
He could but utter " ha !" and " hem !"
  Whene'er he tried to speak.

In vain he sighed, in vain he tried
  To utter words of love ;
The words still hung about his tongue,
  His tongue refused to move.

With widow Gray 'twas just the same,
  The same with widow White,
The words he wanted never came ;
  Cried Joe, " and serves me right !

" The love I checked—poor foolish dolt—
  When I was young and thin,
Now, sunk in fat, is like a bolt
  Which time hath rusted in.

" But here the matter shall not rest,
  I'll act like greater men,
Whose tongues refuse the mind's behest—
  I'll use the surer pen."

Joe wrote a note to Nelly Bell,
  And proffered heart and hand ;
To widows Gray and White as well,
  In terms as warm and bland.

Says Joe, " The first who answers ' Yes '
  Shall soon be Mrs. Brown ;
Should these refuse my lot to bless,
  There's still a chance in town."

Without delay three answers came
    By messengers express ;
Joe read and found them all the same,
    The gist of each was " Yes."

" Now here's," cried Joe, " a pretty go !
    Ah, poor unlucky me !
The law allows one single spouse,
    And I've proposed for three.

" Too great success has crowned my plan,
    Whatever shall I do ?
If I should dare to marry one,
    They'll say I've cheated two.

" I cannot dare this deadly breach,
    With no escape behind ;
I'll write a piteous note to each,
    And say I've changed my mind."

Three piteous notes brought three replies
    More furious each than each ;
Joe read them o'er with tearful eyes
    And heart too full for speech.

Three lawyers' letters followed next;
    Was ever man below
Bamboozled, worried, and perplex'd
    Like poor, unlucky Joe ?

His triple loves were blazed about
    Through all his native town,
And urchins, when he passed, would shout—
    " There's lady-killing Brown !"

The women folks, when he appeared,
    Would call him " rogue" and " cheat,"

And even old companions jeered
And quizzed him in the street.

The lawyers plundered his estate,
The world became his foe,
An Almhouse was his dreary fate,
And death his term of woe.

Ye bachelors, a numerous flock,
Ye spinsters more than they,
Give ear to Cupid's am'rous knock
Ere ye turn old and grey.

Be taught by honest Joseph's fault,
Be warned by Joseph's sin,
Before your love turn like a bolt
Which time hath rusted in.

THE OLD BACHELOR'S SONG.

THERE grew a sweet flower,
  In my garden bower—
Young Love was the floweret's name—
So dear to me, so fair to see,
  That the roses red
  Might have hung their head
With a redder blush for shame,
  And the lilies turned white
  Out of envy and spite,
If placed by the side of the tiny flower
Which budded and bloomed in my garden bower.

Young Beauty's smile was the sun that cheered,
  Young Hope was the morning dew

That fed and fostered, strengthened and reared,
    And tinged with their beautiful hue
The delicate leaves of the tiny flower,
That shed its delights on my garden bower.

But the smile of Beauty was turned away,
    Hope shook his pinions and fled,
And my beautiful flower drooped day by day,
    And now lies shrivelled and dead ;
But its withered leaves until this late hour
Fling their sweet perfume on my garden bower.

THE MARSEILLIAN CAPTAIN'S TALE.

JOSEPHINE.

IKE a dream, a brief romance,
    Was my life with Josephine,
In this pleasant land of France,
    Near the little town of Guines.
While my ship discharged in port,
    I went out to St. Pierre,
To partake the merry sport
    Of its yearly feast and fair.
And 'twas there, in the *ducasse*,
    That I met with Josephine,
Who, amid the merry mass
    Of the beauteous, trode the queen;
Through the mazes of the dance
    I pursued her fairy feet,
Striving now to catch a glance,
    Now a smile supremely sweet,
Till the blissful moment came
    When her eyes were turned to mine,

And betrayed a mutual flame
   Through their lashes long and fine;
For I, too, was young and gay,
   Nor unpleasant to behold,
In that noon of manhood's day,
   When my gaze was bright and bold.
I was marked amid the crowd
   For my manly form and air,
And had oft ere then been proud
   Of my conquests 'mongst the fair;
Yea, had yielded loosened reins
   To my passionate desires,
For within my youthful veins
   Flowed the blood of southern sires.
But a monarch might have smiled
   On this peerless Josephine,
On this humble widow's child,
   Of the little town of Guines,
And a demon have recoiled,
   With the purple tint of shame,
From the thought that could have soiled
   Her untainted heart and name.
Saints! had I a painter's art,
   I could paint her even now—
Flossy, flaxen locks that part
   O'er an alabaster brow;
Eyes of deepest azure, beaming
   With the gentle light of love,
'Neath the silken lashes streaming,
   And the pencilled shades above.
I would tint a cheek with hues
   From the lily and the rose,
When the pearly morning dews,
   In their folded leaves repose;

I would rob the young carnation,
   To give parted lips their glow,
And increase the sweet temptation
   By a dimpled chin below ;
By a throat as white as milk,
   By the charm of swelling breasts,
Bosomed in the snowy silk,
   Like twain turtles in their nests ;
By a form where every fold
   Of the robe should fall with grace,
So that men should cry, " Behold,
   A seraphic form and face ! "
But, though I could thus portray,
   Thus inform my constant thought,
I would cry, " Away ! away !
   All your efforts are but naught.
Art, undo the work of Death,
   Ere you bid my heart rejoice ;
Give this poor creation breath,
   Bid it thrill me with its voice ;
Let it woo me to its arms
   By its dear unconscious wiles,
By its thousand nameless charms,
   Winning words, and witching smiles ;
Let its bosom rise and fall,
   Like the summer ocean's swell,
As it lends an ear to all
   That untiring love would tell.
Bid it meet my raptured gaze
   With the eyes of Josephine,
Give me back my happy days
   In my cottage home at Guines ! "
These are idle words, alas !
   Let them stir my heart no more,

Let me rather strive to pass
  From those memories of yore.
Yet it seems to be my doom
  To be urged as by a spell,
Like the mariner of whom
  Your own Island's bard doth tell, *
To procure a brief repose,
  When the spirit brings me here,
By the pouring of my woes
  Into some lone stranger's ear.
How I glory in it now,
  That, despite my House's pride,
I was true to every vow,
  And made Josephine my bride!
For the brightest spot that shows
  In the widely-chequered scene
Of a life that nears its close
  Is my cottage home at Guines!
There the wingèd moments sped
  As I never knew them flee,
There the gifts of joy were spread
  With a bounteous hand for me ;
There were smiles for ever dear,
  Looks of deep unchanging love,
Tones that fell upon my ear,
  Like the music of the grove ;
Yet the golden coin, the purest,
  Hath its portion of alloy,
And black Care, when bliss seems surest,
  Comes to mix the cup of joy.
Ah ! 'twas sweet to dream and sip,
  Until Care cried, " Dreamer, wake !

---

* Coleridge in the " Ancient Mariner."

You are master of a ship,
    And your fortune's yet to make ! ''
I will spare you all the tears
    With the kisses mixt between,
All the hopes, and doubts, and fears,
    Of our final parting scene.
Fancy me upon the deep,
    Underneath a tropic sky,
Where the winds are all asleep,
    And the waters torpid lie.
It is night, but slumber flies
    From my cabin close and hot,
Yet I shut my drowsy eyes,
    And the present is forgot.
I am borne on Fancy's wings
    To my cottage home at Guines,
And behold mysterious things
    Round the couch of Josephine.
Forms are there I do not know,
    Whispering counsels and commands,
There are stifled sounds of woe,
    Then a child is in my hands ;
It inspires a single breath,
    Turns a feeble gaze on me,
Shuts its languid eyes, and death
    Sets its sinless spirit free.
Josephine !—I see her now ;
    She is lying calm and still,
With the death-damp on her brow,
    And her fingers white and chill.
Swift I spring upon the floor
    With a half-unconscious scream.
Blessed Virgin ! It is o'er,
    This accursed waking dream.

Once again we fall and rise
  On the reawakened seas;
Once again our vessel flies,
  Sprung to life before the breeze.
Wastes of water fade behind,
  Capes and islands rise to view;
Dreams of home invade the mind
  Of the dullest of our crew.
If you e'er were on the ocean
  Till your step became a roll,
And your mind conceived a notion
  That the brine was over all,
You will know with what delight
  We beheld our bark advance,
Till the naked eye could sight
  Our belovëd land of France.
Now the destined port is gained,
  " With a welcome and a will; "
Yet my boding heart is pained
  With a sense of coming ill,
And I drag my tardy feet,
  With increasing doubt and fear,
To the home I left replete
  With a love so deeply dear.
Ah! the cottage door is fast ;
  There is none to heed my call;
Yes, my brief romance is past,
  And despair is over all.
In the little churchyard nigh,
  Underneath the grassy sod,
Child and mother's ashes lie,
  And their souls have risen to God.
I am little skilled in books,
  Nor to theologic schools

Have I ever turned my looks
    For celestial laws and rules ;
But I've read, within the pages
    Of the ocean and the sky,
Lessons never changed through ages,
    Lessons never known to lie;
Read, and recognised a Power
    Who disposes all below,
And in that tremendous hour,
    When I struggled with my woe,
He did not deny relief
    To my great and bitter cry.
For, behold ! to soothe my grief,
    From the late beclouded sky
Burst a sudden, shining star,
    And I felt that *she* was there,
Smiling on me from afar,
    Chiding down my wild despair.
And I bowed and blessed the Power
    Who disposes all below,
And from that benignant hour
    Ceased the keenness of my woe.
Yet I only " bide my time,"
    An unwilling lingerer here ;
For I long to rise sublime
    To that better, brighter sphere,
Where I know she loves me still,
    And rejoices in her heart
When I turn from ought that's ill,
    Or perform a noble part.
She has been my saving grace
    In many a sinful scene,
For I turn from aught that's base
    When I think of Josephine—

Turn from guilty joys away,
　With a loathing and disgust
Speech refuses to convey
　To the ear of brother dust.
For my soul within me cries,
　" I have drunk seraphic bliss,
And for ever must despise
　Such a sordid joy as this !
One who lived in pure delight
　With the peerless Josephine
Cannot stoop from such a height
　To a pleasure base and mean ! "
I am grey, and worn, and old,
　And my race is nearly run.
I have borne the polar cold,
　And the burning tropic sun ;
Where the canvas, rent to shreds,
　Has been strewn on ocean weeds ;
While the cordage snapt like threads,
　And the masts like withered reeds.
In the elemental strife
　I have borne me undismayed,
Freely venturing limb and life
　Where my feeble arm could aid—
Not for gain, nor yet that I
　Deemed my fellows' praises sweet;
But that death, whom others fly,
　Is the friend I long to meet.

THE SALT MAKER'S SONG.

NOTE.—The *Saunier*, or Salt Maker of the North of France, generally drives about the country in a light cart, during two or three days a week, delivering his salt. As the imposts are heavy and the competition keen, his gains are very moderate; but he is generally a jovial fellow, and nearly always singing or talking encouragingly to his horse as he drives along.

GET on, my horse! get on, Brunow!
  Whatever makes your pace so slow?
  I'm sure you had your fill this morn
Of juicy hay and mealy corn.
Get on, my horse! get on, Brunow!

When evening comes there's rest for you;
Alas! my cares are never through ;
How fast so ever I proceed,
There's some one urging greater speed.
Get on, my horse! get on, Brunow !

The tax-collector called to-day,
And asked me when I meant to pay;
The baker, butcher, tailor too,
Declare their bills are overdue.
Get on, my horse! get on, Brunow !

My wife avers the parlour chairs
Are torn and worn beyond repairs;
And for herself, she must confess,
She scarcely has a decent dress.
Get on, my horse! get on, Brunow !

This hat of mine, which once was new,
Has grown uncomely to the view;
This coat, whose years can scarce be told,
Is far from pleasant to behold.
Get on, my horse! get on, Brunow !

The shades of night begin to fall,
And you shall soon enjoy your stall,
For yonder comes my little lad
To have a ride beside his dad.
Get on, my horse! get on, Brunow !

He sees us half a league away,
Deserts his infant mates and play,
And runs to clamber in the cart,
And nestle on his father's heart.
Get on, my horse! get on, Brunow !

THE ABERDONIAN'S TALE.

THE WRECK OF THE OCEAN QUEEN.

OVER the bar and into the tide,
  Out and away on the ocean wide,
  By a cloud of quivering canvas prest—
  Canvas swelled by a breeze from the west,
Out from the harbour of Aberdeen,
To Dantzic bound stood the Ocean Queen.

Then spoke an old tar, " In sooth !" quoth he,
" I don't much fancy this chopping sea ;
The wind is veering fast to the east;
I saw a dozen rats at the least
Leave the vessel and scamper away,
The while careening in port we lay.

This morning, too, as I left the Cove,
Torn from my wife and children's love,
The old dog howled at the cottage door
As he never was heard to howl before ;
And over my path there passed a hare,
Which gazed at me with a wierdly stare.

All omens these which I like not well,
And others too, did I care to tell,
With thoughts of the dear ones left behind,
Lie like a leaden weight on my mind,
And make me wish, still more and more,
That this voyage of the Ocean Queen were o'er."

" Avast!" said the skipper, " stow your jaw!
I've often rounded the gusty Skaw,
With frailer vessel and feebler crew,
And never blenched tho' the tempest blew.
Didst ever behold my cheek turn pale
Midst wrathful surges or raging gale ?

" No stouter ship than the Ocean Queen
Hails from the harbour of Aberdeen,
And you yourself were the first, I know,
To boast her strength should the breezes blow ;
The last to challenge her master's word,
Tho' yards and masts went sheer by the board.

" Then loosen the reefs, and let her flee
Over the waves of the German Sea ;
Let every inch of her canvas draw ;
To-morrow, perchance, we'll sight the Skaw—
In less, perchance, than a week be found
Safe in the port to which we're bound."

        *   *   *   *

And faster and faster the vessel flew,
And fiercer and fiercer the east wind blew,
And higher and higher the billows rose,
And leapt on the deck like vengeful foes,
And louder and louder the Storm-Fiend shrieked
As sails were shredded and timbers creaked.

And wilder and wilder his laughter pealed,
When the smitten vessel lurched and reeled,
Sunk in the terrible trough, or gave
Her shuddering side to the crested wave ;
" Ha, ha! ho, ho!" he gibbered and roared,
When rigging and masts were swept by the board.

He tossed the hull in his savage glee,
He plunged her deep in the seething sea,
Flung her aloft till she seemed to spring
Out of the waves like a living thing;
Caught her again with a giant's strength,
And hurled her forward a cable's length.

A sad and terrible thing, I ween,
This fiendish play to the Ocean Queen ;
A terrible thing to all below,
Thus to be bandied to and fro.
But the hull was firm, and the hatches sure,
And what could the crew, except endure ?

Endure they did, till the dismal night
Was chased by the dull November light,
And a seaman's stable foot could tread
The slippery planking overhead ;
But then, what a sight! it checked their breath,
They were drifting down to certain death !

Nearer and nearer a rocky shore,
Where billows were bursting loud and hoar,
And reefs out-running ledge upon ledge,
Half a mile from the jaggëd edge;
And hope died out at the dreadful view,
From every heart in the fated crew.

At length, with a far-resounding shock,
The vessel struck on a sunken rock—
A moment struggled against the strain,
Then groaned, and crashed, and parted in twain;
And only one of a crew of eight
Survived to tell of his brothers' fate.

He told it me with a faltering tongue,
When he was old and I was young;
And I tell it you, whose vessels sweep
The azure fields of the mighty deep,
And pray you see that the outward bound
From pennon to keel be stout and sound.

Oh, do not trust, for the greed of gain,
Unworthy craft to the faithless main,
Since the stoutest ships that ever sailed,
And men in the firmest courage mailed,
Are only the playthings of seas and skies
When the winds are loose and the waters rise!

THE SAILOR'S SONG.

THERE'S not a girl in all the world
    To match my Mary Ann ;
  Her hair is like the threads of gold,
  Her neck is like the swan ;
And bluer, brighter eyes than hers,
  Have never gazed on man.

Her form is straighter than the reed
    That rises by the rill ;
  Her step is lighter than the fawn's
  Which bounds along the hill.

There is a magic in her voice
Beyond magician's skill.

Right pretty are the maids of France,
Dispute the fact who dare!
And beautiful the maids of Spain,
With bright black eyes and hair;
But ne'er a girl in all the world
With Mary may compare.

Where'er I go she fills my heart—
There's room for none save she;
She is so fair, she is so kind,
So all that best can be;
My love is all for Mary Ann,
And Mary's all for me.

THE POET'S TALE.

PAULINE.

In a humble cemetery, on one of the hills overlooking Rouen, there was to be seen, in the year 1867, an unpretending stone slab bearing an inscription, of which the following is a literal translation :—

"Pauline,

" To her affianced Henry, separated from her by the Conscription, and believed to have fallen in Wagram, his first battle-field.
" Eternal Regrets!
" Pauline, deceased 1832."

Out of the history briefly told in that inscription arose the following verses :—

I HAVE climbed to woo the Muses
High o'er the Norman plain,
On my right a Norman city,
At my feet the winding Seine;

O'er my head a sky where splendour
   And gloom appear at strife—
A sky of cloud and sunshine,
   Like a chequered human life.
And the Muses seem to hear me,
   And to say, with smiling mien,
" String the lyre and tell the nations
   The story of Pauline ! "
So, I sing—who will may listen,
   Or who lists may call me wrong ;
For the Muses' spell is on me,
   And my destiny is song.

Pauline ! Pauline ! I see thee now
   In all thy charms arise,
Thy swelling form, thy raven locks,
   Thy darkly-flashing eyes ;
Thy laughing lips and snowy teeth,
   Thy face of joyous youth,
By fancy's pencil all portrayed,
   Arise in very truth.
The mild and grateful evening breeze,
   Which breathes upon me now,
Is such as oft in other years
   Has fanned thy fairer brow.
Where I am straying thou hast strayed
   Full many a time and oft ;
Where I am sitting thou hast sat
   On this green sward so soft ;
Where I am standing thou hast stood,
   A child of Norman ground,
And turned thy bright admiring gaze
   On all the beauties round.

The city spreading fair and wide,
  The island-studded Seine,
The waving crops, the verdant woods
  Which deck the summer plain,
Have met thy raptured gaze as mine,
  And standing where I stand,
Thy heart hath swelled with honest pride
  In this thy Norman land.
But not an exile and alone
  Thou trod'st these grassy heights;
The loving and beloved was near
  To share thy young delights.
'Twas here the chosen of thy heart,
  Who dreamt to call thee " spouse,"
Young Henry, filled thy willing ear
  With oft-repeated vows.
'Twas here that life's untrodden ways
  In brightest hues appeared;
'Twas here ye schemed your fairest schemes,
  Your airy castles reared;
For youth and beauty, joy and love,
  Concentred all their rays
In one great golden gleam of hope
  To gild life's coming days.
But lo! a cloud obscures the sun
  Upon the verge of night,
And shadows on thy life, Pauline,
  Have hid thee from my sight!
Pauline, I see thee yet again,
  But ah, how changed art thou!
Thy hair is mixed with silver threads,
  ·There's care upon thy brow.
Thine eyes have lost their former fire,
  Thy cheek its former bloom,

Thou hast the languid step of one
    Who journeys to the tomb ;
Thy golden dreams are all dispelled,
    Thy latest hopes have fled,
For he around whose life they twined
    Sleeps with the nameless dead.
A Conscript, he was torn from thee,
    And (sad to be revealed)
Was marched to battle and to death
    On Wagram's fatal field.
And doubt and fear, and groundless hope,
    Slow withering to despair,
And weary years of loathèd life,
    Were each in turn thy share.
Thy cup was bitter to the dregs,
    But thou hast drunk it dry,
And now in yonder lone graveyard
    In kindred earth dost lie ;
Thine epitaph and history thus,—
    " Alas for poor Pauline !
She loved and lost, she grieved and died;
    She *was*, and she *hath been !* "

Red-handed War, we hear thy tramp,
    We feel thy scorching breath,
And love and hope and beauty change
    To woe, and blight, and death!
Thou turnest virtue into vice,
    Rich plenty into dearth,
And tramplest into ruined wastes
    The fairest scenes of earth!
And wherefore givest thou the lands
    To rapine, sword, and flame ?—

That one perchance of thousands ten
  May clutch the bubble, Fame!
His fame ?—It is to mount the breach
  The foremost of the band ;
'Tis steadfast in the ranks of death
  On battle-field to stand ;
It is to lead the crushing charge
  Where foes are thickest prest,
When shot, and shell, and pointed steel,
  Assail each daring breast !
It is to vanquish in the field
  A seeming stronger foe ;
It is to slay and trample down
  And scatter endless woe ;
And ah ! how many brave men fall
  To raise one single name !
To *thousands* toil, and wounds, and death,
  To *one* the hero's fame !

Ye Kings and Kaisers of the earth,
  Of new or ancient line,
I stretch my hands and cry to you
  With all the might that's mine—
Pause ere ye hurl your subject men
  Amidst embattled strife ;
Reflect how many human lives
  Twine round each human life !
What shattered hopes, what breaking hearts,
  What years of grief and pain
For each, how mean soe'er he be,
  To swell your conquests slain !

Do ye aspire to leave your name
  A theme for future story ?

There are—the field of Mars apart—
　A thousand roads to glory !
Go, lessen error, vice, and crime !
　Go, aid the march of mind !
Go, succour, strengthen, elevate—
　Not scourge and slay your kind.
Go, struggle to extinguish wars,
　Make strife and hatred cease ;
Unite to turn the field of Mars
　Into a field of peace.*

* The above was written near Rouen in August, 1867, when the *Champ de Mars* at Paris was turned into a veritable *Champ de Paix* by the great International Exhibition.

THE CORPORAL'S SONG.

SIR Philip Malone to the wars has gone,
　And left his lady-love crying,
"Alas ! and alack ! he'll never come back
　Till I in my grave am lying !
Ah ! never a knight shall have the right
　To sigh at my feet a lover,
But I'll sigh and moan for Philip Malone
　Till pleasureless life be over."

But Philip Malone had hardly been gone
　A month, or but little over,
When there came a knight, Lord Marmaduke hight,
　To sigh at her feet a lover.
He was plain and old, but silver and gold
　Were plenty enough in his coffers,
And the lady thought that she certainly ought
　To close with Sir Marmaduke's offers.

" To die an old maid," she thoughtfully said,
　" Is certainly far from my wish,
And a bird in the hand, with plumage so grand,
　Is better than two in the bush."
So, false to her vows, Lord Marmaduke's spouse
　She quickly consented to be ;
And, truth to declare, there's many a fair
　As fickle and faithless as she.

Long years have gone past, and home at the last
　Sir Philip returned from the wars,
With titles, 'tis true, with honours not few,
　But little save these and his scars.
The wife of another—a wife and a mother—
　He found the betrothed of his youth ;
And what did he do to cause her to rue
　The sad breach of her faith and truth ?

Did he slay, as a foe, her husband ?　Oh, no.
　Or hang himself? drown himself?　Neither.
He bottled his rage, and, cool as a sage,
　Did something wiser than either.
He'd had in the wars quite plenty of scars,
　A surfeit of blood and slaughter ;
So he wiped a tear for the loss of his dear,
　And married his drummer's daughter.

THE COMMUNIST'S TALE.

WHEN dread confusion reigned in France,
    In seventy, seventy-one—
When prostrate in the dust she lay,
    By traitors' arts undone,
Her fairest towns and provinces
    By German hordes o'er-run—

When Paris, pride of Frenchmen's hearts,
    Beleaguered fought and fell—
When Prussian pæans rose to heaven
    With most exultant swell,
And demons seemed to walk the earth
    Let loose from lowest hell—

When war had swallowed up our means,
    The siege destroyed our trade—
When daily bread by honest toil
    No longer could be made,
And Prussia held the throat of France
    Demanding to be paid—

Then deep mistrust of men and means,
    Fierce discord stalked abroad;
The rich averred our rulers drove
    Full tilt on ruin's road;
The poor declared whoever ruled
    They only felt the goad.

A thousand orators arose,
    Each powerful in debate,
Each with his solder and his bolt,
    To tinker up the State;

And each deriding rival claims
  With many-worded hate.

Imperialists, Legitimists,
  Advanced pretentions high;
Two factions of Republicans,
  Gave each to each the lie;
Their rival flags the Tricolor,
  And flag of crimson die.

For me, o'er politicians' claims,
  I racked my weary brain ;
But which was right or which was wrong,
  I strove to see in vain,
. Tho' every leader swore the truth
  Which marked his cause was plain.

Ah, me! it was an evil time,
  A time of wild unrest;
Dissension like a nightmare sat
  On Gallia's seething breast;
Not more by those who hated her,
  Than those who loved, oppress'd.

One morn, beside my fireless hearth,
  I gnawed a fleshless bone,
For other food within the house,
  My wife and I had none ;
Nor had we longer wherewithal,
  On which to raise a loan.

Piece after piece our furniture,
  And (save the clothes we wore)
Our raiment too, piecemeal had gone,
  To swell a broker's store;

And Famine, lean and hollow-eyed,
  Was pressing on us sore.

That morning spake my wife in scorn,
  As wife, however meek,
Oppressed by such a load of ills,
  Might well be driven to speak:—
"The cobbler's wife has fire and food,
  And flesh on limb and cheek,

" And if you had but half the soul,
  Of neighbour *Pere Labouse*,
Ye need not gnaw a fleshless bone,
  In tattered pants and blouse,
With neither fire nor furniture,
  Nor food within the house.

"Of right and wrong you would not care
  To vex your silly head ;
That Faction is the right for us,
  Which soonest gives us bread,
No matter what its flag may be,
  The Tricolor or Red.

" Why should you be so plaguy nice
  In times so out of tune?
I know that wiser folks than you
  Believe in the Commune
As sent to banish all our ills—
  A never-equalled boon.

" And well I know that *Pere Labouse*,
  Who, wont to be so poor,
Now struts a chief among the 'Reds,'
  And scouts the ' Tricolor,'

With such abundance in his house
   As ne'er was known before."

I hung my head without response,
   For very well I knew
That every reason I could urge
   My wife would meet with two ;
And raging hunger's pang besides
   Beyond endurance grew.

No fire, no food, no honest work,
   What better could be done?
Amidst the ranks of the Commune
   That day I bore a gun,
And bravely " looted" sundry shops
   Before the set of sun.

Our leader was a lawyer's clerk,
   A captain of repute,
Avoiding dangers for himself
   And for his men to boot ;
The latest in the battle field,
   The foremost in the " loot."

Ye wives and mothers of the brave,
   Did warriors choose their chiefs,
As we of the Commune did ours,
   Far fewer were your griefs.
Not balls would fly, but bulletins,
   Like lawyer's windy briefs !

Then would a single boastful tongue
   Defeat a powerful foe,
The splutterings of a single pen
   Lay hostile myriads low,

And Hock, Bordeaux, and bright Champagne,
   Instead of blood, should flow.

O, brave Laplume ! we never feared
   To follow where you led,
For never fox had keener nose
   For scenting prey ahead,
Nor ever with a swifter foot
   A coming danger fled.

O, many was the toilsome march
   From which you saved your men,
And many were the fights we won
   Through your audacious pen,
While cheerily we sipped our wine
   In some unnoted den.

But war, by proclamation waged,
   And battles won in print,
Were not enough to pleasure men
   On bloody business bent.
And so against the foe, at last,
   In very deed we went.

'Tis not my purpose to relate
   What conquests we achieved,
Nor how the artful Versaillaise
   Misguided France deceived,
Till Fortune turning from our side
   Their losses all retrieved.

Yet, I aver, we Communists
   Did ne'er sustain defeat,
But only for strategic ends
   Thought proper to retreat,

Until our cunning foes contrived
　　Their leaguer to complete.

And when their waspish legions swarmed
　　Around our luckless town,
Then did our guns and mitrailleuses
　　By thousands mow them down ;
Yet senseless Victory fled from us,
　　Their brutal brows to crown.

Our strongest forts and barricades
　　They captured by surprise,
And when we stretched our arms to them
　　They turned away their eyes,
And savage-heartedly refused
　　To come and fraternise.

O, Liberty! Equality!
　　Fraternity ! so dear
To every Communistic heart,
　　Sweet words which we revere,
Ye fell unheeded on the dull,
　　Debased Versaillian ear.

The Versaillaise, their treacheries,
　　Their butcheries and their rage,
Shall yet descend to evil fame
　　On Communistic page,
And drape their memories in disgrace
　　Through many a coming age.

Fools! fools they were who trusted life
　　To wretches such as those !
Our wary captain better judged
　　The nature of his foes,

And better far, for me, at least,
  Our line of action chose.

Near Jena Bridge, there was a sewer
  Debouching in the Seine,
We oft had marked it as we passed—
  A lofty, vaulted drain,
In summer dry and free from sludge,
  Except in times of rain.

And more than once the brave Laplume
  Had pointed out to me,
That up this sewer a hunted man
  In desperate need might flee,
And hide in safety for a time,
  Till farther flight could be.

And when he saw our ruthless foes
  Throughout the city spread,
And far and wide the flaming sky
  With conflagration red,
Then up this sewer Laplume and I
  In consternation fled.

And up we went, and farther up
  We crept on hands and feet,
While each could hear the other's heart
  In wild excitement beat,
As vaporous stench and darkness joined
  Our horror to complete.

"Laplume ! Laplume !" at last I cried,
  And clutched him like a vice,
" I can't go on ! I won't go on !
  I hear the rats and mice ;

The darkness is like blackest pitch,
    The odour's far from nice !"

" Too true, my friend," replied the brave,
    " But life is very dear,
And if our foes should find us out
    We have the worst to fear ;
And yet—and yet I hardly think
    They'll come to seek us here.

I own our lobby's hardly such
    As suits a Paris dandy,
The roof is rather near the floor,
    The want of light's unhandy ;
But keep your courage up, my friend,
    We're near the stores, and brandy."

The prudent chief! the thoughtful man !
    Well knowing how it fared
Full oft with revolutionists,
    This dismal pass had dared,
And here a chamber in the wall
    With ample stores prepared.

It was a cavern scooped so near
    A grating in the street
That we had air, and glimmering light,
    And heard the passers' feet ;
May never hunted Communist
    Secure a worse retreat.

We even dared when night came on
    And silence seemed to reign,
To raise the grate, and scan the street,
    As far as eye could strain,

Till some commotion made us dive
　　Like rats within our drain.

And we had food, and we had drink
　　From vermin well secured,
But to our residence for all
　　We could not get inured,
For more familiar grew the rats
　　Than could be well endured.

Ah! many a time their shining eyes
　　Right into mine did peep,
And shuddering horror o'er my frame
　　In clammy dews would creep,
To think that one or both of us
　　Might be devoured in sleep.

And drearily the time dragged past ;
　　An hour appeared an age ;
The compass of a single day
　　Beyond what mind could gauge ;
But more than all our worst extremes
　　We feared our victors' rage.

Much did we talk of better days,
　　And much of our escape,
And much invoke the vinous god
　　To aid our plans to shape,
While plenteously 'mongst friends without
　　Versailles was pouring grape.

One evening given to potent draughts,
　　And maudlin, dull debate,
It happened that the drowsy god
　　Had crept upon us late ;

And what took place ere break of day,
  I shudder to relate.

The curses of a Communist
  Upon those rats alight,
They picked my dear companion's bones
  On that unlucky night;
And nibbling at my precious nose,
  They woke myself in fright!

A skeleton lay poor Laplume,
  A fearful sight to see;
Yet I was glad, and very glad—
  So selfish man can be—
To think the rats had eaten him,
  And only nibbled me!

My poor Laplume! I thought of all
  Your escapades and pranks,
And when I searched your secret stores
  And found a hoard of francs,
I bade your skeleton adieu,
  With ardent tears and thanks.

I knew escape was perilous,
  But yet resolved to try,
For in that den another night
  I could not dare to lie;
'Twas better far by hands of man,
  Than teeth of rats, to die.

But, thanks to fortune, and the francs
  Which good Laplume held stored,
In safety I outran the risks
  Of hostile fire and sword,

And still amidst the ranks of men
  My perils can record.

But woe's my heart, for the Commune,
  To proletaires like me,
It offered such immunities
  As ne'er again can be ;
From rents, from taxes, and from debts,
  Its mandate set us free.

It drove policemen from our streets,
  It shut the Court-house door,
It took the riches from the rich,
  And gave them to the poor,
And opened to the mendicant
  The merchant's choicest store.

Old laws and forms of government
  Beneath its censures fell,
Morality, religion too,
  Priest, altar, book, and bell,
The Red Republic sought to tomb,
  And ring their funeral knell.

It was a saturnalia,
  A bloody jest of yule,
In which Parisian proletaires,
  Resolved to play the fool,
Appointed the Commune to reign,
  The Lord of all Misrule.

And nothing now remains of it
  Except an evil name ;
It rose in strife and anarchy,
  And set in blood and flame,
Bequeathing us for heritage
  A legacy of shame.

SONG OF THE FREED CAPTIVE.

I AM free! I am free! as I love to be,
  As the wind on my native hills ;
Free as the bird on the forest tree,
  As the trout in the silver rills !
I am free! I am free! as the booming bee
  Which presses the purple heath ;
Free as the waves of the rolling sea,
  Or the things that sport beneath.

I have burst the doors of my prison-house,
  And flee to the land I love ;
Its soil is under my bounding steps,
  And its glowing sky above ;
And rather than wear a captive's bands,
  Or pine in a dungeon's gloom,
I would basely fall by a caitiff's hands,
  And sleep in a nameless tomb.

THE YOUNG FRENCHMAN'S SONG.

COME over to France, to beautiful France—
The flower-land, the wine-land, the home of romance;
Come, fish in the rivers and sail on the lakes,
Or carelessly ramble through forests and brakes.
Come, saunter on footpaths o'ershaded by trees,
Or sit in the arbours in coolness and ease;
Come, drink the dark wine as it laughs in the glass,
And dance with the maids in the merry *ducasse.**
Nor judge ye them harshly, as wanting in worth,
Though they're swifter to love than the maids of the north.
Though they're swifter to sigh, and swifter to smile,
Their hearts are as warm and as wanting in guile;
Nor yet have their cheeks—have their lips less of charm,
Though Sol may have kissed them with kisses so warm.
Their glances are bright as their own summer's rays;
What maiden can love like a charming *Française?*
Would you live in a land of delight and romance,
Come over to France, to beautiful France.

END OF " TALES OF THE STORM BOUND."

---

* Ducasse, a church festival in the north of France.

Yarns

OF THE

Pentland Firth.

Yarns of the Pentland Firth.

PRELUDE.

THE NORSEMAN.

Most of the inhabitants of the northern shores of Caithness are of
Norse origin, but in no part of Scotland are the natives more strongly
attached to their birthplace. Point St. John, from which our Norseman
is supposed to have taken his survey, overlooks the Pentland Firth,
Orkney Islands, and Skerry Lighthouses, from the Caithness side.

ON Point St. John the Norseman stands alone,
   With Phœbus' setting glories round him thrown,
   And as he turns his gaze on either hand,
   He sees the great, the terrible, the grand:—
The dreaded Pentland's rough and rapid flow,
The wide Atlantic lit with evening's glow,
High Dunnet Head, the Pentland's towering lights,
The Orkney Islands, mountains, capes, and bights,
A lengthened stretch of bay-indented coast,
Whose cliffs arise, a bold defiant host,
From which the shattered might of ocean reels,
Like Phalanx broken on a thousand steels.
These meet the pensive Norseman's gaze by turns,
Warm in his breast the love of country burns;
He weaves his patriot thoughts in rugged verse,
Which thus to winds and waves he did rehearse :—

   "My Northern Clime! my Northern Clime!
      Though cold thy breezes be ;
   Though round my home the fleecy foam
      Is wafted from the sea;

Though late thy vernal flowers appear,
    Thy winters early come,
I would not for a milder clime
    Exchange my northern home.

" I would not give the Orcadian hills,
    The home of fog and breeze,
The battered cliffs that rear their crests
    Above the stormy seas,
The winding creeks, the elfin caves
    Along thy rugged coast,
For all the art-engendered grace
    That softer climes can boast.

" Let Southern prize his fatter fields,
    His sunny slopes and vales,
His leafy groves, whose rich perfumes
    O'erload the languid gales;
His sluggish streams and level meads,
    His plains unmarked and tame,
His crowded towns, where all is art,
    And Nature but a name:

" Give me the bold and beetling crags,
    Where whitening breakers roar ;
The bleak, untrodden mountain steep,
    Where eagles proudly soar;
Give me the beauties sternly grand
    Which Nature's hand doth trace,
Which daring man can never smoothe,
    Nor daring art efface.

" And where's the clime can match the charms
    That now before me lie—

The charms of mountain head and isle,
　　Of blending sea and sky ;
Those scenes supremely beautiful,
　　When winds and waters sleep ;
Those scenes tremendously sublime
　　When storms bestride the deep!

" My Northern Clime! my Northern Clime!
　　He is not son of thine
Who does not love the white sea-mew
　　And the sparkle of the brine.
The man who fears to brave the breeze,
　　Or breast the billow's foam,
Can not be sprung from northern sires,
　　Nor reared in Northman's home."

Thus spoke the Norseman on his rugged shore,
Where tempests howl and waves incessant roar,
Where wide morass and treeless wastes appear,
And winter's reign is lengthened and severe.
On that bare soil, beneath that cloudy sky,
Few beauties meet the Southern traveller's eye,
Yet there the Norseman builds the cherished home
To which he turns where'er his feet may roam,
Nor ever finds in any fairer zone
A land so dear, so beauteous as his own.

A FISHERMAN'S YARN.

THE WITCH'S WIND.

" COME, spin us a yarn, Will," cried I.
   " Yes, spin us a yarn," cried all,
" For here we must ride till the turn of the tide,
   Since the wind won't come at your call."

"I've whistled for half an hour," said Will,
   " Yet the stubborn breezes lag;
Though I've known a hurricane burst like a bomb
   At the simple wish of a hag!"

"Come, tell us about it, Will," cried I.
   " Yes, tell us," cried all the crew.
"Then, here," cried Will, as he lighted his pipe,
   "Goes a yarn that's Gospel true!"

"I was nearly out of my teens," said Will,
   "At home with the Skipper in Mey,
But could pull, I reckon, a stiffer oar
   Than I can at the present day.

" I had stood a hand at Wick, that year,
   And a capital catch we had;
And the Skipper himself had owned his luck
   Was never the worse for the lad.

" 'Twas after the boats had all come home,
   And the crops were nearly ripe,
That the Skipper sat on a Saturday eve
   Thoughtfully smoking his pipe.

" Then slowly struck the bowl on his nail
   Till the ash was wholly out;
His wont, when he schemed or cleared his mind
   Of any perplexing doubt.

E

" 'The Drover shall have the two-year-olds,
   The price he offers is fair;
'Twill cover their cost and keep, I think,
   And leave a trifle to spare.

" ' And the yearling creatures offered me,
   By Magnus Manson, of Walls,
Might be bought a bargain for ready cash,
   To stand in the others' stalls.'

" Thus far, to himself, and then to us—
   My elder brother and me—
' You'll see that the sheets and sails of the yawl,
   Are ready on Tuesday for sea.

" ' We'll start for Longhope with the early flood,
   And possibly may get back
If Magnus Manson and I can trade,
   In course of the ebb and slack.

" ' There's Magnus Manson's cousin, in Gills,
   Will lend us a hand across,
Or if he won't, with Benjamin Wares,
   We shan't be much at a loss.'

" On Tuesday all were ready to start,
   The Yawl in her neatest trim,
And we stood away from the Castle Bay,
   While the day was yet but dim.

" We reached Longhope with as fine a breeze
   As ever had filled a sail ;
But it chopped about to the West Nor'-West,
   And rose to a tearing gale.

" And from Tuesday morn till Friday night,
　Wind-bound in the Hope we lay,
Counting the hours on our finger ends,
　And chafing at our delay."

" Made you no account of the Orkney girls?
　Was there never an island flower
Along the Hope, or the heights of Walls,
　To quicken a lingering hour? "

Will vented a lengthened puff of smoke,
　Winked thrice with his weather eye,
Then forged ahead with his yarn again,
　Vouchsafing me no reply.

" Magnus Manson's cousin, from Gills,
　The Skipper, my brother, and I,
For three days lazily puffed our pipes,
　And sullenly scanned the sky.

" Came Magnus Manson down to the shore,
　And jesting at our distress—
' Why don't you trade for a wind,' asked he,
　' With our neighbour Canny Jess?'

" Said the Skipper, ' I've sailed for sixty years
　And whistled the breezes in ;
I've ne'er been beholden to Witch's wind,
　And I'm now too old to begin.'

" But Magnus Manson's cousin, from Gills,
　My elder brother and I,
Slipt to the shop for a quarter of tea,
　And visited Jess on the sly.

" We asked a light for our pipes; the witch
    Invited us to step ben,
And we saw before us a wrinkled wife,
    Of a good three score and ten.

" A wrinkled hag with a straggling beard,
    And a threatening nose and chin,
And a cast in her eye, that plainly said—
    ' I'm in league with the Man of Sin.'

" She greedily clutched the proffered tea,
    With a chuckle meant for mirth ;
' And you'll want a wind for this,' said she,
    ' To carry you over the Firth ?

" ' Well, first we'll try if your tea be good,
    Then one of yourselves shall run
And fetch me the bucket out of your boat,
    And we'll think if aught can be done.'

" The tea was tested, the bucket fetched,
    The witch herself went ben,
And clucked in the other end of the house
    As you've heard a clucking hen.

" At times a pig would seem to grunt,
    And a cat to caterwaul,
While we shuddered and wished us out of the house
    Riding the Firth in our yawl.

" 'Twas nigh an hour ere the hag returned
    With the bucket in her hand,
And in it three tiny wisps of straw,
    Each girt with a worsted band.

" 'This bucket,' she croaked, 'you'll place in your boat,
    As close to the prow as you may,
And all be ready to start from the Hope
    At the earliest peep of day.

" 'A favouring wind will fill your sails
    Till you've rounded Cantick Head ;
Till the flood has run, and the slack begun,
    But the breeze will then drop dead.

" 'And then you must throw a wisp of straw,
    A single wisp, in the sea;
And another breeze will fill your sails
    Till Gills lie under your lea.

" ' A second wisp must then be flung,
    And you'll scud to Harrow Bay;
But keep, as you love your life, the third,
    Till you've landed safe in Mey.'

" We stowed the straw as the witch had bid,
    And just as the sun appeared,
Down the Hope, with a favouring breeze,
    And round by the Head we steered.

" The wind drop'd dead as we passed the Head,
    A wisp was given to the seas ;
The sails were filled till the masts were bent,
    And we flew before the breeze.

" Down drop'd the wind for a second time,
    And a second wisp we threw ;
Then tacked and scudded as fine a board
    As ever the breezes blew.

" We left the Men of Mey on our lea,
    And down upon Harrow bore ;
And slackened sail at a cable's length
    From the wished and welcome shore.

" Then laughed the Skipper a scornful laugh—
    ' A snuff for the witch !' cried he,
And clutching the hindmost wisp of straw,
    He pitched it into the sea.

" Crack, crash ! went the thunder overhead ;
    Thick darkness fell on the deep ;
And round the boat-like famishing fiends,
    The billows began to leap.

" We rowed like men in the grip of death,
    Still heading, we thought, for land ;
But the angry demons of the deep
    Had taken our yawl in hand.

" And still the more that we urged ashore,
    The further they forced us off ;
Heaving us high on the mountain waves,
    And deep in the dreadful trough.

" Till how we went, or whither we went,
    We neither noted nor knew;
'Twas all that we could to bale the boat
    And keep her from broaching too.

" The thunder bellowed, the lightning flashed,
    'Twas all the light that we had;
The yawl must have perished in any hands
    Save the skilful hands of my dad.

" But just when the strength of all was spent,
  And the hopes of all but o'er,
She suddenly steadied a cable's length
  From the witch's cottage door.

" The tempest ceased, and the sun lit up
  The Hope like a burnished glass;
In our minds alone did a trace remain
  Of all that had come to pass.

" We left the Hope with the breeze of heaven,
  For not for the Orkney's worth
Had we tried again, with a witch's wind,
  To ferry the Pentland Firth."

"Bravo, Will! a capital yarn!"
  Cried I and each of the crew.
"Ah, well!" quoth Will, "you may call it a yarn,
  But I tell you it's Gospel true."

OLD ANNE'S YARN.

THE SWELCHIE OF STROMA.

The Whirlpool, called the Swelchie, is situated at the north-east corner of the Island of Stroma, in the Pentland Firth. It does not rage always, but in certain conditions of wind and tide would infallibly swamp or suck down any undecked vessel entering it. The loss of the boat and crew, which forms the subject of the following "Yarn," occurred early in the current century. The incidents connected with the catastrophe were furnished me by an eye witness, (the same into whose mouth I have put the narrative) and were corroborated by other aged persons in Stroma, and along the Northern Shores of Caithness. In my recital I have endeavoured to retain as nearly as possible the particulars as I received them.

THE Freswick men had bought a boat
  From a builder at Stromness,
And crossed the Firth to fetch her home
  When their land work ceased to press.

When the herring boats were all drawn up
  And the crops were under thatch,
When shoals of sillocks along the shores
  Were the fisherman's only catch—

They reached Stromness on an autumn eve,
  Each man in his trimmest guise ;
And spent the night in a gay carouse,
  Till they saw the sun arise.

At least such rumour reached our Isle,
  And was never since gainsaid ;
But God forbid that a word of mine
  Should wrong the unburied dead !

They left Stromness on a breezy morn,
  When the sun in the east was low,
And merrily coasted Gremsay Isle,
  And scudded through Scapa Flow.

By Hoxa Head and by Herston Bay,
   And close to the Barth they sailed ;
But ere they headed to cross the Firth,
   The wind had lessened and failed.

And the ebb set west in its fullest force,
   For the moon was three days old ;
And the Men of Mey were up in might,
   And the Swelchie swirled and howled.

The sails were doused when they ceased to draw,
   And the oarsmen rowed their best ;
But the boat got caught in the strongest ebb,
   And it hurried them west and west.

We sighted the boat, and knew the risk
   That the struggling boatmen ran ;
If once they entered the Swelchie stream,
   They must perish every man.

Half a mile to the south, and their boat
   Might catch our eddy and wait ;
Less by a length, and the Swelchie-stream,
   Was their sure and certain fate.

Our pilots signalled and shouted hard,
   But the men were surely fey ;
For they handled their tackle, landsmen-like,
   In an odd, unskilful way.

And neared and neared till we knew them all,
   Each face of the fated seven ;
Fast, fast they were in the Swelchie's clutch,
   And we cried for their souls to heaven.

Ah, me ! they could neither pull to land
   Nor out to the smoother sea ;
For the boat was reckless of helm and oar,
   And on to her doom sped she.

Our pilots shouted, our women screamed,
   The boatmen struggled hard,
And the frantic fear upon every face
   Was terrible to regard.

But ever the wilful boat plunged on,
   In spite of struggles and screams ;
For the Swelchie was sucking her in and in
   With the strength of a thousand streams.

And round and round, in the raging whirl,
   The boat and the boatmen flew ;
And nearer and nearer, at every sweep,
   To the yawning vortex drew.

And ropes, and sails, and oars, and masts,
   And thwarts went overboard ;
And jackets and vests in the Swelchie's maw.
   All flung with a swift accord.

For 'tis the thought of our fishermen
   That the Swelchie's mouth will close,
And miss its hold on a human prey,
   Whilst swallowing things like those.

But vainly oars, and masts, and sails,
   And jackets and vests were spent ;
The boat stood up, as it were, on end,
   And down with a plunge she went.

The Swelchie closed above its prey,
    With a plash and a sullen roar;
Nor wreck, nor rag, nor corpse of man,
    Has ever been cast on shore.

I am after seventy years of age,
    And my hair is white as spray,
But I mind how the boat went round and down
    Like a thing that happened to-day.

I am after seventy years to-day—
    I was under a dozen then—
Yet I still can hear the shriek of fear
    That followed the drowning men.

It rose above the surge's dash,
    And the Swelchie's sullen roar;
It startled the whole of the Uppertown,
    And pealed to the Southern shore.

My home is mean, and my fare is coarse,
    I am frail and full of pain;
The joy and pride of my life are past,
    And can never return again.

My friends are few, for the world is cold
    To the aged, poor, and low;
And whenever it pleases death to call
    Right glad shall I be to go.

But I'd rather linger a hundred years
    Behind the last of my kin,
Than die as they did who died that day,
    In the Swelchie's dismal din.

A PILOT'S YARN.

UNCLE DAN, THE PENTLAND FIRTH PILOT.

EXPLANATORY NOTE.—Between the German and the Atlantic Oceans, having the mainland of Scotland on the south and the Orkney Islands on the north, roll the turbid waters of the Pentland Firth. Except about an hour during "slack water," or turn of the tide, the current of the Pentland Firth averages nine or ten knots an hour, and cannot be stemmed by a mere sailing vessel. The pilots, by taking advantage of the numerous eddies, know how to hold their own; but few entire strangers attempt the passage of the Firth without the assistance of a pilot; and before education introduced a better morality, many a shipmaster was muleted in double fees, as in the manner set forth by our pilot in his yarn.

MY Uncle Dan was a moral man,
    And seldom drank or swore ;
  My Uncle Dan was an honest man,
    While he kept his foot on shore.
But, strange to tell of my Uncle Dan,
    Whenever he touched the brine,
His notions always got confused
    On the laws of yours and mine.

On shore, dishonesty shrank abashed
    At the sound of my Uncle's name,
For ne'er was he known to lift a plack
    To which another had claim ;
But, once upon board, such odds and ends
    As landsmen could scarce conceive
Would find their way to my Uncle's pouch,
    And never asked owner's leave.

The skippers who sailed the northern seas
    Knew Uncle's faults to a man ;
But they also knew that their ships were safe
    In the hands of my Uncle Dan ;

For Britain never produced his match
  At steering a vessel to berth,
And none in Caithness better knew how
  To pilot the Pentland Firth.

Bay and creek, and skerry and ness,
  And eddies great and small ;
Ebb and flood, and reef and roust,
  My Uncle knew them all.
The shores and the seas from east to west
  He knew for a hundred miles,
And the wells and flows, and sounds and hopes,
  To the farthest Orkney Isles.

Or east, or west, or north, or south,
  Wherever the wind might veer,
Blow high or low, run ebb or flow,
  My Uncle knew whither to steer.
But to my tale. 'Twas an autumn morn,
  If I do aright remember,
Exactly fifty years ago,
  Come the first of next November.

A smartish breeze was ruffling the ebb,
  An hour and a quarter run,
When over the eastern waters rose
  The sober November sun,
And, rounding Noss head, a gallant barque
  Attracted my Uncle's eye ;
For he knew she signalled a pilot out
  By the red flag half-mast high.

" Get ready, my boys," cried Uncle Dan,
  To myself, and cousins three—

" To Rob o' the Rock," and " Tom o' the Hole,"
 And " Peerie Will," and me.
" There's a pilot required for yonder barque,"
 (And he chuckled and rubbed his hands) :
" A stranger here, I know by his gear,
 And the awkward way that he stands.

" Get out in haste, and pilot him west,
 For the highest fee that you can ;
But leave a shot in the locker, my boys,
 'Twill be needed for Uncle Dan.
Run him up the way of the ' Men of Mey,'
 And tell him to stand to sea,
And then make off, for fear of squalls ; "
 And my Uncle redoubled his glee.

We launched our boat, the Mary Jane,
 And dashed across the tide,
Till we reached the barque, made fast a rope,
 And climbed the stranger's side ;
We found the barque of Jonathan's build,
 And her master, a swaggering blade,
" Guessed " he hadn't seen a " clearance " like ours
 Since he entered the timber trade.

He reckoned our " squires " didn't thank their sires,
 Nor much approve of the " spec' "
That cleared their "lots" of their timber plots,
 And he squirted the juice on the deck.
He screwed us down, and lower down,
 Begrudging our meanest fee ;
But I got charge of the Yankee barque,
 And west away stood we.

We rounded the rocks of Duncan's Bay,
  And skirted the " Western Bore,"
Standing now upon Stroma Isle,
  And now upon Canisbay shore ;
Tacking here with the breeze abreast,
  And there with the breeze abaft.
From eddy to ebb, with little way,
  But a wondrous show of craft.

And we left him west of the " Men of Mey ;"
  But little the Yankee " guessed "
That the wind and tide would soon unite
  With a force he could never resist.
He fought them long, but in spite of his teeth,
  He lost upon every tack,
For the westerly wind and the eastering flood
  Were carrying him swiftly back.

And down he went upon Swona Isle,
  Where he narrowly 'scaped a wreck,
Down, till he easted Skirza Head,
  And my Uncle stood upon deck.
Nor failed my Uncle to find a berth,
  Where the barque at anchor could ride,
Until he could pilot her west the Sound
  With the flow of the westering tide.

He sorely blamed the " lubberly swab "
  Who'd played the pilot before,
And cleverly pocketed odds and ends
  From out of the Yankee's store.
But Jonathan's " eye-teeth had been cut,"
  For a Yankee 'cute was he ;

And he fathomed our plans and Uncle Dan's
  Ere he entered the open sea.

And, asking my Uncle down below,
  He plied him so hard with grog
That the old man's tongue outran his wits,
  And his brains were lost in fog.
He drank and drank, till at last he sank
  With a heavy gurgling snore,
And lay completely spirit-logged
  On Jonathan's cabin floor.

He lay—he knew not how long he lay—
  Entranced in his drunken sleep ;
Nor if 'twas the tide or the Yankee's barque
  That carried him out to the deep.
But, lo ! when he opened his drowsy eyes,
  A 'wildered man was he,
To find himself in his little boat
  Far out on the open sea.

Outstretched in a punt of nine feet keel,
  Unmeet for the slightest gale,
With naught to shield his shivering frame
  Save a shred of tattered sail ;
Without his pickings, without his fee,
  With never a pipe to smoke,
With a racking head and a parching throat,
  My Uncle Dan awoke.

He started up and gazed around,
  With a wild, bewildered stare ;
The barque was gone, and he was alone,
  With the ocean everywhere.

He looked to the east—the cloudless sky
    Gave hopes of a tranquil night ;
He looked to the west—the setting sun
    Went down in a blaze of light.

He looked to the north, he looked to the south,
    But as far as the eye could sweep,
Around and around the only bound
    Was the meeting of sky and deep ;
With never a boat, with never a ship,
    With never a floating thing,
Save only he and his tiny punt
    In the midst of the mighty ring.

He had battled the " Bores of Duncan's Bay,"
    He had tossed in the " Men of Mey,"
He had weathered the wrath of wind and wave,
    Till his hair was scanty and grey.
The raging winds and the roaring floods,
    He had battled them like a man,
For there wasn't a braver stept in shoes
    Than my brave old Uncle Dan.

But now, though he sat on a smiling sea,
    On an evening calm and mild,
His head drooped over his hopeless breast,
    And he wept like a sucking child ;
For how could he pass the dreary night
    Afar on the open sea,
In the sprites of the deep, the ghosts of the drowned,
    In the Finmen's company ?

He wasn't without his trust in Heaven—
    Your seaman is seldom so—

Though he oft forgets the Power that saves
  When the storm hath ceased to blow ;
Though he bid religion pass to-day,
  And call again to-morrow ;
Though he's oft a thoughtless, dissolute dog,
  He's seldom an Atheist thorough.

Your blinded advocate of chance,
  Whom the churchmen cannot reform,
Who laughs at faith, and sneers at hope—
  Put him out to sea in a storm.
Put him far at sea in an open boat,
  And alone, like my Uncle Dan,
And I'll lay you my yawl to a schooner's punt
  You would find him an altered man.

My uncle thought on his friends at home,
  The wife he might ne'er see more,
And wrung his hands, and wept and prayed,
  As he never had prayed on shore.
'Twere long to tell how he lay becalmed
  On the broad Atlantic's breast,
Or number the risks of his tiny bark
  When a breeze sprang up in the west.

'Twere sad to hear of his raging thirst,
  With nothing to quench its fire,
Or the hunger that gnawed his vitals up
  With the fangs of fierce desire.
Enough to say that a second day
  And a third dread night had run,
Ere a coaster picked my uncle up
  At the rising of the sun.

Nor ever again was my Uncle Dan
　　The pilot he'd wont to be ;
He would never climb to a stranger's deck,
　　Nor hear of a double fee.
He pulled an oar with a feebler stroke,
　　And steered with unsteady hand ;
He was ever the last to put to sea,
　　And the first to spring to land.

He never went west of the "Men of Mey,
　　Nor into the open seas,
But he shivered and shook in a nervous fit,
　　Like a sail in a ruffling breeze.
Some twenty years have passed away
　　Since my uncle stowed the oar,
And hoisted sail, to stand, as we trust,
　　For a fairer, happier shore.

And this was the last advice he gave
　　To myself and my cousins three—
To "Rob o' the Rock," and "Tom o' the Hole,"
　　And "Peerie Will," and me:
"Let Conscience stand at the wheel," he said,
　　"And Honesty heave the log;
Keep a sharp look-out on a Yankee ship,
　　And be sparing of Jonathan's grog;

" Beware of the wicked one whose nets
　　Are spread for the soul of man,
And whenever you think of a double fee,
　　Remember your Uncle Dan."

———◦╬◦╬◦———

THE AUTHOR'S YARN.

THE LAST CRUISE OF THE DWARF.

The Dwarf, a small boat of about ten feet keel, was the property of several partners, one of whom was represented by Finlay MacLeod, a youth of about seventeen years of age. A larger boat had been purchased by the "Company," and the Dwarf was sold to be employed as a "lighter" at Wick. A few days previous to the departure of the Dwarf from Canisbay, I accepted the invitation of Finlay MacLeod to have a farewell sail in the little boat. Caught by a sudden squall, we ran before it, as described, with unshortened sail, and it was the opinion of Mr. John Gibson, my nautical "guide, philosopher, and friend," that we had been in imminent danger of running our tiny craft to the bottom of the sea. So momentous an occurence had, of course, to be commemorated in verse. "The Last Cruise of the Dwarf" found its way into *The N rthern Ensign*, and, slight as the thing may be, I believe its non-appearance among my "Yarns of the Pentland Firth" would be considered a grave omission by some of my friends in the "far north."

IT was Saturday, the nineteenth day
   Of the pleasant month of June,
And the sun o'er the Kirk of Canisbay
   Proclaimed it the hour of noon ;
A gentle breeze from the south-sou'-west
   Invited us out to sail ;
So gentle it was that we never dreamt
   Of its bursting a tearing gale ;
When we launched the Dwarf at the "Old Distil,"
   And west away stood we,
With a wind that bellied our single sail,
   But barely ruffled the sea.
Finlay MacLeod took rudder in hand,
   And I got charge of the sail—
I, who had never, in seaman's phrase,
   Been a mile from a brown cow's tail!
The Red Rock passed, and the Black Hole passed,
   And scouring across the Bay,
Right speedily fleeted the little Dwarf,
   Till we reached the Men of Mey.

Then the wind it veered, and a black cloud peered
   On the brow of the western height;
Cried Finlay MacLeod—"Look out for squalls,"
   And Finlay MacLeod was right.
For scarce had we put the Dwarf about,
   On the homeward tack to stand,
When over the Bay, like a thunder-clap,
   The black squall blew from the land.
"Sheet home! sheet home!" cried Finlay MacLeod;
   "Hard home it is!" shouted I;
As through the waves, like a wingèd thing,
   Our vessel began to fly.
" Ho, here she goes!" cried Finlay MacLeod;
   "But it's all that the Dwarf can do."
I looked a-head, and the roaring sea
   Was terrible to my view.
"No fear! no fear!" cried Finlay MacLeod;
   "But I wish that we could reeve!"
I looked abaft, and the bubbling brine
   Was wetting Finlay's sleeve.
And the sky grew blacker over head,
   And stiffer the tempest blew,
But through the foaming waters the Dwarf,
   With her sail unshortened, flew.
She cut the waves as her prow had been
   Not of timber, but burnished steel;
She dashed them off like a man-of-war,
   Though only of ten feet keel.
" Well done, brave Dwarf!" cried Finlay MacLeod;
   "Let the tempests rage their fill;
We'll soon be out of their fury's reach,
   For yonder's the 'Old Distil!'"
But the black clouds burst, and the big drops gushed
   From the fountains of the sky;

And before the Dwarf had touched the shore
    Not a stitch of our clothes was dry.
Yet we drew her high on the pebbled beach—
    For we've neither pier nor wharf—
And thus had Finlay MacLeod and I
    Our last cruise in the Dwarf!
For the men of Wick have heard of her,
    And thither she's bound to go,
To ply midst the billows of their Bay,
    When the wild nor'-easters blow.
For the Wickians know that the gallant Dwarf,
    O'er the crested waves will spin,
When even the life-boat can't put out,
    And the steamer can't put in.

LOST AT SEA IN A FOG.

THE STROMA MAN'S YARN.

The inhabitants of the island of Stroma bring all their peats, or turf fuel, from the mainland, and chiefly in the summer months, when darkness is scarcely perceptible, but dense night fogs are of frequent occurrence in those high latitudes.

THE morn had arisen in cloudless light,
    And the noon been warm and dry;
But heavy dews began to fall
    As the set of day drew nigh.
Thick fogs crept over the western main
    And down on the Orkney hills,
Warning my brother John and I
    To start from the haven of Gills.
A Stroma man would have said we chose
    To cross at an awkward time;
For the flood was only three hours run,
    And the moon was in her prime.

But we feared the fog and trusted the wind—
    A breeze from the south-south-east—
To carry us over and into the tail
    Of the eastern eddy at least;
And thus, about nine o'clock at night,
    On the twelfth of last July,
From the haven of Gills for Stroma Isle
    Stood my brother John and I.
Our boat was down to the water's edge,
    With a heavy load of peats;
Fore and aft, from timbers to thwarts,
    Till we scarce could reeve the sheets.
But west away to the Men of Mey
    Our course was clear and quick;
And there we met with a raging flood
    And a fog exceeding thick.
The wind dropt down from a steady breeze
    To unfrequent, fitful blasts;
Down, till the lately bellying sails
    Flapped idly round the masts.
And then we rowed with might and main,
    But we numbered only two;
The wind was dead, and the fog was dense,
    And east, with the flood, we flew.
We missed the Isle and the eddy too,
    And still went drifting east,
Till the boat began to heave and pitch,
    And the sea to foam like yeast.
"If you love your life," cried my brother John,
    As he hastily shipped his oar;
"If you love your life, pitch out the peats,
    Or we'll swamp in the Western Bore!"
And the boat was cleared as she ne'er had been,
    Nor ever again may be;

But we rose and fell on the heavy swell,
    And never shipped a sea.
And soon we were drifting smoothly on
    But as swiftly as before;
Yet we sat in silent thankfulness
    To have passed the Western Bore.
Nor did we now attempt to row,
    Though we sat with oars in hand;
We were just as like to pull out to sea
    As we were to pull in to land;
For the wind had dropt, the flood run down,
    And the fog obscured the light;
No compass had we, and thus you may see,
    How we lost our bearings quite.
So we drifted away, or lazily lay,
    With a dull and drowsy motion,
As we rose and fell with the ceaseless swell
    Of the never-slumbering ocean.
And still as the lingering hours dragged past,
    And we drifted lazily on,
Not of doubt or of fear, but of hope and cheer,
    Spoke I and my brother John.
Each had his doubts, you may well conceive,
    'But his doubts were unexprest;
Each had his fears, you may well believe,
    But he lock'd them in his breast.
I own that I started once in fright,
    In the midst of a dozing dream,
And cried to my brother John to row,
    For we were in the Swelchie-stream.
And we rowed perchance for half-an-hour,
    Till smoother seas were found;
And we lay again in the open main,
    With our misty curtains round.

And once my brother roused me up,
    And bade me ply my oar,
For he knew the land was close at hand
    By the breakers' constant roar.
But we sat for the most in dull suspense,
    And waited the dawn of day,
When haply the glorious sun might shine
    And the fogs might fly away.
It was cold indeed, but scarcely dark,
    Through the whole of the tedious night,
For the only sign that day had broke
    Was a change in the line of light.
And at last the sun displayed his face,
    Yet high in the east was he,
Ere ever the misty curtain rose,
    Revealing the tranquil sea.
And we found ourselves in the western main,
    A league to the west of Hoy;
But the flood was bearing us steadily east,
    And we hailed our home with joy.
I do not say that we suffered much
    From either fatigue or fright,
Nor yet that we ran a deadly risk
    In a tranquil summer night.
I have known of men who have dared as much,
    For a double share of grog;
But still it's far from a pleasant thing
    To be lost at sea in a fog.

"LITTLE AGNES."

THE FISHERMAN'S DAUGHTER.

IN the island called "the Mainland,"
   Largest of the Orcadian group,
On a little plot of plain land
   Lying near "The Fishers' Hope,"
Stood, in years long since departed,
   Honest Magnus Manson's cot.
Magnus, ah! a better-hearted
   Never net nor cod-line shot.
Daring Magnus! still the herring
   Found in him their fellest foe ;
Still the bottle-noses erring
   'Mongst the inlets felt his blow.
Strong, and brave, and wise was Magnus,
   Fisher of the olden style;
And his daughter, "Little Agnes,"
   Was the beauty of the isle.
"Little Agnes," so her father,
   So the neighbours called her all—
"Little," from affection, rather
   Than because the maid was small,
For among the Scottish nation
   The diminutive endears,
And has often slight relation
   Or to stature or to years.
Whether full or empty handed,
   Still with equal power to please,
To his cottage, when he landed,
   Went our "Toiler of the Seas."
Agnes still had smiles to greet him,
   Words of welcome for her sire,
Comfort everywhere to meet him,
   Grateful food and grateful fire.

Never wearied him with cravings
    For attire above their lot,
Ever made their scanty savings
    Deck themselves and deck their cot.
Peace, content, and joyous laughter
    Shared that home unknown to guile.
Happy Father! happy daughter!
    In their misty northern isle.
Sad it was that the deceiver
    Ever found an entrance there;
Sad that e'er he found believer
    In a maid so pure and fair.
Forced by some marine disaster,
    Wherewithal she could not cope,
Lo! a ship, a tall three-master,
    Sheltered in the "The Fishers' Hope"—
Lay for many weeks together,
    Safe within its land-locked bay,
Until fairer wind and weather
    Let her rig and sail away.
And her Captain, young and handsome,
    Skilled in every pleasing art,
Bore a captive none could ransom—
    Agnes Manson's guileless heart.
Lightly spoken, lightly broken,
    Faith and troth of gallant gay,
Backed by fitting true-love token,
    Gave he, ere he sailed away.
Yet the luckless maiden never,
    Never saw her lover more;
And a weariness for ever
    Hung around her island shore.
Life for her had lost its gladness,
    Life for her was settled gloom,

And its never-flitting sadness
   Weighed and crushed her to the tomb.
Anxiously the loving father
   Strove to raise the drooping maid,
Would have died of hunger rather
   Than that she had wanted aid—
Aid of doctor, aid of cordial,
   Aid of aught the earth could give,
To avoid the fatal ordeal,
   Bid her smile again and live.
And the maid herself would gladly,
   For his sake, have stayed her doom ;
But they lengthened swiftly, sadly,
   Did the shadows of the tomb.
And she drooped as droops the lily
   When the vernal Zephyr flings
Vapours frequent, white, and chilly,
   Frosty vapours from his wings.
Drooped and drooped, but ne'er accused,
   Closer clutched the prized love-token,
Till the silver chord was loosed,
   And the golden bowl was broken.
Then they laid her down to sleep,
   Near the great church of St. Magnus;*
Nor can tempest's fiercest sweep
   Break the rest of "Little Agnes."

* The Cathedral of Kirkwall.

MAN THE LIFEBOAT!

At Wick, in the month of September, 1857, I was an eye-witness
of the events which I have endeavoured to commemorate in the following ballad. Captain Tudor, since deceased, was harbour-master at the
time, and, as the herring fishing was just at its height, there were many
thousands of strangers in the town.

" MAN the lifeboat!" The words at first
    Where whispered by a few.
"Man the lifeboat!" from mouth to mouth
    The cry of omen flew.
It pealed from thrice three thousand throats
    On Pultney's grassy slopes,
To sinking hearts in yonder ship
    It bore reviving hopes.
"Man the lifeboat! but who would dare
    To launch on such a sea,
With death before and death behind,
    A-weather and a-lea?
Three days a tempest from the east
    Had lashed the German waves,
And many gay and gallant tars
    Swept down to ocean graves.
Three days ago yon helpless hull
    Careered a gallant bark,
Her timbers firm, her rigging sound
    And cheerful as the lark,
Her sailors sang their merry songs,
    Their liquor gaily quaffed,
Till swoop'd the Demon of the storm,
    And smote her fore and aft.
Then went the rigging by the board,
    The vessel ceased to steer,
And floundered, helpless, in the seas,
    While death to all seemed near.

Three dreary days, the waif of chance,
　　She drifted to and fro ;
Her crew, with rum and horror wild,
　　Awaiting fate below.
But after noontide on the third
　　The storm began to lull,
And then the raging Bay of Wick
　　Received the battered hull.
The Bay—ah ! there the waves leap'd up,
　　Bent round their crests and broke,
While at their roar along the shore
　　A thousand echoes woke.
The main was wild, but wilder yet
　　The billows of the Bay,
And only chains and anchors now
　　Might swift destruction stay.
For should the vessel touch those waves,
　　That moment were her last ;
The shuddering crew the dangers view,
　　And forth the anchors cast.
Hurrah ! hurrah ! the anchors bite,
　　The ship may yet be saved ;
Ye waves have vainly lashed her sides,
　　Ye winds around her raved !
But ever from the open main
　　Huge rollers strike the ship,
And force her farther in and in
　　At every heave and dip,
Until to gazers from the shore—
　　Ten thousand now are these—
She seems to hang upon the rim
　　Of those white-crested seas.
" Man the lifeboat ! " 'twas then the cry
　　From all the shores burst out ;

But daring seamen viewed the Bay,
    And shook their heads in doubt.
Down came the captain of the port
    And strode along the shore ;
A Tudor he, whose pedigree
    Was traced to kings of yore.
And he was worthy of his name
    And royal pedigree,
For never trod on British soil
    A braver man than he.
And first he viewed the tossing ship,
    And then the shrinking crowd,
And then addressed the seamen round
    In dauntless tones and loud—
" My lads, shall brothers drift to death
    While we make idle moan?
Put out the boat!—I'll find a crew,
    Or board the ship alone!"
Not swifter coward fear invades
    The band whose leader flies,
Than at the captain's dauntless words
    Did hope and courage rise.
Men ran the boat upon the rocks
    That dip to meet the wave;
The first that sprang upon her thwarts
    Was he, that captain brave.
And promptly followed to his lead
    Her complement of men,
The deftest steersman of the port,
    And sturdy oarsmen ten.
Strong, willing shoulders shoved her off,
    She leapt amidst the foam,
And bounded o'er the crested waves,
    As ocean were her home.

She passed the ship, swung round, and neared
   To seize the ready rope,
While from the shore there pealed a cheer
   Of mingled joy and hope.
Short-lived delight!—as swift as thought
   A monster billow rose,
Bent round its crest, and boat and ship
   Enfolded in its close;
As if the Demon of the Storm—
   The Dragon of the Bay—
Had leaped upon the daring men
   Who sought to wrest his prey.
The ringing cheer became a wail,
   Or died on every lip,
When that dread billow swallowed up
   Alike the boat and ship.
The wave rolled on, the ship arose ;
   With streaming clothes and hair
The crew around the broken mast
   Clung, grouped in grim despair.
The boat arose; three gallant lads
   Were struggling in the sea,
And far and wide the oars were strewn,
   A-weather and a-lee.
"Ho, fling the buoys!" the buoys were flung;
   Two gallant lads were saved,
But high and higher o'er the third
   The billows plashed and raved.
He struggled long, but sank at last
   Beneath incessant shocks;
Whilst swiftly drifted in the boat
   Towards the jagged rocks.
But, lo! a floating oar was caught,
   And towards the river's bed

The sturdy steersman's dexterous arm
  Right firmly kept her head.
She drifted through the raging surge,
  She reached the crowded strand;
The solid ground again received
  The drenched and lessened band.
But only for a breathing space;
  Their task they re-began—
Forced out to that ill-fated ship,
  And rescued every man.

I've heard of men on battle-fields
  Who smote their foes like grain
Which falls beneath the reaper's scythe
  When harvest clothes the plain;
And I have heard their praises sung
  Until my heart was sick;
The braves my Muse would rather sing
  Are braves like those at Wick;
Not men who smite their fellow-men
  On fields of mortal strife,
But men who from the jaws of death
  Have snatched a brother's life.

END OF "THE PENTLAND FIRTH YARNS."

NOTE.—I cannot conclude " Yarns of the Pentland Firth," without
expressing my gratitude to Mr. John Gibson, fisherman, and occasional
pilot, now or lately residing in the parish of Canisbay, in the County
of Caithness, whose nautical knowledge was always at my service, so
long as I was in a position to avail myself of it, and for lack of which,
I fear, many errors in respect of winds and tides may have crept into
those ".Yarns," which it has been impossible for me to submit to him
for correction or approval.

A Rapid Rhyme

OF

`

A Merry Time;

Being some account of the Second Annual
Sports of the Sheffield Scottish Athletic
Club, done into verse, on the day on
which the said Sports were held,
namely, June 22nd, 1874.

The Scottish Sports.

INTRODUCTORY NOTICE.

In the year 1874 the Sheffield Scottish Athletic Club, numbering above 200 members, under the Presidency of Councillor H. F. Crighton, resolved to make extensive preparations for their Annual Sports. The athletic talent of the Club, assiduously trained, was supplemented by professional skill of varied character from "our native North," and a grand gala-day was widely advertised. The result was a monster gathering in the Bramall-lane grounds, and a very successful day's amusement until the immense concourse of spectators in some mysterious way broke through the barriers which had been erected to separate them from the performers. After this unfortunate occurrence the remaining part of the programme was only partially carried out, and with much inconvenience to the performers. As Poet Laureate to the Club, the writer had promised to read at the dinner, given under the auspices of the Club, in the Cutlers' Hall, immediately after the Sports, a rhymed account of the proceedings of the day, but the break-down of arrangements at Bramall-lane threw the dinner so late that the reading could not take place. At a subsequent meeting, the Club adopted the "Rhyme" by acclamation, and caused it to be neatly printed for circulation among the members.

ARGUMENT.

Invocation.—Description of the showery morning and subsequent clearing-up of the weather.—The gathering.—The march from the Royal Hotel, Old Haymarket, to Bramall-lane.—The Scottish bagpipes.—Glance at the spectators assembled at Bramall-lane.—The Sports.—The bursting of the barriers.—The finale.

PART FIRST.

AWAKE! O, Muse of Pindar,
    That sang the Grecian games,
The runners and the wrestlers
    Of great historic names;

The men of bone and sinew,
  Of courage, skill, and might,
Who bravely stood for fatherland
  In many a famous fight:
Assist me, Muse of Pindar,
  To sing the glorious day
When our Athletic Club went forth,
  Bedight in grand array.
That day arose in splendour,
  The glorious sun on high,
His fairest radiance scatter'd wide
  To burnish earth and sky.
That day, from field and forest,
  Rich bursts of music rung,
As if the feather'd chorists all
  Their harps anew had strung ;
But ever as the morn advanced,
  The thunder showers came down,
And wreaths of smoke and murky cloud
  O'erspread the gloomy town:
The anxious Scot survey'd the sky,
  Or tapp'd his weather glass,
And tho' the earth was parch'd and dry,
  He pray'd the rain might pass.
And, as in answer to his prayers,
  The clouds were roll'd away,
And cheer'd and freshen'd by the showers,
  Outburst the glorious day.
That day will live in memory
  For ages yet untold ;
Within the annals of our Club
  That day will shine in gold.
'Twas June the twenty-second,
  In eighteen seventy-four,

When Sheffield saw the gallant Scotch
    Towards her centre pour;
From street and square they sally,
    A great and goodly train,
To march from Norfolk Market Place
    Away to Bramall-lane,
To run and wrestle, leap and dance,
    A score of ways to show
Which has the arm of greatest strength,
    The nimblest heel and toe.
The Elliotts and the Wilsons
    Have heard our Club's appeals,
The Irvines, Stobies, Kemps, and Grants,
    The Murrays and McNeils;
The Tears and McIntoshes,
    The Simpsons not behind,
The Hawleys, Hendersons, and Youngs,
    The men of might and mind;
The Pattersons, the Innises,
    The Corries, Cleggs, and Blairs,
The Spiers, the Ushers, Duffs, and Boyds,
    The Fosters, and the Fairs:
The Cummings and McKenzies,
    The Bruces and the Browns,
The Herons, Marshalls, Trains, and Milnes,
    From this and farther towns;
The Hyslops and the Hastings,
    The Gilmours and the Gows,
The Lindsays, Robertsons, and Gunns,
    The Baillies and the Dows,
The Campbells and McEwens,
    Allured by honour's spells,
The Cowans, Robinsons, and Rudds,
    McDowalls, Doves, and Bells;

The Urquharts and the Davidsons,
　The Parkers and the Prests,
The Turners, Housleys, Smalls, and Smiths,
　The Bissetts, and the Wests,
Throw care and commerce all aside,
　At ledger and at till,
Let simpering girls and 'prentice boys
　Do business as they will.
Bid craftsmen's strokes unheeded ring
　On metals and on logs,
Fling writs and warrants to the winds,
　And physic to the dogs,
And march to Bramall lane to prove
　Their prowess in the field,
And show themselves the sons of sires
　Who knew not how to yield.
They are coming! they are coming!
　By highway and by rail,
On foot, on horse, in coach, and car,
　The currents never fail.
From Glasgow and from Edinbro',
　From Manchester and Leeds,
And fifty smaller towns arrive
　The men of doughty deeds.
The merry maids and matrons,
　In silks and satins dight,
Their faces radiant as the morn,
　Their eyes the stars of night,
From north and south, from east and west,
　Wherever life can be,
The human streams are pouring in
　To swell the living sea;
Amidst them all, our President,
　Our counsellor and head,

The famed umbrella* laid aside—
    The cruel carter's dread—
In bonnet, sporran, kilt, and plaid,
    The costume of his clan,
Our noble Crighton takes his place,
    The leader of our van.
O, never from our country—
    Our own beloved north—
A braver heart, a truer heart,
    A warmer heart came forth.
And near him, in the vast array,
    In medalled pomp we see
Great Dinnie, Fleming, and McNeil,
    And nimble-toed McPhee—
Athletes whom our Britannia,
    Whom all the world, doth know,
They come to-day for doughty deeds,
    And not for empty show.
Nor must the Muse omit to mark,
    Amidst the front array,
Dunlop advance, with sword in hand,
    As best befits the day—
Dunlop,† who at our Club's appeal,
    Hath left our native land,
And brought with him, to grace our sports,
    His gay and gallant band.
But hark! the pipers all strike up,
    Before us roll the drums,
I hear a thousand voices shout
    "The Scotch procession comes!"
Pipe of the Scottish mountaineers,
    Your accents loud and shrill

* Councillor Crighton had some weeks previously chastised with his umbrella a carter who was beating his horse unmercifully in a public part of Sheffield.

† Lieutenant Dunlop had come from Glasgow, bringing with him the pipers of the 105th Lanarkshire Highland Volunteer Brigade.

Through all my heart, through all my veins,
  Through all my being thrill.
The faces round me fade away,
  The scene before me flies,
My native glen, my cottage home,
  Auld Scotia's hills arise!
The auld kirkyard appears again,
  With rude memorials spread,
The gloomy graves have rendered back
  My nearest, dearest dead.
I hear my father's living voice,
  They crowd around me all—
The friends above, whose dust I heard
  The kindred dust let fall!
My mother gives me greeting warm,
  I mark her joyous face,
I 've leapt o'er intervening time,
  And intervening space.
Be still my heart; down, down, my sighs,
  Pipe of the mountaineers,
Awaken mirth or martial ire,
  Not thoughts for grief and tears!
Recall how at Coomassie late
  Your martial music peal'd,
When Afric's swarthy children heard,
  And trembling fled the field;
Recall to us how Britons once
  In distant Lucknow pent,
By every form of direful death
  Which savage men invent,
Heard safety in thy welcome strains,
  Upraised the drooping head,
Felt hope revive in every heart,
  Whence every hope had fled ;

And felt again within their veins
    The glowing currents run,
As foes dissolved at thine approach
    Like mists before the sun!
Recall the fierce Crimean fights,
    The field of Waterloo,
Where Scottish valour, fired by thee,
    Unnumber'd odds o'erthrew;
Recall my wanderings long ago
    Amidst the Scottish hills,
The leafy woods, the roaring floods,
    The gently murmuring rills;
Recall the lightly bounding step,
    The bright and beauteous head;
Bring back the young, the fair, the gay,
    But bring not back the dead!
Down, down, my heart! cease, cease, my tears!
    Away delusive dreams!
Once more I tread the stony streets
    Amidst the living streams.

———————— ⚬⚬ ————————

PART SECOND.

FROM street to street we roll along,
    A great and goodly train,
We reach the field of peaceful strife—
    The famous Bramall lane.
And the people—ah! the people,
    How they swarm and buzz and hum,
We are filled to overflowing,

But the cry is still "They come!"
  Horny-handed sons of labour,
    Wealthy squires and learned dons,
They are streaming in in rivers,
    Orinocos, Amazons.
Ne'er when England's pick'd eleven
    Against Yorkshire's best competes,
Was such gathering, squeezing, crushing,
    As to see the Scotch athletes.
Men in kilts and knickerbockers,
    Doeskins, tweeds, and corduroys,
Gentlemen of birth and breeding,
    Coinless roughs and ragged boys!
And the ladies—how describe them?
    I have struggled, panted, toil'd,
But hyperbole is baffled,
    Poor comparison is foil'd!
At it, yet again, my Pegasus,
    You can but try and fail;
Hold your breath, and strain your sinews,
    Over ditch and hedge and rail!

  *   *   *   *   *

As summer lawn is girdled round
    By many-flowered parterre,
The living circle round the green
    Is dotted by the fair;
The modest daisy lifts the head,
    The roses bud and blow,
The pinks and marigolds shine out,
    The bright carnations glow;
Bloom on, bloom on, ye human flowers,
    Amidst the living hosts;
Bloom on, unscathed by scorching suns,
    Unnipp'd by early frosts.

*   *   *   *   *   *

But while the Muse surveys the fair,
   The merry sports proceed;
Already, nimble-footed youths
   Have signalised their speed:
A Baillie and a McIntosh
   Have taught us how to walk;
Nor yet could Corrie's splendid spurt
   Their just ambition baulk.
A Hastings, a McKenzie,
   Have shown us how to run;
Nor yet could Marshall snatch away,
   The laurels they have won.
The Dinnie, and the Fleming too,
   Have each put forth their strength;
The former thrown the heavy shot
   A never-equalled length;
And Gilmour, of our Scottish Club,
   Hath well sustained his name;
Though far behind the giant pair,
   Of world-extended fame.
And now the vaulter, pole in hand,
   Advances, runs, and springs,
And rises o'er the airy bar,
   As if his feet had wings;
'Tis Hastings now; 'tis Thompson now;
   "They do not leap, but fly!"
So shout the crowd, with plaudits loud,
   Which rend the upper sky.
Again come on, like hunted deer,
   The runners in the race;
And Hanbidge, Pinder, Lindsay, prove
   The men of swiftest pace.

Again they throw, again they leap,
Again the great athletes
Far, far outstrip our common men,
And shame their smaller feats;
Though well for men of common mould,
Our youths sustain their part,
And throw with arms of pith and power,
And leap with grace and art.
And now, ye wrestlers, stand forth!
Ha! sound the trump again!
Will none advance to shake a fall
With Scotland's champions twain?
Where art thou, man of Attercliffe?
Come forward, venturous Blair; *
Advance, and meet the Scotch athletes,
And grapple if you dare!
In vain, in vain the challenge rings,
No venturous Blair stands forth,
Alone are grappling on the green,
The giants of the North;
See how they struggle for the grip;
See how their limbs entwine;
Behold agility and grace,
With giant strength combine.
Now Dinnie throws, now Fleming throws,
Thrice do they grapple fast;
Thrice tug and strain, but Dinnie stands,
Twice victor at the last.
What stirs the mighty multitude?
Why do they sway and bend?
Why rolls the lower circle's rim
To crush the upper end?

* A Mr. Blair, from Attercliffe, had entered his name for the Wrestling Match, but failed to appear at the moment of trial.

Assist me, lions of the Press—
　　Ye swift reporting men—
Apply to this ill-starr'd event,
　　Your deeply piercing ken:
Within the compass of your minds,
　　The whole affair embrace;
Explain, expound, expose it all,
　　How did the thing take place?
Deceivers! jugglers! mountebanks!
　　Your skill is mere pretence!
Stand forth, Philosophy,* my friend,
　　My more than second sense;
Thou seest, explainst, exposest all,
　　Conception, throes, and birth;—
The weight which press'd the upper end
　　Upheaved the lower earth.
Upheaved the earth, and forward hurl'd
　　The swaying, surging mass;
And forced it on the upper end,
　　Till class extinguished class.
Oh! never more let multitude
　　Nor management be blamed,
Since thou hast thus, in Mother Earth,
　　The real offender named.
Thanks, thanks to thee, Philosophy,
　　For none besides could tell,
How order all at once was changed,
　　To this confused pell-mell.
But where are ye, ye men in blue?
　　Exert your vaunted power:
Wave, Robert, wield your truncheon now,
　　Behold the day and hour!

---

* While the writer was cudgelling his brains how to account for the breaking-down of the barriers, a spectator, with a merry twinkle in his eye, observed to another near him, that no doubt the unfortunate occurrence, like the bursting of the Water Company's reservoir at the " Sheffield Flood," was occasioned by a " landslip."

Like mighty dam that bursts its banks,
   And rolls resistless on,
The multitude o'erspreads the field,
   And all control is gone.
Yet still the persevering Scots,
   Play on the tangled game;
And brave competitors come forth,
   To wrest a wreath from fame:
And fain, right fain am I to sing
   Each feat of skill and speed;
But here my order-loving Muse
   Refuses to proceed;
Like that instructor of my youth,
   Long freed from teacher's woes,
Who always made instruction cease,
   When'er confusion rose.
Though Milnes, and Brown, and many more,
   The list of victors swell;
Their gallant feats, my stubborn Muse
   Leaves other bards to tell.
One final "spurt" will she put on,
   One final deed rehearse;
One feat of strength, for greater ne'er
   Was told in prose or verse.
Oh, ne'er since mighty Samson,
   As Holy Writ relates,
Strode off in pure derision
   With Gaza's ponderous gates;
Oh, ne'er since great Goliath shook
   The iron-headed spear,
Which sent through Israel's trembling ranks
   A thrill of rage and fear;
Oh, ne'er since Hercules wielded
   The club which none withstood—

The club which quell'd the Hydra
   And monsters of such brood:
Since Milo raised the struggling ox
   Above his shoulders broad,
And round the Roman race-course,
   'Midst thundering plaudits strode—
Oh, ne'er was greater feat of strength
   By wondering mortals seen,
Than that display'd when Dinnic raised
   The caber from the green.
With graceful ease he lifted up
   The caber high in air,
Strode backward and strode forward,
   A moment poised it fair,
Then centering all the mighty strength
   Which none save he can show,
He heaved it up, and whirl'd it round
   In one tremendous throw!
My song is done—a rapid song,
   A careless song I know,
Unequally the numbers came,
   Unequal they must go.
Tho' critic, with his gange and rule,
   Should measure every line,
Declare my numbers inexact—
   Abhorrent to the "Nine,"
Tho' sage should shake the sapient head,
   And bigot fiercely blame,
The world declare my "crude attempt"
   Unworth reward or fame,
Unpraised, unheard, neglected—I
   To Poesy's skirts would cling,
For Nature gave me, at my birth,
   A ceaseless need to sing!

Miscellaneous

Poems.

Miscellaneous Poems.

PRELUDE.

'NEATH cares—an ever growing load—
The paths of penury I've trode
For many years with aching feet;
Yet, I have stooped along the way,
To pluck a flower or leafy spray,
And found their fragrance sweet.

The daisy, or the buttercup,
The smallest gem that lifteth up
To heaven its shining face,
Hath made my burdens lighter seem,
A brighter radiance round me gleam,
Each gloomy thought to chase.

And I have striven to cull a few,
And humbly offer unto you,
Whoso may choose to take
Those simple flowers, for ye may find
In them a balm to cheer the mind,
Or soothe the body's ache.

PANEGYRIC ON THE ENGLISH LANGUAGE.

WHAT passion ever soared beyond thy reach,

Strong-pinioned, eagle-sighted English Speech?

What thought, conception, many-sided plan,

Was e'er engendered in the soul of man

But thou couldst seize, with talons large and strong,

And bear where greatest peoples thickest throng?

Thee Chaucer, Shakespere, Milton, Byron used,

And into thee their mighty-minds transfused.

Bards, sages, orators, surpassed by none,

Have swelled thy splendours while they raised their own.

Not learned Greece, nor widely-ruling Rome,

Had warmer words for country, friends, and home;

Had nobler words of justice, truth, and right;

Had braver words when Freedom armed the fight.

No modern speech can boast a vaster store

Of all things valued most in human lore.

Earth's greatest lands, least islands of the sea,

Her countless tongues all tribute bear to thee;

And thou to every nation, land, and clime,

Giv'st back rich thought and sentiment sublime.

DUNOTTAR CASTLE

Is a ruin on the Kincardineshire coast. The Castle was once the seat of the Keiths, Earls-Marshal of Scotland; but in the reigns of Charles II. and James II. it was used as a State prison, and is chiefly memorable for the horrible sufferings of the Covenanters incarcerated in its vaults.

WHERE stands beside the German Sea,
    A ruin old and grim;
A remnant of antiquity
    And feudal ages dim—
A relic of barbaric power,
When Despotism had its hour.

Upon a little Cape it stands,
    Far-showing o'er the brine,
Sore rent by Time's unsparing hands,
    Nor yielding scarce a sign
That there the great of earth abode,
And well-nigh regal splendour glowed.

Rank weeds are waving in its halls,
    Whose canopy's the sky,
And sea-birds, perching on its walls,
    Emit their dreary cry,
Mixt with the everlasting roar
Of breakers on the rocky shore.

Unscared, the coney burrows there,
    Where hoary Time hath seen
The high-born dame, and maiden fair,
    In jewels and silken sheen,
The haughty cavalier whose sword
Leapt from its scabbard at a word.

But those whose festive joyance rung
    Above the deaf'ning wave,
For whom the minstrel's harp was strung,
    The beauteous and the brave,
All, all have perished like a dream,
And desolation reigns supreme.

Yet still remain the vaults below,
    By slimy things possest;
Once doleful scenes of every woe
    That wrings the human breast,
Long-cherished Hope's expiring sigh,
And Torture's fierce or feeble cry.

When man, for no unholy deed,
    Was pent in dungeon's gloom;
When mere attachment to a creed
    Might cost a martyr's doom,
With all the thousand agonies
Inventive cruelty could devise.

In noisome damp and mire they pent
    The Covenanters there,
Till it became a punishment
    To breathe the fetid air;
Till strong men wrung their hands and cried,
And feeble, drooped, despaired, and died:

Till many longed and prayed to die,
    And when their prayers were vain,
Blasphemed the Power who could deny
    A period to their pain;
And cursed their ruthless enemies
As fiends, let loose in human guise.

But Heaven may suffer tyrants long,
   And evil laws prevail,
Oppression rioting in wrong,
   While wretched captives wail;
At last the vials of wrath shall burst
And sweep from earth the race accurst.

True, man may grind his fellow man
   In bondage and disgrace;
But ever since the world began
   The history of our race
Attests that love of liberty
Though crushed, can never, never die.

And when to desperation driven,
   The long oppressed arise,
The avengers of offended Heaven—
   Its lightnings in their eyes—
Shall despots, who bestride the world,
In ruin from their seats be hurled !

And desolate as yonder pile
   Shall be the tyrant's hearth;
The dwelling-place of reptiles vile,
   A hate-spot on the earth;
And history shall embalm his name
In everlasting scorn and shame.

THE PASSAGE OF THE RED SEA.

FROM the land of their bondage, oppression, and woe,
   To a fair land of promise the Israelites go;
But the hardened Oppressor begins to repent
That fear should have forced his reluctant consent;
For the hand that chastised him no longer is felt,
And he ceases to think of the blows it hath dealt;
He thinks of the slaves, of the jewels he hath lost,
And he summons his captains, he marshals his host,
His chariots, his horsemen, in numbers they be,
Like the stars of the heavens, like the sands of the sea;
While many the helpless, the warlike but few,
Of those whom the mighty of Egypt pursue;
And dire is the terror pervading their mind
For the sea rolls before and the foe shouts behind ;
But courage, O, Israel!—no cause for dismay—
For the depths of the ocean shall yield you a way ;
See Moses, your leader, outstretching his rod,
At the voice of Jehovah, the might-giving God!
See the billows arising a wall on each hand,
And the channels of ocean as dry as the land!
March onward, O, Israel, for God shall to-day
Prove his arm all-resistless to save or to slay.
On come the Egyptians; their victims are gone,
But the waves yawn apart, and the word is—"On, on!"
The chariots, the horsemen, swift onward they rush,
And swift speed before them the bands they would crush;

On the slaves who, submissive, have bent to his yoke,
Proud Pharaoh will rivet the bonds they have broke;
The masses of water may threatfully frown,
But the prey's in his grasp, and the day is his own!
Ah, Pharaoh, remember the plagues of thy land,
They came, and they went, at Jehovah's command.
Remember that morning of horror and wail,
When the flower of thy Kingdom lay lifeless and pale!
. Who armed the destroyer and guided his sword?
Remember, and quake at the power of the Lord!
Every heart sunk in dread, and rolled every eye,
When the billowy bulwark was loosed from on High;
But the yell of the conflict, when foes rush on foes,
Were a dulcimer's note to the shriek which arose,
As inward the waters, on left and on right,
Swept, whelming the King and his warriors of might.
Thus vainly are thousands equipt for the field,
A thread is the corslet, a cobweb the shield;
All pointless the arrow, and powerless the sword,
When opposed to the puissant arm of the Lord!

LINES SPOKEN AT THE BANQUET GIVEN TO GENERAL SIR
GEORGE BROWN, AT ELGIN, SEPT. 11TH, 1855.

FROM the far land of battle, from victory he's come,
    To the friends of his youth, to the land of his home ;
From defending the right 'gainst aggression and wrong,
In the cause of the weak, 'gainst the arm of the strong ;
From the dread heights of Alma, from Inkerman's fight,
Where he scattered the foe in the flower of his might ;
From siege, and from breach, and from red-reeking plain,
Where the arrows of death fell thicker than rain,
The good ship hath borne him in peace o'er the wave,
For God stretched his arm o'er the head of the brave.
Yes, back to his country in triumph he's come,
Though not like the victor to vanquishing Rome.
Far higher and nobler the trophies he brings
Than breastplates of captains or vestments of kings,
Than thousands of captives to crouch at his heels,
Than monarchs enfettered and dragged at his wheels.
Enfeebled by sickness, and wasted with wars,
He comes to his country with wounds and with scars ;
But he comes with the boast that he ever hath been
The Soldier of Freedom, of Country, and Queen.
He comes with the boast that his duty was done—
That wherever she pointed, he fearless led on.
He comes to us covered with glory and fame,
And his land with her heroes hath numbered his name !

LINES Spoken by the Author, at a BANQUET given
at the Launch of the Trading Vessel, named
" THE VENTURE," at Speymouth, Morayshire.

SUBLIME are the oak-ribbed monsters,
   Which bulwark our land's liberties ;
Which make us revered among nations,
   Our Island, the Queen of the Seas.

A terrible sight is the war ship,
When, heaving old ocean below,
And rending the skies with her thunder,
She belches forth death on the foe.

And still, when Ambition grasps conquest,
When War spreads his wings on the blasts,
Be our Navy the dauntless defender
Of the glory she wrung from the past.

Be she prompt as of yore to defend us
From tyranny, insult, and wrong ;
Be her white wings for ever expanded,
To shelter the weak from the strong.

Yet give me the handmaid of commerce
That wafts to our shores from afar
The riches that clothe Peace in splendour,
The thews and the sinews of War.

And such is the vessel we've witnessed
Glide into the waters to-day ;
And never a tighter or fairer
Was launched from the yards of the Spey.

And here's to the gallant ship " Venture,"
And here's to her Captain and crew—
Long, long may she walk the blue waters,
Long they be the dauntless and true.

And long may her owners have reason
To reckon auspicious the day
When first they beheld the ship, "Venture,"
Step forth from her berth on the Spey.

———

PLUSCARDEN.

WHOEVER goes to Morayland,
 Should visit Pluscarden ;
In all the regions of the North
 There's not a fairer glen.
Contented toil is busy there
 Amidst the pretty farms ;
And nature, with a bounteous hand,
 Hath scattered countless charms.

A streamlet murmurs down the vale,
 And soft, the summer breeze
Wafts grateful odours o'er the glen
 From scented flowers and trees.
The woods around are musical
 Through all the summer long,
And overhead the sky is charmed
 With merry bursts of song.

A grand historic ruin is there,
  With ivy overgrown—
A monument of priestly power
  In years and ages gone;—
An Abbey fallen to decay,
  Where monks made goodly cheer
On fat sirloin, and juicy fowl,
  And haunch of fallow deer.

The chattering sparrows build their nests
  Amidst its ivy leaves;
The bats within its chambers flit
  In stilly summer eves.
The very owl might roost at will
  Beneath the crumbling roof,
And neither monk nor abbot rise
  To utter stern reproof.

That ivied pile, those chestnut trees,
  That poplar standing nigh,
So tall it looks as if its top
  Were up against the sky;
There is a charm around the whole
  A certain nameless grace—
A kind of holy sadness flung
  O'er all the lonely place.

And all the glen is full of charms;
  No matter where you roam,
There is a spell on every spot
  Endears it like a home.
Methinks when I am sick at heart,
  And worn with vexing care,

'   If I could flee to Pluscarden
    I'd find a solace there.

I own that I beheld the glen
    With Rosa by my side—
A youthful maiden, flaxen-haired,
    Rose-mouthed, and azure-eyed.
Perchance it was her joyous face,
    And soft bewitching eyes,
That made me find in Pluscarden
    An earthly paradise.*

The following lines refer to the late James Trail Calder, the
Caithness Poet. They appeared under a *non de plume*, in one of the
local newspapers, when Mr. Calder was struggling, oppressed by age
and stinted means, to get his History of Caithness published.

POOR poet of the Pentland Firth,
    I almost weep to see
Unquestioned genius, sense, and worth,
    Meet such neglect in thee !

Long years of toil, what scant reward
    They bring thy latter days !
What comfort cheers the aged bard ?
    What meed but empty praise ?

I know the poet's wreath of fame
    Is cherished more than gold,

* The Glen of Pluscarden, with its fine old Priory, lies in the Parish, and about
five miles west from the Burgh of Elgin.

And dearer far his deathless name
  Than hoards of wealth untold.

I know that genius flings its beams
  To charm the drearest spot,
And well I know the poet's dreams
  Are sunshine to his lot.

But ah ! the more the bard enjoys,
  The keener does he feel,
When cold neglect hath stilled his voice,
  And frailties o'er him steal.

If genius paints the homely fair,
  And elevates the low,
It lends a keener edge to care,
  And magnifies each woe.

Neglected bard, it wakes my fears
  To court the Tuneful Nine,
Lest I should meet in after years
  As hard a fate as thine.

Yet when I fling my spirit down
  Through ages now unborn,
And see thee live in bright renown,
  Ah, then I cease to mourn.

Thy name shall live—I cease to weep—
  I strike the lyre in trust—
Yes, live when Mammon's minions sleep
  In long-forgotten dust !

ADDRESS.

LINES SPOKEN ON THE OCCASION OF THE PRESENTATION OF
A SILVER BUGLE AND PURSE OF SOVEREIGNS TO THE
FIRST CAITHNESS ARTILLERY VOLUNTEERS BY THE LADIES
OF THE PARISH OF WICK, JANUARY 14TH, 1861.

THERE rose a cry throughout our isle,
 That danger loomed around—
A dread that foot of foreign foe
 Might tread on British ground.

And English, Scottish hearts were roused
 At dread of war's alarms;
And prompt arose the British youth
 To train for deeds of arms.

From merry England's southmost shore,
 To Scotland's northmost isle,
Spontaneous tramped our gallant lads
 In martial rank and file.

Our fathers saw the sight with pride;
 It stilled our mothers' fears;
Our sisters gave their grateful hearts
 To British volunteers.

Despotic powers abased their voice
 To accents mild and tame;
And greatest still o'er all the great
 Stood Britain's matchless name.

And if her valour thus shines out
 On misty, vague alarms,

What daring would her sons display,
    Should Freedom call to arms!

Our towns would vomit fighting men,
    Our hills would pour them down,
The feeblest hand would grasp a brand,
    To strike for Queen and Crown.

Before the tramp of foreign foe
    Should sound in British ears,
He'd have to meet our gallant fleet,
    And face our volunteers.

Before the yoke of foreign foe
    Were pressed on British soil,
He'd have to fight the *hindmost* man
    Within the British Isle.

And none would sooner stand to arms,
    For glory all athirst,
Nor meet their foes with stouter blows
    Than the gallant Caithness First.

The first and last upon the field
    In Scotia's grand review ;
The first and last in Britain's need
    They'd be, to dare and do.

Their Silver Bugle—Beauty's gift—
    Would sound a charge so clear,
'Twould fire each Scottish heart with hope,
    Chill every foe with fear.

MY REASONS FOR JOINING THE NATIONAL
EDUCATION LEAGUE.

The " National Education League " did not accomplish all that the more sanguine of its adherents expected of it; but it doubtless attained to an important place among the forces whose converging result was the " Elementary Education Act, 1870." However, the zeal of the writer of the following verses would certainly have been considerably abated if he could have foreseen that the new educational machinery would be employed, as it has been, to crush out of existence hundreds of thousands of efficient self-support'ng schools, and burden tax and rate-payers with the education of a class well able to pay for themselves.

 WANDERER from a northern land,
　　Whose hills are bleak and bare,
Whose fields repay the toiling hand
　　With doubtful crops and spare,
I came to England's broader fields,
　　More genial clime and soil,
Where every cultured acre yields
　　A richer meed to toil.

I saw her old baronial halls,
　　Amid their fair domains ;
The fruits of countless folds and stalls
　　On all her fertile plains.
I saw her towns and cities vast,
　　Her commerce carried wide,
A ceaseless current, full and fast,
　　Wherever men abide.

I saw her wealth, in copious streams,
　　From countless sources flow ;
A power surpassing all my dreams;
　　'Gainst indigence and woe.
" Oh, what a glorious land ! " I cried,
　　" None wretched here can be ; "

A thousand thousand tongues replied,—
  " Give answer, what are we ? "

I turned from fashion, rank, and wealth,
  To noisome streets and lanes,
Where wretched forms, in rags and filth,
  And sin-polluting stains,
Were clutched within a demon's gripe,—
  Dull Ignorance his name,—
Who dragged alike the green and ripe
  Through scenes of sin and shame.

His shadow, like a murky cloud,
  Obscured the minds of all ;
And evil minions in a crowd
  Were ready at his call,—
Intemperance, Unthrift, and Sloth,
  Gaunt Hunger, Greed, and Lust,—
Who seized their victims, nothing loath,
  And ground them to the dust.

Oh, brothers ! I have witnessed sights
  " To make the angels weep ; "
They've haunted me for days and nights,
  And poisoned food and sleep ;
And I have marvelled how the great,
  The rich, the wise, the strong,
The pillars of the church and state,
  Have suffered them so long !

And when I saw a band advance,—
  With dauntless words and plain,—
Declaring war on Ignorance
  And all his baleful train,

I gave them welcome, warm and true,
   I stretched my hands to heaven,
And cried, " To you, ye faithful few,
   May all success be given !

" God strengthen you in heart and hand
   To work a work sublime,
To win the weapons for a land
   Which battle Vice and Crime ;
To light the torch which shall illume
   To justice, truth, and right ;
To chase the waves of mental gloom,
   By floods of mental light.

" God speed ye ! for ye seek to raise
   The fallen from the mire,
And in the bosoms of the base
   To kindle heavenly fire ;
To lead the children of the poor
   From sights of evil name,
To halls where Science spreads her store
   And points the way to fame.

" God speed to you ! go, speed the day
   When armëd strife shall cease,
And bloody-handed War give way
   Before celestial Peace ;
When nations, taught by reason's voice,
   Shall struggle most to gain
The triumphs which make hearts rejoice,
   And lessen human pain.

" God speed to you ! go forth and win
   The noblest fight of all,—

The fight where Ignorance and Sin
    Shall be the foes to fall.
And fellow-men, by these enchain'd,
    In manhood's might shall rise,
Rejoicing in the freedom gained
    Through your sublime emprise.

" God speed ye ! for ye seek to ring
    The knell of bigot hate,
And rival sects together bring,
    With spirit truly great,
To strive for high and holy ends,
    By means without intrigue :
The wise, the good, will be your friends,
    And God will speed the League ! "

THE CORNY TOE.

INTRODUCTION.

Mesdames, Mesdemoiselles, Messieurs, my Readers, I have "struck ile !" My poetical fortune is made. Once upon a time, I had the honour to submit a sample of my rhyming ware to a certain learned Society. Two distinguished members of the august body remarked on my performances adversely. The first condemned *all* poetry. "When Nature began to arrange her herbs, flowers, plants, trees, &c., in circles, squares, triangles, pentagons, polygons, and other regular mathematical figures, then he would believe that pentameters, hexameters, rhyme and rhythm were forms of speech natural to man, or worthy of being cultivated by him ; but, for himself, he held it as axiomatic that, if a man had anything good to say, he said it in prose. If the fervour of his mental temperament drove a man to express his thoughts in verse, and a modicum of sense were still left him, it would be blank verse he would employ. If he resorted to rhyme—and he (the speaker) believed nothing except rhyme had been submitted to the Society that night—well, common politeness kept him, on the present occasion, from expressing his opinion on rhyme; he would observe merely that no great poem ever had been, or ever could be, written in rhyme!" And the learned speaker resumed his seat, leaving, or wishing to leave, on the minds of his auditors, the impression that the nearest lunatic asylum was the poor rhymster's only fitting abode. The second philosopher did not concur entirely in the sweeping condemnation uttered by his distinguished colleague. "He believed the age of poesy was past. Former poets had observed and depicted all the phenomena of nature, and had seized and, so to speak, cystalized in their verse every gem of poetic thought." Readers, I was completely stunned, mentally crumpled up, like the spoiled sheet, which the editor wrathfully consigns to the fire-place, or to the waste-paper basket, and would have crept home broken-heartedly to that obscurity from which I ought never to have emerged, had it not been that the President of the Society—a real philosopher, a *savant* of world-wide reputation—soothed, encouraged, and metaphorically patted me on the back; yet, I went forth from the hall of audience, a sadder if not a wiser man; and for many days was I sore troubled in mind, well knowing that in the sadly down-trodden field of poesy, I had not yet lighted on an unnoted flower, an unearthed nugget, an undiscovered gem. One day, I was hobbling dejectedly over a solitary, stoney road, suffering from an unmitigated corn on the small toe of my left foot; suddenly, happily the thought, the *afflatus divinus* struck me. *Eureka!*— I had found it!—the subject never yet treated by any versifier, dead or living! I invoked the Nine Muses—each aided me—not with a verse, a stanza, or a canto, no, but with a twinge! In nine twinges I sang the "Corny Toe!" and "Ossian hath received his fame!" *Sublimi feriam sidera vertice!* I have struck a cord of feeling that will vibrate to the pedal extremities of booted and shoed humanity to the last generation, and I shall sit under the shade of my own laurels, secure from the shafts of the scorner henceforth and for ever.

1st Twinge.

THE Toe! the Toe! the Corny Toe!
    It causeth its owner a world of woe;
    It cripples his steps where'er he may go;
    It plagues his life like a mortal foe;
    And whenever he sues for peace, cries "No!"
      That Toe! that Toe! that Corny Toe!

2ND TWINGE.

He's cottoned and coddled that toe for years!
He's cut it with razors, with knives, and shears,
Till out from his eyes ran rivers of tears,
Evoking little, however, save sneers;
For seldom, how seldom a soul appears
 To sympathise with that Corny Toe.

3RD TWINGE.

He's read for it recipes old as the hills,
He's poured for it cash into drugsellers' tills,
Paid for it scores of chiropodists' bills,
Madly gulped for it powders and pills;
But there it remains the worst of his ills,
 That Toe! that Toe! that Corny Toe!

4TH TWINGE.

He's tried it with plasters, lotions, and soap,
Big boots and shoes, to give it full scope;
The leaves of the ivy have led him to hope,
But, apart from every figure and trope,
These remedies only foster the crop,
 On the Toe! the Toe! the Corny Toe!

5TH TWINGE.

He's hunted the valleys and mountain tops,
For every species of herbal crops,
Dived into every manner of shops,
For simples and compounds, in solids and drops;
By every manner of cuts and chops
He's tried to reduce it, but up it pops;
It grows, it grows, and it never stops,
 That Toe! that Toe! that Corny Toe!

6TH TWINGE.

Time over him passes with rapid wing,
And there is not a change he knows to bring
Through summer, autumn, winter, or spring,
But that corn preludes with an ache or sting,
Making its owner unmusically sing—
  "That Toe! that Toe! that Corny Toe!"

7TH TWINGE.

It has thrown a chill on his best emotions,
And troubled the flow of his heart's devotions;
It has fairly confused his clearest notions
On every question of salves and lotions,
Drastics, tonics, pilules, and potions,
  That Toe! that Toe! that Corny Toe!

8TH TWINGE.

How the anti-vivisectionists rail
If a dog or cat, a frog or a snail,
Shall under the battery or scalpel wail;
But oh! would they only study the tale
Of the corn that sticks like a riveted nail,
The tears from their eyes would flow without fail,
By the bowl, the basin, the bucket, or pail,
  For the Toe! the Toe! the Corny Toe!

9TH TWINGE.

The worst I have wished the worst of my foes
Is a pair of tight boots upon corny toes;
Then to watch and triumph over his woes,
As limping over the pebbles he goes,
With the tears trickling down the sides of his nose;
Far worse than the bastinado's blows
  Is a Toe! a Toe! a Corny Toe!

THE WIDOW'S DETERMINATION.

THEY bid me leave my native land—
　　The land so dear to me;
And mine shall be a richer home,
　　Beyond the Atlantic Sea.

"Forget!" they cry, "these rugged hills,
　　These moorlands bleak and bare;
For smooth the lawns, and broad the fields,
　　And rich the verdure *there*.

"Ay! *there* luxuriant plenty springs,
　　Spontaneous, from the the soil
Which *here* the niggard earth denies
　　To never-ending toil.

"And health, and wealth, and happiness,
　　Are all in store for thee,
Wouldst thou forsake this sterile glen,
　　And cross the smiling sea."

True, true the Western World may be
　　The glorious land they say;
But still it is the "Stranger's Land,"
　　And oh, 'tis far away!

True, there the fattening flocks may feed,
　　The fields luxuriant wave;
But here my father's lived and died,
　　And here's my husband's grave.

And here my children saw the light,
　　And here in joyance trode;

Here two in childhood, one in youth,
   Gave back their souls to God.

And here I've lived, was loved, and wed,
   And here in joy and tears,
In plenty and in penury,
   I've numbered three score years.

This glen beheld my virgin grace,
   And sees my furrowed brow;
This glen must be my last abode ;
   I *cannot* leave it now !

LETTER

FROM AN EMIGRANT'S CHILD IN AMERICA TO HER GRANDMOTHER
IN SCOTLAND.

" GRANDMOTHER, they tell me you live far away,
   Where the bright sun is seen at the dawning of day;
   That you live in a cottage beside a green wood,
   Contented and cheerful, and kindly and good.
They say you are cheerful, but when your thoughts roam
Away to your children, so far from their home,
And then from your eyes do the briny drops fall,
As you think upon mother, on uncle, on all.
But grandmother, dear, a time may yet be
When I may come over the waters to thee—
Those waters they speak of, so deep and so wide,
That great wooden houses are borne on their tide;
And father and mother, and brothers will come,
And all live together in one happy home.

And uncle will come, when he comes from the land
Where he gathers the gold that will make him *so* grand!
O, yes! he will come, and ne'er go again
So far, far away, to give grandmother pain;
For our days will be spent in sunshine and glee,
When all have come over the waters to thee.
But should we not meet while our home is on earth,
Nor ever sit joyous around the same hearth;
Should we never see *you*, nor your home by the wood,
Like you, we shall try to be cheerful and good.
Then grandmother, dear, we shall meet when we die,
In the home of the happy beyond the blue sky."

THE HILLS WHERE I WAS BORN;

OR,

A VOICE FROM THE WEST.

THE hills where I was born—Oh, yes!
  I see them in my dreams—
    Their rugged peaks, their shaggy slopes,
      Their wildly dashing streams.
The lapwing hovering o'er the marsh,
  The lark at early morn—
I see them all, as when I trode
  The hills where I was born.

The cottage and the cottage green,
  Where I was won't to play,
To revel in the joys of youth,
  The livelong summer day.

The gamesome lambs, the grazing herds,
  The fields of waving corn;
I see them all, as when I trode
  The hills where I was born,

I left my hills long years ago,
  My friends and cottage home,
And crossed the broad Atlantic waves,
  In western lands to roam;
Where lordly plains extend afar,
  And stately forests rise;
Where giant rivers roll their floods,
  And mountains pierce the skies.

And I have shivered in the blast,
  And sweaten in the sun;
And by my own unaided arm,
  The stranger's gold have won;
And wealth would win me flattering smiles,
  Where cold neglect and scorn
Were all my portion, when I left
  The hills where I was born.

Afar from friends and fatherland,
  I see my coming doom—
The stranger's hand must lower my head,
  And fill my exile's tomb.
Nor thence shall idle grief be mine,
  For bootless 'tis to mourn;
Tho' but in death can I forget
  The hills where I was born!

THE DYING COTTAGER'S REQUEST.

O, TAKE me out! take me out once more,
    To gaze on the setting sun,
And feel his parting beams, before
    Life's lingering sands be run.

Take me out to see the clear blue sky,
    And to feel the balmy breeze;
To hear the laverock's song on high,
    And the thrush in the planting trees.

Fain, fain would I see the trees once more,
    With their leaves of bonnie green;
For months, the length and breadth of this floor
    My longest walks have been.

And O, would you carry round my chair,
    And turn my face to the West,
And let me sit for a little there,
    Before I go to my rest?

For the heather moor hath charms for me;
    I would see the broomy knowe,
The cattle out on the flowery lea,
    And the horses at the plough.

I would see the corn, I would see the grass,
    If it yet begins to wave;
For before the months of summer pass,
    'Twill be green above my grave.

I would see the scenes where my early hours,
    Flew faster than words can tell;

I would see the little wayside flowers,
  And bid them a last farewell.

O, take me out! take me out once more,
  To gaze upon earth and sky;
And then, when my brief survey is o'er,
  You can carry me in to die!

MY SOCIAL CREED.

HORNY handed son of labour,
  Let me grasp thy hand in mine;
  If thou art an honest neighbour,
  Fear thee not that I'll decline
Thy grimy hand in mine to take,
And give it friendly shake for shake.

For I, too, have been a worker,
Almost from my cradle bed,
And I trust no labour-shirker,
Though a toiler with the head;
And at times my work hath been
Than thine own, perchance, less clean.

God forgive me! evil passions
Many times have forced me wrong;
Lucre's slave, or senseless Fashion's,
I have followed with the throng,
When I should have stood, with steel
Stiffly-backed, for human weal.

These are blots in mine escutcheon;
Sloven work in thine will be;
Do not think there is not much in
Slips like these for thee or me;
He who soweth evil seed,
Evil fruits will reap indeed.

He who worketh stoutly, truly—
Smiting smith or struggling bard—
Though he suffer *Here* unduly,
There will meet with due reward:
This my Gospel is and Creed—
Whoso will may leave or read.

Honest Worker (noble title!)
Let me grasp thy grimy hand;
Thine are deeds as worth recital
As the bravest in the land;
Rather would I laud thy labours
Than thy tensil-titled neighbour's.

Titles are but worth the having
When they are the stamp of worth;
Gained by fawning, crouching, slaving,
They're the meanest gauds of earth.
Honest Worker, thou mayest stand
With the highest in the land.

IN DEFENCE.

THEY tell us grandly that the age
 Of poesy has gone by,
That crystallised upon the page
 Of former poets, lie
All gems of thought—the rich, the rare,
The brilliant, exquisite, and fair.

Ah ! bounteous Nature, is it thus ?
 Have former poets wrung
Thy treasures out, and left for us
 No beauties to be sung ?
Not so ; thy gems—a boundless store—
Shall last our race till time be o'er.

For never, never can the bard
 Exhaust the gems of thought
Whilst thou, before his keen regard,
 Dost spread thy pages, fraught
With pictures old, yet ever new
In figures, grouping, shade, and hue.

Not ever once, while man retains
 His changeful form and soul,
While changeful foliage decks the plain,
 And changeful seasons roll,
Shall tuneful poet lack a theme
Whereon to pour the lyric stream.

No ! while the gracious God above
 So blesses earth below,
So long the hymns of grateful love
 From minstrel lips shall flow,

To join the ceaseless harmonies
Which mount in tribute to the skies.

But those with eyes that cannot see,
　　And ears that cannot hear,
And souls which poets' minstrelsy
　　Can neither stir nor cheer,
To hide their own defective powers,
Must needs proclaim decay in ours.

———

The following is a reproduction, in verse, of the account of an actual occurrence which took place on one of the Belgian railways, some years ago. The Belgian Press unanimously lauded the conduct of the points-man, and the King awarded him an honorary medal.

THE POINTSMAN;

OR, AFFECTION AND DUTY.

THE pointsman stands by the railway side,
　　With a father's pride and joy,
To gather the smiles and watch the sports
　　Of his handsome three-years' boy,
Who merrily plays between the rails,
　　Reclined on the sunny ground,
With the flow'rets culled by his father's hand
　　From the flowering borders round.
The whistle screams in the pointsman's ear,
　　And following fast behind,
The rush of a sweeping train comes on
　　Like a mighty, rushing wind !
The rails in his charge are out of line,
　　What, what shall the pointsman do ?

Death to his child or all in the train,
  He must choose betwixt the two !
He flies to his post—the rails are right,
  With a rush the train goes by ;
The father turns to look for his child
  With a tear-beclouded eye.
"O, father," cries the smiling boy,
  " I was not at all afraid ;
I knew that God is for ever near,
  And always ready to aid,
So I laid me down, as I do at night,
  To put myself in his care,
And every one of the cars had passed
  Before I finished my prayer. "

———

THE YOUNG BRITON'S REPLY TO OLD BRITISH CROAKERS.

WE meet with croakers who aver
  That Britain's star goes down ;
That in her hand the trident shakes,
  And on her head the crown.
Yea, that her sons and daughters born
  Combine to bring to shame,
Not to uphold and magnify
  Her ancient honoured name.

We say to cravens such as these—
  "Go, chase your fears away !
Britannia's glorious name shall last
  Till earth's remotest day.

For not, although this isle should sink
　　In circumjacent sea,
Should Britain's grand historic name
　　And glories cease to be.

" There's not a zone which feels the beams
　　Of heaven's benignant sun,
Where Britain's high emprise hath not
　　Undying glories won.
We've graved our names on northern hills,
　　And burning southern plains ;
The sovereign people of the west,
　　Whose blood is in their veins.

" Who smote their giant forests down,
　　And taught their soil to bear
The waving crops, the grazing herds,
　　The towns and mansions fair ?
Flesh of our flesh their fathers were,
　　Their speech is one with ours,
We are not rivals, we for rule
　　But twin fraternal powers.

" Our sway is wide in Indian climes,
　　Where sacred rivers flow ;
'Tis owned in equatorial isles,
　　Where spicy breezes blow.
No empire's arm is stretched so far ;
　　No tongue of man hath taught
To wider climes a purer faith,
　　Or more exalted thought.

" The rod is wrung from tyrants' hands,
　　Unfettered every slave ;

Sweet freedom made the right of all
 Where'er our banners wave.
Beneath our sway the freer man
 More nobly walks abroad,
In soul elate with higher thought,
 More love to man and God."

We tell the croakers, one and all,
 That Britain stands sublime ;
Nor shall her growing glories cease
 To match the march of time.
The sacred trusts our sires have left
 We'll guard with jealous care ;
The laurels planted by their hands
 Shall prouder laurels bear.

The conquests by their valour won
 We'll labour to increase,
Not through the arts of murderous War,
 But through celestial Peace.
We'll strive to make Britannia shine
 In all that's good and wise—
A star to show the tribes of men
 The pathway to the skies.

THE BATTLE OF AGINCOURT.

THE sun hath set on Agincourt,
    The rain descends in floods,
As Henry and his war-worn bands
    Encamp amid the woods;
And far as Henry's eagle eye
    Can pierce to left or right,
His Gallic foeman's twinkling fires
    Invade the reign of night.

God help thee, England's daring King!
    Farewell to thy renown,
If thou and thy diminished host
    Be barred from Calais town,
And through the plains of Agincourt
    A passage thou must clear;
A hundred thousand French lie there,
    In warrior's choicest gear.

And while the boist'rous jest and song
    Amuse thy fresher foes,
Thy wearied troops on moistened earth
    Shall court a vain repose;
And when the gray October morn
    Shall creep o'er Gallia's land,
On, on her locust host shall pour
    To crush thy wasted band.

The gray October morn hath broke,
    But still the locust host
Hath not advanced a hand-breadth yet
    Beyond their vesper's post.

Not, surely, that their feeble foe
  Hath moved their hearts to fear,
Say rather that they scorn for such
  To mar their morning's cheer.

Then thus, at length, with patience spent,
  Out spoke the English King,
"Now, may the Holy Trinity
  Salvation to us bring!
No longer shall we idly wait
  Those craven sons of France;
Upon them with your bended bows,
  Strike home with sword and lance!"

Know ye how the noble racer,
  By heel admonished, springs,
And leaves the starting post behind
  As if his feet had wings!
So darted England's warriors forth,
  When Henry gave the word,
So rushed against their tardy foes,
  With cross-bow, lance, and sword.

Have ye seen the reapers' sickles
  Mow down the bearded grain,
When autumn's mellow hues are spread
  O'er all the fertile plain?
So fell the flower of Gallia's host,
  The foremost men of France,
Beneath the flights of English shafts,
  Before the English lance.

Have ye seen the mountain torrent
  Bear down the broken wrack,

When autumn rains hath lent it force
    To sweep its foaming track ?
Like mountain-torrent England's host,
    Like wrack did Gallia's might,
Her princes, peasants, horse, and foot,
    Sweep down the tide of flight.

Not Cressy's field, nor Poictier's,
    E'en then renowned in story,
Was fought against superior odds,
    Nor gained with greater glory :
A hundred thousand strong at morn
    The Gallic army lay,
Scattered and flying, wounded, slain,
    Were all ere noon of day.

Our swords to ploughshares we would beat
    With willing hands, I trow,
And only strive with neighbour States
    In peaceful commerce now ;
But let our rivals not forget
    Our fathers' deeds of yore;
Nor yet that sons of hero-sires
    Still guard Britannia's shore.

THE SUMMER BONNET.

JUNE, 1875.

I talked to my wife on an eve in June,
 For I felt in the talking humour,
With the birds round our cottage all in tune,
 And nature dressed as a " Bloomer."

I talked unto her of the public good,
 And of party trick and juggle ;
Why the Liberals fell, and the Tories stood,
 In the last Election struggle.

I talked unto her of the liquor trade,
 And impending legislation,
And showed her the recent advances made
 In the matter of cremation.

I talked of Moody and Sankey, men
 Who have made a grand commotion ;
And, changing the subject, I talked again
 Of the latest " Yankee notion."

I talked unto her of the liberal arts,
 About painters, and their pictures ;
And to prove that I was a man of parts,
 Was liberal in caustic strictures.

I talked of the peoples 'neath Eastern skies—
 Their language, manners, and dresses,
And the changes which might perchance arise
 From the Russians' late successes.

I talked of books and of authors of note,
 Of editors and their papers ;

I dipped into physic, and dared to quote
   Some recipes for the vapours.

I talked of explorers in Afric's clime,
   Of Livingstone and of Baker ;
But she sat in a day-dream all the time,
   Nor could speech of mine awake her.

I gazed in her face, for I felt alarmed,
   Since my mind conceived a notion
That she had been into a statue charmed,
   All powerless of speech or motion.

But she rose at last, to my great relief,
   And left the room without speaking ;
While after her I, like a midnight thief,
   With a noiseless step went sneaking.

She entered her chamber, and straightway went
   To a tiny box within it,
And over an object it treasured, bent
   Her beautiful head one minute.

Then raising her eyes as in ecstacy,
   Her face with a glow upon it,
She cried with a deep and delighted cry,—
   " What a love of a summer bonnet !"

A NEW YEAR'S RETROSPECT.

IN the valley where my being
  First received its vital motion,
Runs a dark and rapid river
  To the all-absorbing ocean.

On which river's bosky margin,
  In the days long since departed,
I and other young companions,
  Thoughtless, gay, and single-hearted

As the gamesome mountain lambkins,
  Sporting on the neighb'ring heather,
Played our merry pranks and gambols
  In the sunny summer weather.

One from out the many frolics
  Of those truly golden ages
Rises even now before me,
  Fresh on memory's faded pages—

We would launch upon the current
  Of that river, dark and wavy,
Bits of bark and broken branches,
  And baptise the whole—"our navy."

Then along the margin running,
  We would·watch, with gaze extended,
O'er the fortunes of our " vessels,"
  Till the course of each was ended.

Some would lag from the commencement
  Amongst weeds and waifs entangled ;
Some would vanish in the rapids ;
  Some on rocks be dashed and mangled.

Few would keep the middle current,
   And 'twas still a thing of wonder
If these reached the goal we set them,
   Otherwise than far asunder!

Where are we who played so gaily
   By that river, dark and wavy?
We are stranded, shattered, severed,
   Like our childhood's mimic "navy!"

Cast together on Life's river,
   In the days long since departed,
Far is each who keeps the current
   From the friends with whom he started.

Some have gone he knows not whither,
   Leaving neither sign nor token,
Some have passed him, some have lingered,
   Some have perished—wrecked and broken!

Thus we drift, we few survivors,
   With diversity of motion,
On our scattered waves of being
   To Eternity's vast Ocean.

LIFE AT HIGH PRESS RE.

WITH yearnings and strivings,
  And heavings of breast,
With throbbings of pulses,
  And wildest unrest,
Impelled, or impelling,
  On! onward, headlong,
Each chasing his object,
  We hurry and throng.

On farther, still farther!
  Up higher, still higher!
Down deeper, still deeper,
  Lies what we desire.
" Had I but yon object,
  My struggles should cease,
But while, it lies distant,
  For me there's no peace."

No steed is so rapid
  As human desire,
Not one, though we've harnessed
  Wind, water, and fire;
Not one, though we've broken
  The lightning to bear
Our thoughts to earth's limits
  Through ocean and air.

We toil and we struggle
  With hand and with head;
We sweat for a pittance—
  A morsel of bread ;

For honours, for riches,
    Fame, pleasure, or power,
For bubbles which glitter
    And burst in an hour.

No resting contented—
    A something remains
To pluck from enjoyment
    Or add to our gains.
The more we have treasured,
    The more do we want;
And onward, still onward,
    We struggle and pant.

We rifle the treasures
    Of earth and of sea;
And, grasping of knowledge,
    As riches are we;
We'd scale the Empyrean
    If ladders were given,
And pluck out the heart of
    The mystery of heaven.

But, lo! in the middle
    Of manifold schemes,
Of well-ordered projects,
    Or bedlamite dreams,
The bolt of Death smites us;
    None, none, can deliver,
And the spirit returns
    To be judged by the Giver!

THE MYSTERY.

SOUL, which vivifies this frame,
　　Much I long to know
Whence at first you hither came,
　　Where at last you'll go?

Is this feeling—is this thought,
　　Which no eye detects—
By our subtle juncture wrought—
　　Physical effects?

Soul, who art the body's queen,
　　Governor of all,
Shall you cease when this machine
　　Dust to dust shall fall?

Tell me, if you ever wist
　　Since you sojourned here—
Tell me, did you pre-exist
　　In another sphere?

Are you the Divinest's breath
　　Breathed in me at birth?
Shall you, on the body's death,
　　Pass again from earth?

Are you on your trial now,
　　As the many think?
As you good or evil sow,
　　Shall you soar or sink?

Shall you, for your errors here—
　　Errors, ah! too rife!—

Sink from base to baser sphere,
  Vile to viler life?

Or at once be plunged in woe,
  Passing mortal ken,
At the moment when you go
  From the haunts of men?

By Another's suff'rings free,
  Blood of sinless spilt,
Ransomed from the penalty
  Due to human guilt,

Shall you at a bound attain
  To supernal bliss,
Never more to suffer pain,
  Think or act amiss?

Or in spheres which meet our eyes,
  Strewn through airy space,
Shall you high and higher rise,
  As you grow in grace,

Till you reach the bright abode,
  See the radiant brow
Of the everlasting God,
  Dimly visioned now?

Mystery of mysteries!
  Questions all are vain;
Never did our wisest wise
  Make your being plain.

Only the Creative Power
  Knoweth what and whence

He will, at the fitting hour,
 End our dread suspense.

We must wait and work till then,
 Work in humble trust;
God will justly deal with men—
 Soul and sordid dust.

— · —

THE STATESMAN'S DREAM.

THE statesman flung himself down depressed,
 In his chamber all alone—
" A thankless, wearing struggle at best,"
 He said to himself with a groan.

" I could not do all that my friends desire,
 Were I thrice as clever and strong ;
And hour by hour opponents conspire
 To prove that my actions are wrong.

" They watch my words as well as my acts,
 Fling clouds on my clearest views;
Give an ugly twist to my fairest facts,
 And all virtues to me refuse."

The Statesman's head on his bosom sank,
 While sleep on his senses stole;
And lo! in the Land of Dreams, he drank
 A draught from a golden bowl.

A draught that gave him power to sweep
  Adown through the future years,
And look behind, from an airy steep,
  On his former self and peers.

And he seemed to see himself arise
  From envy and slander's slime,
As an eagle soars through cloudless skies,
  In a glorious summer's prime.

And he seemed to hear a voice anear—
  "Thou hast bravely borne thy load,
Hast spent thy might to further the right,
  And thy future is with God."

And he waked refreshed, and went his way,
  To the struggles of his lot;
Nor all through life to his dying day,
  Was that cheering dream forgot.

A GLORIOUS DEATH. (?)

SOLDIER lay, in the gairish day,
    Amidst the dying and dead,
  While the skylark soared, and merrily poured
    His melodies overhead.

The soldier lay on the battle field,
  In sorrow and bitter pine,
For the fateful ball that caused his fall
  Had crashed through the soldier's spine.

"And this," he said, "is honour's bed,
  And this is a glorious death—
To lie with none to give you aid,
And pray as you never before have prayed,
  For power to resign your breath!"

And here an ancient crone drew nigh,
  With an evil face and a ruthless eye,
And ended his pangs with a stone,
  And rifled his clothes, with sundry oaths
That gold within them was none.

"And this," she said, "is honour's bed,
  And this is a glorious death!"
As she left him to lie with his face to the sky,
  A corpse on the crimsoned heath.

But "Io triumphe!" pealed afar,
'Midst all the pomp of glorious War—
  And away with melancholy!
A splendid victory had been won,
And helmets gleamed in the summer sun,
  "Io triumphe!" was the cry!
  "Io triumphe! victory!"
  Rolled aloft to the summer sky,
With *Te Deums* grand and holy!

OUR COLLEGE EXCURSION.

INSCRIBED TO W. A. HARDY, ESQ., NOTTINGHAM.

DO you remember that auspicious day—
How long ago I do not care to say—
When you and we—a troop of merry boys
And sadder masters—did, with joyful noise,
From Ecclesall to Froggatt Edge repair,
'Neath summer skies and fragrance-teeming air;
And how the wingèd hours above us flew,
Till Vesper sprinkled earth with cooling dew?
That day to me remains a sunny spot
In mem'ry's landscape, nor by you forgot
May wholly be; so that I have believed
The rapid rhyme I wove, by you received
Benignly, might perchance, in leisure,
Recall that summer day of guileless pleasure.

———

'TWAS on the twenty-ninth of May,
I do remember well,
A sweet, serene, and sunny day,
When our excursion fell.
Our masters smiled, our laughter rang,
In prospect of the fun,
And clearing out the hampers, packed
With ample ham and bun.
To Froggatt Edge, in Derbyshire,
Our merry troop was bound,
All in a chaise and omnibus,
With steeds that spurned the ground.
At one o'clock we started off,
With many a ringing cheer;

And ne'er a master bade us cease,
   Nor sought to look severe.
And some had whips, and some had canes,
   And some, upon the sly,
Concealed pea-shooters in their clothes,
   To pelt the passers by;
And two—but silence as to this,
   For this school-law debars—
Why, two at least, were known to have
   A meerschaum and cigars!
And some within the omnibus,
   And some without did ride;
But more, to stretch their youthful limbs,
   Did gallop by its side;
And in and out, and all about,
   Like monkeys in a show,
We climbed and leapt, and ran and frisked,
   With joyous youth aglow.
From Ecclesall to Froggatt Edge
   Our merry party flew,
And halting at the Chequers Inn
   A moment's breathing drew.
Then hither thither burst away
   The scores of nimble legs;
The only power to call us back,
   The power of ham and eggs.
Away! away o'er moor and rocks,
   Through fields and forests green;
Above, below, we gaily go,
   'Midst many a charming scene.
We saw the rugged mountains rear
   Their rocky crests in air,
And wondered what Titanic hands
   Had piled such masses there;

We saw the Derwent winding on
   Through Derby's lovely dales,
'Twixt woods that flung their fragrance forth
   To scent the summer gales.
We gazed upon the grassy slopes,
   Where grazing herds were rife,
The villages and pleasant farms,
   Instinct with busy life.
We turned our gaze to east and west,
   O'er many a fairy nook,
And, spying Chatsworth Hall, exclaimed—
   "How nice to be a Duke!"

'Tis brave to climb the rugged steeps,
   Where heath-cock hoarsely screams;
'Tis sweet to roam through leafy woods,
   And sit by purling streams;
But all the charms that Nature spreads,
   How fair soe'er they be,
Must yield their place, with hungry youth,
   To ham-and-eggs and tea.

And thus it was we turned our backs
   On each bewitching scene,
And sought again the Chequers Inn
   When appetites grew keen.
We drop the modest curtain o'er
   The clatter and the din,
And vast consumpt of victuals at
   Our little "Wayside Inn;"
For words were weak to show how high
   The piles of food were reared,
How manfully they were attacked,
   How swiftly disappeared.
But only *you* can comprehend
   The bustle and the noise

Who've tended at the feeding of
  A troop of hungry boys ;
You, you alone, can realise
  The floods of milk and tea,
The piles of buns, of ham-and-eggs,
  That *were* and ceased *to be* ;
The piles and floods that disappeared ;
  And still the cry was "give !"
For youth, you know, must live and grow,
  While age needs but to live.
Suffice it that, when tea was o'er,
  We took our homeward way,
Delighted with the glorious feed,
  And pleasures of the day.
And often we review the whole,
  And linger o'er each sport,
Lamenting that a holiday,
  So pleasant, was so short.

                BY YOUNG AGAIN.

THE GROCER'S DAUGHTER ;

OR,

THE EXPERIENCES OF A POETICAL BACHELOR.

I FELL in love when I was young,
  And loved, with all my heart,
A girl who had a witching tongue,
  And dresses wond'rous smart.
I twined her many a loving rhyme,
  I studied Werther's *woes*,
And wrote her tales I thought sublime,
  In sentimental prose.

Perchance my prose was wretched ill,
  My rhymes as poor as this;
But yet my diction, thought, and skill,
  Were praised so much by Miss,
That I did really think such men
  As Byron, Burns, and Scott—
Should I go on to wield the pen—
  Must quickly be forgot;
And wondered why the world went round,
  Just as at other times,
Nor stood, in reverence profound,
  To listen to my rhymes!
Alas for youthful poet's dreams,
  And trustful lover's too!
Alas for all who write their themes
  To maidens like my "Loo!"
Loo's father had a country inn,
  A grocer's shop kept he,
And dealt in whisky, rum, and gin,
  Tobacco, snuff, and tea.
And oft, behind the counter, would
  My true love take her stand,
For she was dutiful and good,
  And quick of tongue and hand.
Nor Hamlet's mother had more thrift,
  (As true as I'm a sinner!)
Who, from a funeral feast, made shift
  To save a marriage dinner.
For "dear Louisa," in the shop,
  Made use of my poetics
For wrapping soda, starch, and soap,
  Cathartics and emetics.
My tales in prose—my cherished tales
  Of friendship, love, and war—

Made bags for tacks and paling nails,
    Wrapt pots of glue and tar.
'Tis true that in her breast love's flame
    Burnt like a new-snufft taper,
While thus she spread her lover's fame,
    And saved her father's paper.
Yet, in my uncommercial mind,
    No grateful feelings glowed,
To meet with love and thrift combined
    In such a novel mode.
With burning wrath did I behold
    My valued written stuff
Round Jack or Jim's tobacco rolled,
    Or holding Donald's snuff.
Nor ever have I felt, since then,
    So much unlike a hero;
The ink did stagnate in my pen,
    My spirits fell to zero.
Small grocers' daughters I forswore
    From that time and forever;
My tales—my finest tales—I tore,
    And burnt my rhymes so clever.

THOUGHTS ON THE ALARMING DECREASE OF THE MALE SEX, AS SHOWN BY STATISTICIANS, AFTER CENSUS, 1871.

WE'RE dropping off, we masculines,
    While women-folks increase;
I wonder how the world will wag
    When we entirely cease!
I wonder how the sweeter sex
    Will fare when we are gone,

Or how they'll fill the posts of life,
 And brave its ills alone.

I wonder if they'll deck themselves
 In as superb attire,
When we're no longer left to gaze,
 To flatter, and admire!
For whom will maids display the charms
 Which we no more behold?
On whom will matrons lay their wrongs,
 With ne'er a man to scold?

I wonder if they'll ever feel,
 When we are quite extinct,
That many were the faults of ours
 At which they might have winked!
Ah! will they ever come to feel
 That we're a grievous loss,
And vow if we would but come back,
 We ne'er should find them cross?

I wonder if they'll e'er regret
 The wrongs they made us bear,
And mourn the coldness and disdain
 Which drove us to despair!
And oh! when we are far removed
 From all our mortal ills,
I wonder very much indeed
 Who'll pay their "little bills!"

Oh! ladies, darling ladies!
 Do pause a bit, and think
How very, very near yourselves
 Might be to ruin's brink

If we should vanish from the earth !
  As sure as you're alive
The strongest minded of your sex
  Could not for long survive.

We're dropping off, we masculines,
  As statisticians show;
Fair ladies, do be warned in time
  Before the remnant go.
Don't struggle, as you struggle now,
  To snub and humble man,
But aid, exalt, and cherish him
  By all the arts ye can.

———

LINES

SENT WITH A PRESENT TO A YOUNG LADY ON HER MARRIAGE DAY.

(Written by request of the donors of the present.)

AS bright be the years of thy future, fair bride,
  In all that is beauteous and best,
As a sweet summer-day, whose sun seems to glide
  Through seas of repose, to the west.

May he who has won thee in womanhood's morn
  Be faithful and loving through life ;
And smiles of contentment for ever adorn
  The home where he leads thee as wife!

May storms of adversity pass o'er your heads,
  Like blasts o'er the oak-shaded flowers,
Which, after the tempest, look up from their beds,
  Refreshed and revived by the showers !

May the hopes of your hearts, on this happy day,
   Be all realised in your lot ;
Yet ne'er 'midst the blessings which brighten your way
   The Giver of blessings forgot!

Thus blest in yourselves, and a blessing to those
   Whom Fortune may gather around,
Through life's tranquil day to its late, happy close
   Mayest thou and thy chosen be found!

In this modest offering—these prayers for your weal—
   We all in this dwelling unite,
And send you these verses our thoughts to reveal :
   May they carry our message aright!

———

ODE TO THE POET.

HAIL! creature of the lofty head,
   Scarce earning for thyself a crust of bread
      To keep together soul and body ;
  In Fancy's realms thou walk'st with gods sublime,
  But on the unromantic shores of Time
      Thou art no mate for " Lord Tom Noddy."

Thou walk'st in beauty 'midst celestial spheres;
Unrivalled music greets thy raptured ears ;
     Seraphic figures flit around thee ;
On earth, in raiment fashionless and bare,
In dwellings which misfortune's children share,
     Neglected and despised, I've found thee.

The mighty mysteries of the universe
Thou striv'st to grasp, and solve, and wouldst rehearse
    Their secrets to the ears of mortals ;
But through misconduct of thine own affairs—
Thy buyings, sellings, and such petty cares—
    Grim Want sits ever at thy portals.

When patrons seek to further thine advance,
How soon, how very soon they look askance !
    Thou wilt not stoop an inch to please them.
When Fortune offers riches to thine hand,
Thou art away in distant Wonderland,
    And dost return too late to seize them.

But few of us do measure out the span
Of three-score years and ten—the space to man
    Allotted by the dread Supernal.
And well for thee our sands so swiftly run,
For sadder lot than thine were surely none,
    Were life on earth for thee eternal.

For aught that unpoetic eyes can see,
More wretched than Tithonus thou wouldst be
    If doomed to similar existence.
Thou dost appear of all the human race
Least fitted for thy human dwelling-place ;
    Thou soar'st above with such persistence.

Before these realistic times began,
Thy predecessor was a God-sent man—
    A boon, a blessing to terrestrials,
A Prophet, Preacher, Seer, and Sage in one,
For whom heaven's portals always stood undone,
    To give him entrance to celestials.

And still methinks 'twere good for worldly men
To listen to thy teachings now and then,
    Nor hold thee wholly in derision.
Who knows, but in thy commerce with the skies,
Some gleams of wisdom from the Great All-wise
    Might reach them, also, through thy vision ?

Farewell, O Poet !   Mystery to me ;
If most to pity or to envy thee
    Is still to me an unsolved riddle ;
When I consider thee, full oft I think
'Twixt creature and Creator thou'rt a link—
    A Jacob's ladder stationed in the middle.

THE POET'S MISSION.

IN his native Scottish valley,
    Underneath a summer sky,
Wandering lone, the youthful poet
    Saw a virgin form draw nigh ;
From her lips of peerless beauty,
    Heard this sweet raphsodic cry:—

" Joy for ever! I have found thee, the minstrel sought
    so long!
Joy for ever ! I have found thee, thou darling Son of
    Song!
I, I the Goddess Poesy, my mantle o'er thee fling,
And consecrate thee Poet; my son, go forth and sing !
I spread before thy vision Creation's wondrous plan,

'Tis thine to read the golden scroll, and teach its
    truths to man.
I bid the thousand voices of ocean, earth, and air,
To thy poetic spirit their messages declare.
The odours of the forest, the blushes of the rose,
The colours of the rainbow, their secrets shall disclose:
The human heart and passions shall show themselves
    to thee ;
Of Nature's vast arcana I bid thee hold the key ;
The wings of thought shall bear thee wherever thou
    wouldst go—
To highest heights above thee, to deepest depths
    below;
Nor even starry Science, despite her piercing ken,
Shall penetrate so deeply the ways of gods and men.
Go forth, my son, and fear not thy mission to pro-
    claim;
Sing not for filthy lucre, sing not for idle fame,
But sing the thoughts within thee, howe'er the gales
    may blow;
Reprove the wicked lofty, commend the noble low;
Declare the truths thou knowest, though dearest
    friends deny,
And never lend thy genius to consecrate a lie.
I cannot give thee riches; my son, thou must expect
In penury to labour, to sing in cold neglect;
While nerves of keen sensation shall vibrate in thy
    frame,
And in thy restless bosom shall glow a heart of flame.
The lightest praise shall thrill thee, the lightest
    censure sting ;
Thy soul to souls congenial with painful love shall
    cling ;
The woes which calmer mortals can calmly, firmly
    brave,

Shall wring thy soul with anguish as bitter as the
    grave ;
But if thou wilt be faithful thy mission to fulfil,
My presence shall support thee through all extremes
    of ill;
And thou shall win for guerdon the poet's laurel
    crown,
And even help thy country to better her renown ;
And when thou shalt be gathered with kindred dust
    to lie,
Then shall thy name be written 'midst the names
    that cannot die!"

SCOTLAND REVISITED.

MY northern hills—auld Scotia's hills—
    I see your summits rise,
And tears that will not be repressed
    Are starting in my eyes,
As mem'ries of departed years,
    Of friends I shall not find,
Of early dreams and baffled hopes,
    Are rushing through my mind.

When last my country's heather hills
    Receded from my view,
Right many were the friends I left;
    Alas! they now are few!
The grasping grave hath gathered some
    Within its icy fold,
And some are exiles, like myself,
    And some are changed and cold.

The faithful few who still remain
  As changed, I ween, are they ;
The hoary locks are hoarer still,
  The raven mixt with grey;
The chubby boy and infant girl
  Are man and maiden now,
And care has stampt his traces deep
  On many a youthful brow.

My cottage home deserted lies,
  Its walls in crumbling heaps ;
And o'er the neighb'ring hamlet's site
  The reaper's sickle sweeps ;
Our grove of mingled larch and firs,
  Our grand aerial pines,
All, all have fallen and lent their trunks
  To form the " Sweeping Lines."

The engine's rush and whistle's scream
  Have reached our very glen ;
The deer and fox have fled their haunts,
  And given them up to men.
I know that utilitarians think
  'Tis vastly better so ;
Yet sadly, sadly do I miss
  The scenes of long ago.

I cannot find my former haunts ;
  The road hath changed its course ;
The winding river doth not flow
  With half its wonted force ;
The mountain loch and tarn are dried,
  And hushed the murmuring rills ;
All, all are changed, save only you,
  Auld Scotia's heather hills ! -

THE POET'S MISSION.

SHE spoke, and passed from vision
   To some celestial zone,
While silent stood the poet,
   As statue cut in stone,
Until within the valley
   He found himself alone.
Then rose his voice in rapture,
   The woods and rocks among,—
"Sweet Goddess, I believe thee!
   Why did I doubt so long?
Sweet mission, I receive thee,
   Henceforth my task is song!"
And he sang, and singeth ever,
   Sings in pleasure, sings in pain,
Watching, waiting for the glory—
   Must he always wait in vain—
Promised by the fleeting vision
   Which inspired his youthful strain.

THE POET'S KINGDOM.

I NEVER am lonely, the muse is my friend,
And thousands of fancies my footsteps attend,
That people the moments, which toil leaves to spare,
With countless creations unspeakably fair.

I cannot feel poor, for my kingdom is spread
Beneath me, around me, and over my head;
I've cornfields and vineyards, rich meadows and streams,
And rule, without rival, my kingdom of dreams.

The spirit of Beauty converses with me
From star-spangled sky and sun-gilded sea ;
And cherubim, stealing the voices of birds,
Address me in language surpassing all words !

The great of all ages, in action and thought,
By dainties untempted, by flatteries unbought,
Come into my dwelling, and sit by my side,
With never a semblance of shyness or pride.

The Greek and the Roman, the German and Frank,
The foremost in wisdom, the highest in rank,
With those of my country most widely renowned,
As guests in my poor little chamber are found.

A worldling might enter with practical looks,
And see in my chamber but books—faded books ;
But back to their heroes my vision extends,
And they speak to my heart the language of friends.

Rich dullards pass by me with impudent scorn,
For coinless my purse is, my raiment long-worn ;
And not for their eyes is the splendour which gleams
Round a child of the muse in his Kingdom of Dreams.

Enchained to their Lucre—the god of their love—
The wing's of the spirit ne'er lift them above ;
They hear not those accents so dulcet and clear,
Which ring at this moment thus, thus on mine ear,—

" Go, string the lyre, Poet, and gladden the earth !
I, Hope, shall go with thee, who smiled on thy birth ;
Faith, Honour, and Justice, thy steps shall attend,
The Fancies surround thee, the Muse be thy friend.

" Go, soothe the racked bosom with accents of love,
Speak peace to the wrathful, point sinners above,
Make use of thy gifts for the good of thy kind,
And yet shall thy brows with bays be entwined.

" Mere minions of Mammon, poor drudges and slaves,
Shall slumber unhonoured, forgot in their graves,
When thou shalt have risen and written thy name
In letters of light on the pages of fame ! "

My fare may be homely, my labours be rude,
Misfortune pursue me with all her fell brood ;
But, cheerful and hopeful, my strains shall ascend,
While God shall vouchsafe me the Muse for my friend.

The wealthy may pity, the haughty despise,
My claims raise the smiles of the mammonish wise ;
But my lot they might envy, though lowly it seems,—
I'm a lord ! I'm a prince, in my Kingdom of Dreams !

———

HISTORIC DEATHS.

CHARLES IX. OF FRANCE AND SOCRATES.

MY fancy, roaming o'er the past,
    Two vivid visions saw ;
One filled my mind with dreadful thoughts,
    And one with holy awe.
First, in a royal chamber I,
    'Midst fawning courtiers, stood,
And saw a royal sufferer writhe,
    Perspiring burning blood.

I marked him writhe, and toss, and glare,
  With fear-distended eyes,
And gathered from his fevered lips,
  Those conscience-smitten cries :—

" Those evil, evil memories
  Of treachery, rage, and gore,
Of desperate fight, and mangled slain,
  They haunt me evermore.
Great gouts of blood are on the walls,
  The roof, the floor, the bed,
And from myself at every pore
  Are gushing, rank and red.
The Huguenots! the Huguenots !
  Around my bed they throng,
Now cursing me with dying gasps,
  Now chanting doleful song.
Infernal phantoms glare on me—
  Hark, how they shriek and yell !
Are all the fiery fiends let loose
  To drag me down to hell ?
Ah, mother, mother ! why didst thou,
  Through all my sireless youth,
For ever guide my feet to tread
  The ways of base untruth ?
My reign hath been an evil reign,
  A cheat, a crimsoned lie !
My life hath been a cheerless life,
  My death—I cannot die !
The sacred pyx, the crucifix,
  The priests have lost their power ;
All holy thoughts abandon me,
  Grim horrors rule the hour ;

The pains of hell have seized on me,
　　The fiends surround my bed,
My boiling blood is struggling out
　　To join the streams I've shed.
The Huguenots! the Huguenots!
　　With Henry of Navarre,
With all their dead and living hosts
　　Are threat'ning vengeful war.
The pains of hell have seized on me,
　　The fiends surround my bed;
All, all combine to curse my soul,
　　The living and the dead.
I cannot live! I dread to live!
　　I cannot, cannot die!
The flames of hell have seized on me,
　　And scorch me where I lie!"

The horrid vision fades away,
　　The cries of anguish cease,
I leap o'er space and time, and tread
　　The shores of classic Greece.
Through queenly Athens, far and wide,
　　I wander at my will,
'Midst miracles of sculptured art
　　And architectural skill;
And all through Academus I,
　　Through the Lyceum, walk,
And by Ilyssus' famous stream
　　Where sages roam and talk.
But where is Sophroniscus' son,
　　Athena's sagest sage?
Why doth he not in wise discourse
　　Ingenious youth engage?

And why do I, unquestioned, pass
    " Uninterviewed " along,
A stranger, all unnoticed, pass
    From whispering throng to throng ?
" To-day he drinks the hemlock's juice,
    His hour must needs be near."
" I wonder how he'll meet his death ? "
    Such whispers reach my ear;
But stilled all other sounds of speech—
    Impulsive grief or mirth—
As when a storm hath spent its rage,
    A hush o'erspreads the earth.
And lo ! in prisoned cell, I stand
    By Sophroniscus' son,
The poison circles in his veins,
    Its work is well nigh done ;
And yet amid his weeping friends,
    He, only he, is calm,
And pours into their aching hearts
    Such words of soothing balm :—

" Now why should I begrudge, my friends,
    Or wherefore fear to die ?
Before us all, or soon or late,
    That certain fate doth lie.
And sure we should account him blest
    To whom the gods allow
To sink so tranquilly to rest
    As I am sinking now ;
To die condemned, yet innocent,
    With conscience calm and clear,
Regretted by the wise and good,
    With sorrow all sincere;

To die before disease and age
    Combine their double force
To waste the strength and leave the frame
    An animated corse ;
To die before those evil nights,
    When sleep is woo'd in vain,
And painfully the sands of life
    Drop, weary, grain by grain;
To die and go—Ah ! friends, methinks
    I see, as in a trance,
The curtain of the future move,
    And lift at death's advance.
The Island's of the Blest appear,
    Celestial scenes arise,
Departed heroes beckon me—
    The brave, the just, the wise.
There Nestor, Homer, Hesiod,
    Ah ! far more than I can tell
Extend their arms, and smile to me—
    Farewell, my friends, farewell !"

Thus Socrates, the Wise, expires,
    And thus do mankind still
Their best instructors misconstrue
    And persecute and kill.
By poison, crucifix, and sword,
    By cord, and axe, and fire,
By slow starvation, cruel neglect,
    Earth's worthiest expire ;
But better live a Socrates—
    Like him resign life's breath—
Than reign a Charles, in perjured pomp,
    And die a Charles' death.

WALLACE BEFORE HIS JUDGES.

FROM the prison they have led him,
    Crowned, in mockery, as a king;
But his eye is still the eagle's,
    Though they've clipt the eagle's wing.
He is chained and guarded surely,
    But his steadfast soul is free,
And to charges, taunts, and insults,
    Thus defiantly speaks he :—

"Leader I of outlaws, never!
    Foremost I amidst a band
Sworn to shed our dearest heart's-blood,
    Or to free our native land
From our spoilers, our oppressors—
    The invaders of our rights—
Ever swarming to the northward,
    Thick as Egypt's locust flights.

"I a traitor to King Edward?
    By the Rood, I never was!
For I was not born his subject,
    And I never owned his laws.
True it is, I've slain my hundreds
    Of his armed invading hordes;
True, I've burnt his castles, wrested
    From their lawful Scottish lords.

"And restore me to my mountains,
    Give me back my trusty brand,
And the few who still are faithful
    To our own beloved land.
I would smite, and slay, and spare not,
    Tripling each reproachful deed,

Whilst a single loathed invader
   Lived to ravage north the Tweed.

"He who slew my dearest kindred,
   Drove the remnant to the rocks—
Me and mine, to seek for shelter
   With the eagle and the fox.
The enslaver of my country,
   The destroyer of my race,
Bids me crawl, like beaten spaniel,
   Lick his feet, and sue for grace!

"Ye have power, and may condemn me
   To the vilest form of death;
But your king, I have defied him,
   Do, and will with my last breath.
I am helpless in his clutches,
   Let him work his wrathful will;
Patriot hearts will beat for Scotland,
   Patriot arms defend her still.

"Feet and hands your chains may circle,
   But as free as when I trod
On my native Scottish heather
   Shall my spirit rise to God.
Stretch the rack and rear the gibbet,
   Tear this body limb from limb;
There's a God above who judges,
   I will sue to none save Him!

"Caledonia, O my country!
   I shall play my final part;
I shall die the death appointed,
   With thy name upon my heart.

But, behold the future opens!
  Joy of joys! my eyes can see
Patriot falchions flashing round thee—
  Caledonia, thou art free!

"Tyrants' minions cannot rule thee,
  Tyrants' laws can never bind,
For a patriot's heart is glowing
  In thy weakest, humblest hind.
'Midst the nations, I behold thee
  Free and great, and glorious rise;
And my name with thine shall mingle,
  While thy granite mountains rise."

BESSIE.

OUR Bessie was as beautiful
  As daisy—flower in May ;
What time it lifts its dewy head
  To greet the king of day.

The old would linger as she passed,
  Enchanted by her grace;
The young would walk a mile about
  To look upon her face.

Her wavy hair and azure eyes,
  Her rosy mouth and chin,
Seemed all too sweet and beautiful
  For any child of sin.

A radiance with her presence went,
   A gladness seemed to dwell,
Which lifted gloom and discontent
   As by a magic spell.

The poor forgot their poverty,
   The sorrowful their grief,
The sorest sufferer felt her come
   An angel of relief.

She moved among us for a time,
   Unspeakably fair—
A golden bird, a gleam of light,
   A thing beyond compare.

She moved among us for a time,
   And then returned to God;
But earth and we seemed bettered through
   Her beauteous brief abode.

All loveliness, all gentleness,
   All innocence and glee,
As if her mission was to teach
   How joyous life might be.

We sorely missed her from our midst;
   But e'en when tears were rife,
We thanked the heaven for lending earth
   So beautiful a life.

ODE TO LIBERTY.

SWEET Liberty !
   Dear Liberty !
   Far dearer yet wert thou to me,
   If I could find but two agree
   On what thou art or ought to be.

Our politicians all declare
Thou art a gift beyond compare—
   The choicest given
   To man by heaven ;
   And in thy cause
   They heap up laws,
Till, like Tarpeia at the gate,
Thou needst must sink beneath the weight
Of shields above thee flung by those
Professing friends, but acting foes.
Bards call thee goddess, call thee queen,
Yet never shade of shade hath been
   Impalpable as thou.
Not one has courted more than I
That presence thou dost still deny
   To every prayer and vow.
Thou ridest not upon the wind ;
The freest, fiercest, is confined
   By laws it must obey.
In vain the waves their currents pour,
They cannot pass the rocky shore
   · Which rudely bids them stay.
In vain would flooded river roll
O'er meadow green and wooded knoll,
He, too, is under fixed control,
And must not overleap the goal
   And limit of his way.

The moral and the physical
Firm fixëd laws alike enthrall,
And these extend their sway o'er all
Creation's actions, great and small;
    In vain my scrutiny.
Nor yet in matter nor in mind
Thy form Protean can I find,
    If form belongs to thee,
      Dear Liberty!
      And can it be
That thou art a nonentity —
A mere chimera of the brain—
When millions, on the battle plain,
Have poured their blood like winter rain,
    Their lives for Liberty.
Yet I have drunk Pierian springs,
Have borrowed fancy's swiftest wings,
To range o'er all created things
    In bootless quest for thee.
If thou art more than empty name,
Pray how dost thou attest thy claim
    To entity?
Which certainly must be,
If dreamers have not lent at thee.
For East and West, and North and South,
Thy praises are in every mouth;
And if I could but realize thee,
None would more belaud and prize thee.
    But O! belauded Liberty,
      Thou from me
      Dost ever flee.
Nor have I mind nor corporal seeing,
If thou hast or hast not being.

MRS. MATTHEWS' BABY.

WE'VE got a baby at our place,
 The tiniest little creature ;
Each limb a paragon of grace,
 A model every feature.

I ne'er, in all my born days,
 Did meet with such another ;
And then it has such winning ways,
 And isn't a bit of bother.

It is the gentlest, sweetest mite
 That ever was created;
No pencil could portray it right,
 No tongue could overrate it.

Don't think, because I'm its mamma,
 I prize the mite unduly ;
Because its sober, staid papa
 Thinks it a treasure truly.

The way he's got to handle it
 Would make a Turk admire him ;
He'll kiss, caress, and dandle it,
 As if it ne'er could tire him.

And every neighbour who drops in
 Is eloquent in praise of it;
The very sternest it can win,
 Just by the looks and ways of it.

Why, even Mrs. Martha Gunn,
 For all she is so spiteful,

Has been to see the little one,
   And owns it is delightful.

And yet, whene'er I get a dress,
   A cloak, a hat, or bonnet,
She's certain sure to call express,
   And pass her strictures on it.

But, baby—well, what could she say,
   Or what could any other?
She could not take the fact away
   That I am baby's mother.

And as for baby, darling pet!
   What woman could resist it?
Why, not a man has seen it yet
   That has not seized and kiss'd it.

Ah! 'tis a babe of babes the pink,
   And not a bit of bother;
In all the world I do not think
   There can be such another.

Some mothers may think theirs as sweet,
   And sweet to them they may be;
But sure I am they can't compete
   With our unequalled baby.

THE GROANS OF A GRUMBLER.

"I said, in my haste, all men are liars."

Comment by an old Scotch Divine—"Ay! ay! ye said that i' yer *haste*, did ye, Davie, man? Deed gin ye hed been here ye might ha'e said it at yer *leisure*."

I READ in the world's wide page,
  And mark a war upon Truth—
A certain hatred and rage
  Against the simple and sooth—
Youth claiming the wisdom of Age,
  Age aping the graces of Youth.

The hair on the maiden's head,
  (Mainly, by purchase, her own),
Must be the raven or red,
  Which Fashion chooses to don,
May be plant or animal bred,
  It matters not where it is grown.

Nor is it only her hair
  That woman borrows or buys;
But her teeth, so pearly fair,
  The splendid light of her eyes,
And her figure, rounded and spare,
  May be nothing but purchased lies.

Nor only Matron and Maid
  Traffic in craft and deceit;
'Mongst Manhood, in every grade,
  Brazens the liar and cheat,
From Monarchs in purple arrayed
  To peddlers that peddle the street.

In metal, timber, or stone,
  What is there honestly made?

True workman, where have you gone ?
Has each abandoned his trade,
That swindlers may lord it alone,
And villany's game may be played ?

The trader, accounted fair,
  Mingles the better and worse ;
Turns a good and wholesome ware
  Into a poisonous curse ;
Nothing for buyer's health doth care,
  If he may put gold in his purse.

Only trust what Quackery saith,
  And who need sicken or die ?
Who so willeth may hold his breath—
  A lease for Eternity—
Snap his fingers in face of Death,
  And the buffets of age defy.

Comes there a politician here,
  'Tis with a purpose and plan—
'Tis with a certain panacea
  For all the evils of man !
Was ever Speaker more sincere
  Since the functions of speech began ?

He is the friend of your class ;
  Lives for the weal of your town ;
Toils for the good of the mass,
  The stricken, and the trodden down—
You'd see, if his breast were of glass,
  The good he seeks most is his own.

In Shem, in Japheth and Ham,
  Are needless pain and distress—

The wolf devouring the lamb ;
    The greater crushing the less ;
Ambition, Interest, and Sham,
    In the Bar, the Pulpit, and Press.

Pretension and wordy cram
    In wisdom and learning's seat,
Scamping, shoddy, and sham,
    Where ever we turn our feet ;
And crimes which cry to the great " I Am,"
    For punishment sudden and meet.

O, world ! what have you to give,
    That is the thing which it seems ?
O, justice ! where do you live,
    Out of the kingdom of dreams ?
Shall I never rejoice at the sound of your voice,
    Nor bask in your beautiful beams.

IS IT NOT BEAUTIFUL IN GOD'S WORLD ?

MUCH I have paced this world around,
    And of its toil and care,
Its pains and sorrows, still have found
    Mine own an ample share ;
But yet I've met in every sphere
A joy to charm, a friend to cheer.

When clouds above my head were dark,
    When billows swept the deck,

When Fate appeared to doom my bark
    To sure and speedy wreck,
The sun has shown his radiant form,
Dispelled the clouds, and chased the storm.

I've met with men, who call the world
    The dwelling-place of tears,
An orb, by God in anger hurled,
    Beyond the brighter spheres,
Wherein His will is clearly shown,
His love to every dweller known.

To me the world is ne'er a place
    Abandoned to despair,
For tokens of its Maker's grace
    Surround me everywhere ;
And " Clouds of Witnesses " appear
To prove his presence ever near.

Each season of the changeful year
    Can bring me fresh delight;
E'en Winter hath his brow severe
    With crystal glories dight;
The Spring, in verdant buds arrayed,
Awakens song in sun and shade.

The Summer, clad in leaves and flowers,
    With fruitage in his hands,
'Mid genial warmth and fresh'ning showers.
    Walks o'er the smiling lands ;
And Autumn, crowned with golden grain,
Heaps generous plenty on the wain.

Methinks that murmurs must offend
    The dread Creative Power,

Whose countless benefits descend
  On earth at every hour ;
And blind, methinks, that man must be,
Who fails those benefits to see.

If man to man were only just,
  And grateful to his God,
Still bearing with a pious trust
  Each Heaven-appointed load,
Methinks that this terrestrial ball
Might still be beautiful to all.

SCOTCH GREETING TO THE PRINCE OF WALES.

On the visit of their Royal Highnesses the Prince and Princess of Wales, to Sheffield, in 1875, at the request of the Scottish Arch Committee, the author endeavoured to express the feelings of the Scottish residents in Sheffield towards the august visitors in this greeting :—

SONS and daughters of the north,
  From our Scottish homes come forth,
  Loyal still to loyal worth.
    We, amidst the gathered gay,
Would our Prince and Princess greet
With all honours that are meet ;
All that hearts with love replete,
    Can through feeble words convey.

Nor of power or high degree
Blinded worshippers are we ;
'Tis our joy in you to see
    Lustrous worth and rank allied ;

And so fair a light hath shone
From your Royal Mother's throne,
That her House is dearly known,
   Wheresoe'er the true abide.

Queenly Mother, Princely Sire,
None have set examples higher,
Better fitted to inspire
   Noble purpose in the breast.
Have we need to cross the brine,
Name the Royal Danish Line,
When amidst us here doth shine
   She who patterns all its best?

Ye inherit lofty place,
Majesty and winning grace;
In yourselves and in your race
   Be your parents' virtues found;
And (but distant be the day)
When your hands the sceptre sway,
We so willingly obey,
   Spread the climes of earth around.

May your righteous rule increase
Every art of joy and peace!
May the faithful never cease,
   Round your justice-pillar'd throne!
May the wisest homage bring,
Highest bards your praises sing,
And your greatness earth enring,
   To the farthest peopled zone!

On yourselves and loved ones all,
May the Lord of great and small

Bid the richest blessings fall,
    That an Empire's heart desires!
Pray we, children of the North,
In our native land, or forth,
Loyal still to loyal worth,
    Like our Caledonian sires.

SPRING.

NOW do the feathered tribes again
    To pour the joyous vocal strain
        There tuneful throats unite;
The balmy air, the budding grove,
Are resonant with lays of love
    From morn till dewy night.

Again the nimble swallow flies,
Intent to catch, by swift surprise,
    Her airy insect-food;
The cawing rooks again prepare,
'Midst branches rising high in air,
    To hatch their sooty brood.

The toilsome bee, betimes abroad,
Is bearing home the golden load,
    Her hoarded thrift to swell,
Unconscious that voracious man
Will mar her economic plan,
    And plunder life and cell!

The fisher, rising with the lark,
O'erhauls his sails, retrims his bark,
    And pushes from the shore;

And now securely plies his trade,
Where winds and waves their revels played,
   With plash and deaf'ning roar.

The shepherd leads his woolly bands
To graze on verdant pasture lands,
   Where, thoughtless of the knife,
The lambkins on the sunny banks
Indulge a thousand sportive pranks,
   In joy of recent life.

Now doth the the daisy lift its eye
To greet the smiling vernal sky,
   No more by storms o'erspread ;
And where the purling waters run,
The yellow cowslip to the sun
   Uprears her modest head.

The brawling streamlets hush their voice,
To listen while the meads rejoice,
   The woods their notes prolong ;
While hill to hill its gladness tells,
And fair Creation's bosom swells
   With universal song.

Six thousand years* have passed away
Since man beheld the orb of day
   His vernal radiance fling :
Not till that orb with age grow dim
Shall raptured poets cease to hymn
   The glories of the spring.

---

*Something less than 6,000 years, according to Christian chronology, but our muse refuses to be bound to an exact observance of arithmetical numbers, being sufficiently trammelled by harmonic numbers.

AN AUTUMN LAY.

THE leaves are dying on the trees,
Or falling in the autumn breeze,
The fields are shorn of fruit;
The feathered tenants of the groves,
Which made them lyric with their loves,
Are parted now, or mute.

They go in other lands to sing
The glories of another spring,
Another summer's praise;
To build their feathered homes anew,
'Neath milder skies of brighter blue,
And suns of warmer blaze.

The powdered snows will soon descend,
The leafless forest boughs to bend,
And robe the world in white;
The clouds will drive along the skies,
The howling winter winds arise,
And riot in their might.

The brooks, their tuneful voices lost,
Encircled in the arms of frost,
Will pause in icy sleep;
The rivers under winter's reign
Will bear their tribute to the main
With melancholy sweep.

But yet it is not Nature's plan
That all shall then be gloom to man;
Across the frozen lake,
Behold the hardy skaters bound,
Whilst Echo to the shores around
Repeats the mirth they make.

Behold the Christmas Tree arise,
Adorned with many a showy prize
    To tempt the joyous child;
Behold the smiling Christmas board,
Where sparkling wines are freely poured,
    And smoking dainties piled.

When tempests rave with loudest din,
Behold the cheerful hearth within,
    Where sits respected Age,
And pours in childhood's eager ear
The tales of wonder, love, or fear,
    Commixt with counsels sage.

To him who knows to live aright,
Each season has its own delight,
    Though each must bring its care;
Nor would the soul, contented here,
Aspire to win a brighter sphere
    If all below were fair.

———

PEACE AND WAR.

AMIDST the sons of men I walk alone,
  For me the wealthy and the great despise,
Companionship with fools I will have none,
  And when I seek communion with the wise,
They shake their heads, and say to me, "Begone!
  Thou tread'st the earth, thy head is in the skies."

And thus, perchance, it hath been mine to hear
  Seraphic sounds, to other listeners mute,

And sights of wonder to mine eyes appear
Whose being sober Reason doth dispute—
Must I be deaf and blind lest equals jeer,
And silent where I cannot quite confute?

I will not! for a spirit cries to mine—
"Thou hast thy talents, strive not these to hide;
Yea, talents which, for purposes divine,
The Mighty Master doth to thee confide."
Such high commands I hear nor can decline,
Peal forth my song however men deride.
 *   *   *   *   *

Behold the Spirit shows to me a land
Wide, beauteous, fertile, wealthy, and content,
Her peasant cultures with a willing hand
His acres cursed by no oppressive rent;
Her learned men, her rulers in command,
Are all on schemes of wise improvement bent.

At all her ports the vessels come and go;
Each town is busy as a summer hive;
No dearth of aught her smiling millions know,
Nor yet for sordid ends alone they strive;
In every breast fraternal feelings glow,
Religion, learning, arts and science thrive.

"O, happy land!" I cry with joy elate;
"O, people wise to understand the cause
Why nations sink, or flourish rich and great,
Beyond the limits of inane applause!
O happy I to find at last a State
Where truth and justice make and sway the laws.

"O, Ruler, who hath wisely banished war,
And all the fiends that follow in his train,

The fruits of honest industry to mar,
    And scatter ruin on the peaceful plain,
Thy simple staff outshines the victor's car
    In triumph borne from thousands crushed and slain."

Scarce had these words escaped my lips, when, lo!
    A cloud, no bigger than a human hand,
On far horizon's verge began to show.
    And fast and far its dusky wings expand,
Until it dimmed the sun's meridian glow,
    And darkened over all that peaceful land,

It spread and blackened till it blinded all;
    Confused, beclouded, stumbled to and fro,
The monarch, noble, peasant, great and small,
    In mental darkness deep as shades below;
Each sound without their trembling souls appal,
    In every neighbour starts a mortal foe.

"War! war!" cries one, and through the land resound
    The wildest rumours, dreadest of alarms;
"War! war!" cry all, "the nations threaten round—
    To arms! brave citizens, to arms! to arms!
Repel the foe beyond those limits bound,
    And revel wide in victory's splendid charms."

If equal madness on their neighbours fell
    I know not, for the spirit did not teach;
But these arose, aggression to repel,
    And swiftly hurled defiance each to each;
Blow met with blow, yell answered savage yell,
    And fiendish fury found its highest reach.

And thus two peoples each the other hewed
    With all the fellest implements of strife,

While battlefields with mangled slain were strewed ;
   Great ghastly wounds and helpless maimed were rife ;
Dire famine pinched, fierce pestilence pursued,
   And all the evils that embitter life.

Proud palaces and splendid cities blaze;
   Destruction, plunder, baleful crimes increase,
Till nations round in holy horror raise
   Their hands, and cry in name of heaven to cease!
Then pause the combatants in stunned amaze,
   And either side, exhausted, welcomes peace.

Each paused exhausted, gazed around, and grieved
   To see the evil each on each had wrought;
And all for what?   It scarce could be conceived
   What one refused and what the other sought;
And now so easily was peace achieved,
   The wonder was they ever could have fought.

Their rage extinguished and their arms resigned,
   They build anew their homes in ruins laid,
To honest arts anew direct their mind,
   And re-unite the broken links of Trade.
Can years of peace and industry combined
   Efface the havoc months of war have made?

"What struggles these! what sufferings worse than
      vain !"
   When all had passed, I cried, in sad surprise ;
"How long shall war his dismal part sustain,
   And brothers mangle brothers in such guise?
Speak ! spirit, speak ! and make your answer plain "—
   The spirit answered—" Until man grow wise."

AN EXHORTATION.

BROTHER, help your weaker brother
　　O'er life's rugged way;
Wherefore place before each other
　　Causes of delay?
Stumbling-blocks enough are strewn,
Tho' ourselves should scatter none.

Brother, raise your weaker brother
　　Sinking in the mire;
Strive within his breast to smother
　　Lawless, low desire.
Even he may yet be woo'd,
Won to actions great and good.

Sister, do not loathe your sister
　　Tho' her feet have slid—
Alas! you know not how she miss'd her
　　Footing as she did;
A gentle word, a look of love,
Might yet direct her steps above.

Willing, hopeful, cheerful toilers,
　　Shutting from the breast
Pride and envy, and such spoilers
　　Of our scanty rest;
Loving many, hating none,
Comrades, let us journey on.

MORNING THOUGHTS.

LO! the rosy morning gleams,
   Through its golden portals,
Calling from the Land of Dreams
   Slumber-strengthened mortals
Back to fortunes dark or fair,
Sweet content or carking care.

Back to work calls you and me,
   Let us up and do it;
If but honest work it be,
   We shall never rue it.
Honest work gets honest pay
At the Master's reckoning-day.

Look abroad ere you begin,
   Think an earnest minute ;
You will find that every sin
   Hath a poison in it,
Which doth wide and wider pass
Till it taint the social mass.

Whence are desolating wars,
   Save from mad ambition ?
'Tis dishonesty which mars
   Faithful toil's fruition.
Selfish greed of earthly gains
Multiplies and whets our pains.

Discontentment, hate, and strife,
   Tyrannous oppression,.
Woe and weariness of life,
   All the vile succession
To the wretched bosom known,
Springs from sin, and sin alone.

Could we banish from the earth
    All our errors olden;
Take that rule of heavenly birth,
    Frequent called the Golden,*
As our guide in all we do,
Paradise would bloom anew.

Every worthy action lives,
    Generates another,
Through the impulse which it gives
    To a fainting brother.
Seeds of good, howe'er minute,
Spring and carry golden fruit.

Oh! that unto us this day,
    From benignant heaven,
Strength to turn from sin away,
    Love of good were given!
Then might our imperfect light
Guide an erring brother right.

Then might we ourselves be glad
    In the consolation
That our lives their uses had
    In our day and station;
Then might look in humble trust
For the portion of the just.

* Whatsoever ye would that men should do to you, do ye even so to them."

MAY SINGERS.

POET, poet! why so gloomy
  All the blessed day,
'Midst a thousand chorists singing,
'Midst a thousand anthems ringing,
  'Midst the flowers of May?
Poet, join the vocal throngs,
Pour like them your vernal songs,
  Joyous be as they.

"Querist, querist! I am gloomy;
  Need I tell you why?
Who will listen to my singing,
When such melodies are ringing
  Over earth and sky?
Yet within my breast are pent
Floods of song demanding vent;
  I must sing or die."

Poets find their joy in singing,
  Like the birds that fly.
Sing, your sadness will depart,
Gladness steal upon your heart,
  Joyance light your eye.
Sing, it is your nature's need;
Sing, regardless who may heed;
  You must sing or die.

RECOLLECTIONS OF A VISIT TO LINN OF PETER CULTER, on July 19th, 1877.

ONCE, only once, oh, Culter Linn!
  I stood upon thy brink;
Once listened to thy roaring din,
  But had no power to think,
For mazy memories of the past
Which rushed upon my brain so fast.

I saw thy waters writhe and plash
  Betwixt their ramparts twain,
Leap down, whirl round, and onwards dash,
  As seething as my brain.
I saw and heard, but nothing more;
All thought fled back to days of yore.

Yet wert thou then in all the pride
  Of waters full and strong,
What time I stood thy stream beside,
  And wished to weave a song,
At friendship's half expressed desire
That I for thee should string my lyre.

Above thee verdant woods inclined,
  Fair fields around thee lay,
And calmly down the west declined
  The setting orb of day;
Wild flowerets kissed thy foaming feet,
Or in thy spray drank nurture meet.

The scene was worthy of a stave
  From louder lyre than mine;
But then the Muse no promptings gave,
  No power to weave a line.

My soul was far in other years,
In commerce with her young compeers.

Friends stood beside me—one of youth,
   And one through him made dear—
And we did talk of thee, in sooth,
   And all the landscape near.
But aye, the past arose between,
And shadowed all the present scene.

The very friends who led me there,
   Although they little dreamed,
Themselves the chain electric were,
   By which so densely streamed
The memories of departed years—
Dead hopes, dead joys, and dead compeers.

Dash down thy rocks, oh, Culter Linn!
   Around thy basin rave,
Another harp their praise must win
   Who would extol thy wave.
What time I stood upon thy brink,
My brain whirled round, I could not think.

THE RING.

"I will a plain unvarnished tale deliver."—SHAKSPEARE.

'MONGST our tents, with childish laughter,
   Played the Sergeant's little daughter;
Round her neck we spied a string,
   And thereon a tiny ring;
   And a whisper passed about—

"'Tis a talisman, no doubt!"
But the Sergeant answered "no!
Comrades mine, it is not so:
Listen, and I will declare
Why I hung the trinket there—
We fought the foe at Bushire;
We fought with little to fear,
For their forts were merely mud,
Their arms as old as the Flood,
And quickly their backs we saw,
And followed with loud hurrah!
But one of the rascals turned,
The prime in his matchlock burned;
Our Captain fell on his face,
We raised him out of the place,
We bore him back to his tent,
Alas! life's current was spent!
But his glazing eyes he cast
On me, ere the spirit passed—
"Take this to Ellen," said he,
"This ring and message from me—
Tell I died with her name"—
No further syllable came.
The ring that the Captain gave
I bore upon field and wave,
But ne'er his Ellen have found
Above nor under the ground.
So, when our infant was born,
On a smiling April morn,
Though I had wished for a lad,
I saw the girl and was glad.
We'll call her "Ellen," I said,
For sake of one who is dead.
And round her neck, with a string,

I fastened the Captain's ring.
A foolish fancy I knew,
But yet what more could I do?
No other way could I find
To ease the thought in my mind,
That I must obey my Captain's Command,
Who fell at Bushire, on the Persian strand,
While leading the troops of our native land."

ASPIRATIONS.

I.

LET me live my little day,
   Till my sun of life shall set,
So that come when come it may,
   Death's demand for nature's debt.
I may pass and leave behind,
   When I quit this earthly sphere,
Some memento to my kind,
   That I was not useless here.
Some recorded thought or deed
   That should swell the sum of good,
Satisfy a craving need,
   Soothe a soul to milder mood;
Raise a brother sunken low:
   Somehow leave upon the scene,
Somewhat of a brighter glow,
   Because I myself have been.

II.

Let me live amid the beautiful
   Art, and nature's fairest flowers,

To my great Creator dutiful
   Until my latest hours;
Never shirking aught of labour
   He hath ordered for my share,
Never laying on my neighbour
   More than I myself would bear;
Never sinking downward weakly
   Under man's insult and scorn,
Bearing bravely, bearing meekly
   Ills that must perforce be borne;
Looking to the future, rather,
   Full of hope than timid fear,
Trusting to my Heavenly Father,
   My hereafter and my here.

———

THE SCOTTISH EXILE'S SONG.

KNOW ye the land whose mountains blue
   In rugged grandeur rise
Until their peaks are lost to view
   Amidst the misty skies;
The land where "wimplin' burnies rin,"
   Between their "gow'ny braes,"
While gaily in the summer sun
   The sportive lambkin plays?

Know ye the land where winter's reign
   Is lengthened and severe,
Yet ever to the toil-worn swain
   Are winter's evenings dear;

For Ramsay, Burns, and Scott are read
    Around the ingle's glow,
And young imaginations fed
    With tales of long ago.

Know ye the land where Ossian sang
    Amidst the rocks and caves,
And still around the mountains hang
    The memories of his braves;
The land where hill and dale is rife
    With names of old renown,
When hero-life, in freedom's strife,
    Was poured ungrudging down?

Know ye the land which never bore
    A tyrant's hateful reign,
Whose hills and glens from shore to shore
    Unconquered still remain,
Whose sons in battle's reddest shocks
    Have stood for Fatherland,
Unyielding as the granite rocks
    That guard their native strand?

Know ye the land whose children roam
    In all the climes of earth,
Yet prize o'er every foreign home
    The land that gave them birth?
Its sweet remembrance ne'er depart,
    How far so e'er they stray,
It bears for them the warmest hearts
    Beneath the Solar ray.

'Tis still the land where bosoms glow
    With love's divinest flame,

And men esteem o'er all below,
　A fair and honest name;
The land whose children ne'er forget
　The paths their fathers trod,
The land where true religion yet
　Uplifts the soul to God?

OMNES.

That glorious land, we know it well,
It hangs on memory like a spell—
'Tis Scotland where our kindred dwell!

THE "SPECIAL'S" RIDE.

The following is a transcription of a private letter from Mr. Archibald
Forbes, the celebrated special correspondent, familiarly describing his
ride from Ulundi to Landman's Drift, Maritzburg, etc., in July, 1879.

ULUNDI was won ; and in heaps on the plain
　The Zulus lay wounded, or mangled and slain,
　Or chased by our horsemen they fearfully fled,
　While the blaze of their kraals lit the sky overhead.　.
　When Francis, my friend of the *Times*, and I wheeled,
　And galloped our horses away from the field—
　For we might, if we scribbled our fastest, make shift
　To send by Guy Dawnay our news to the Drift.

At the laager I scribbled a hasty dispatch,
Then sped to head-quarters Guy Dawnay to catch.
Was he starting ? Oh no, and conceive my surprise
To hear Colonel Crealock's, Lord Chelmsford's replies,
To draw their dispatches they waited, they said,

Returns of the missing, the wounded, and dead.
There was this to be done ; there was that to decide;
" Then I'll start, and at once," I impatiently cried.

My purpose scarce uttered, I knew it absurd,
But what would you have, sirs ? my word was my word ;
Though it was not so much my own packet, I swear,
As the news of the fight that I hungered to bear,
For I chafed that head-quarters should be so supine
Regarding dispatches more weighty than mine ;
And thought that Sir Garnet should know with next sun
That the Zulus were conquered, Ulundi was won.

So I turned from head-quarters without more delay,
Got a horse I could trust, both for pluck and for stay,
Told my friends I would bear any message they had,
Refused—though they call me foolhardy or mad—
Refused to be turned from my purpose or mood,
Though the last to entreat me was Evelyn Wood,
Who gave me message to send to his wife,
When I swore I would venture for death or for life.

Lord Chelmsford conveyed me a packet as well,
And I turned from the camp as the dusk of eve fell,
Gave my chestnut the reign, and with sweltering stride,
He sprang on his gruesome and wearisome ride.
Along the rough steep I directed his flight,
For I knew we were speedily losing the light,
And I wished to get over the worst of the ground
Ere the night of Zululand encompassed us round.

No road could be seen but confused wagon tracts,
And o'er the dark sky spread the cumulus wracks ;
Faint tracks on the ground, and faint light in the sky,

The pathway was crooked, the bushes were high;
But forward my good horse directed his head,
His limbs like a brave steeplechaser's outspread,
And speedily, steadily, onward he tore,
As if death pressed behind him and life lay before.

"Foolhardy," perchance! and my rashness I owned,
When the black night around me so fearfully frowned,
When the head of my horse was a prospect too far,
When I dared not strike match for soothing cigar,
Lest the bushes above or the hollows below
Might send me the murderous fire of the foe;
When a marsh might engulf, or a precipice check,
Or my chestnut might stumble, and break legs or neck,

'Twas a road, 'twas a ride for endurance and pluck,
But I cheered my horse forward and trusted to luck,
Peered down to the tracks with the carefullest heed,
Made sure my revolver was ready at need,
Kept every sense strained, lest a sudden Zulu,
Should spring from the bush and my mission undo;
For the news of Ulundi, should I come to grief,
Another must carry more late to our chief.

May I ne'er in emergence be served by a worse
Than my mount in Zululand, my mettlesome horse,
But somehow, he galloped aside from the track,
And it baffled my efforts to pilot him back.
For the blackness of darkness encompassed us round,
And the rank grass untrodden waved thick on the ground,
So I reined him in softly, and soothed him to stand;
For I knew there were marshes, deep marshes at hand.

The rest for a moment to both was a boon,
But I sat like a statue and waited the moon;

Sat waiting and watching, prepared for the worst,
If a beast or Zulu from the bushes should burst;
Sat there on my chestnut as still as a stone,
With my wounded knee aching, limbs chilled to the bone,
Believing the moon had forgotten her hour,
Like a pilgrim whom travail and sleep overpower.

I dare say, as usual, the moon kept her time,
For her great yellow disc did at last show sublime ;
And my chestnut and I turned our backs on the swamp,
And mounted the slope to the next British camp,
Where my friend major Uptcher, gave welcome as true
As Briton gives Briton, where Britons are few—
As friend gives to friend, who comes from afar
With news that their country has conquered in war.

With my friends at the camp I delayed a brief space,
Till a horse was got ready my horse to replace ;
For my spirited chestnut had done a brave heat,
But I left him at Entongeneni dead beat,
Got an escort two stages to pilot me right;
Then rode by myself the long bitter night,
The only adventures the loss of the track,
And painful endeavours to work my way back.

From Entongeneni I freely confess
That the risk from wild beasts and wild Zulus was less,
But how I got forward I scarcely can tell,
As the morning advanced and the blinding fogs fell,
When the ruts of the Wagons had oft to be found
By crawling and feeling all over the ground ;
But another long spell of the journey dragged past,
And welcome, Fort Marshall was reached at the last.

Thence kind Colonel Collingwood sent me away
Refreshad and remounted as morning broke grey,
And steadily, wearily, onward I rode,
Till fiercly above me the burning sun glowed,
Rode steadily on, and to cut the tale short,
Made Landsman's Drift ring with the welcome report,
At two on the fifth, 'neath the blaze of the sun,
That the Zulus were vanquished, Ulundi was won.

The miles of my ride were a hundred and ten,
The hours I spent over it twenty, but then
Consider the halts, and the wanderings astray,
How they robbed me of time and out-lengthened the way:
Consider the fogs, and the darkness profound,
Consider my weight, and consider the ground,
And in spite of Detraction, there still will abide
The fact of a stiffish and hazardous ride.

And sometimes I think, as I smoke my cigar,
Of a medal-perchance at the end of the war;
For next to Port Durnford for fear of delay,
I carried Sir Garnet the news of the day,
And Sir Garnet was pleased to commend my dispatch,
Which others with escorts and guides did not match;
For to get to Port Durnford I'd somehow contrived
Two days ere details from Lord Chelmsford arrived.

And worse than my first was my second long bout,
For I got to Maritzburg so nearly played out,
So famished, so muddy, so wretched in plight,
That my oldest friend there did not know me by sight;
And the worst was the fasts, and the physical strain,
Were no sort of use as a newspaper gain;
Had I stayed at Ulundi for every detail,
My packet had gone just the same by the mail.

I know there are many who scoff, and declare
That I make a tall talk of a puny affair;
I know there are thousands, and thousands besides,
Who prate of more daring and dangerous rides;
But I tell you that ride, ere I rode it again,
I'd be shot at a couple of hours on the plain,
Though the missles of battle fell round me as fast
As hail round Ben Nevis in winter's stern blast.

END OF MISCELLANEOUS POEMS.

Sonnets.

Sonnets.

TO GENERAL GRANT,

EX-PRESIDENT OF THE UNITED STATES OF AMERICA.

I.

O CLANSMAN—for the broad Atlantic flood
Can not wash out our clanship from thy blood !
I give thee cordial greeting, not because
Thou smot'st thy country's foes with victor's sword,
Nor that thou sat'st to consummate her laws,
A chief more potent than despotic lord ;
Nor that a mighty people's free applause
Hath followed thy, perchance, too niggard word.
All these are honours lofty in degree,
And such as noble natures dearly prize ;
Yet not for these I chiefly honour thee,
And seek, while louder plaudits rend the skies,
To bring such tribute of my minstrelsy
As, albeit small, thou may'st not quite despise.

II.

O, valiant captain, ruler firm and sage,
For this I do the most revere thy name,—
Foredoomed to live on history's brightest page,
Midst those thy country girds with fairest fame—
That thou didst ne'er ambition's battle wage,
Nor lend thine aid to further tyrant's aim.

I honour thee that thou hast wielded might,
The range of human freedom to increase,
The fetters from the bondsman's limbs to smite,
And bid the wrongs of stern oppression cease ;
That, faithful guardian of thy country's right,
Thou also art the steadfast friend of peace,
And nobly hast, since thy career began,
Upheld the common brotherhood of man.

BRITISH LOYALTY.

I.

OUR loyalty is not an empty name,
   Nor senseless worship of a favoured race ;
We do not bend the servile knee to fame,
   A noble presence, nor a beauteous face,
Far-stretching power, nor high exalted place,
   Nor all of these combined our homage claim ;
Though each may have its own attractive grace,
   We loyal Britons venerate the throne
Because it symbolizes perfect right.
   The Minister may err through lack of light
Or perverse mind ; our Sovereign stands alone
   In absolute perfection, guarded round
By laws as by a panoply of might,
   Wherein no chink for error can be found.

II.

And when to this, as in our cherished Queen,
   Are added gifts to grace the highest sphere—
As charms of person, complaisance of mien,

Exalted virtue, piety sincere;
When every child has, like the parents, been
Endowed with all the graces that endear,
What wonder though exulting crowds are seen
When one of royal lineage doth appear?
What wonder though the roughest sons of toil
In courtesies with polished courtiers vie?
And hinds who till, with lords who own, the soil,
Combine to raise their plaudits to the sky
In welcome, such as Sheffield late hath shown
To those who stand the nearest to the throne.

TO MISFORTUNE,

ON SUSTAINING A CONSIDERABLE PECUNIARY LOSS, AUGUST 4TH, 1874.

AH, grim misfortune! why dost thou so oft
Impose thy hated presence upon me?
In lowest cellar, or in highest loft
Thou still pursuest wheresoe'er I flee,
Why come from those who walk in raiment soft
To dwell unasked with one of low degree?
The Courts of Greece and Naples, France and
Spain,
By turns sustained thee little time ago;
I pray thee do return to Courts again;
It soils thy dignity to stoop so low,
To haunt a bard and turn his soothing strain
To harsh discordance, unharmonic woe.
Fie, fie, misfortune! go where splendour gleams,
And leave the bard a crust and tranquil dreams.

SONNET

ON READING A VOLUME OF CARLYLE'S ESSAYS AND REVIEWS.

CARLYLE, men say thou'rt scarcely orthodox
   When tried by common theologic rules,
Though thou wert born within the land of Knox,
   And nurtured in her churches and her schools.
When Faith was forced, and held by double locks,
   Alike within the pates of wise and fools,
So men declare of thee; but when I read—
   And I have read thy books since early youth—
I sink my " Catechism " and my "creed,"
   And feel, with thee, a yearning after truth,
A love of honest word and manful deed,
   A scorn of all that is not sage and sooth,
Such as theologist did ne'er impart
   To what, perchance, he 'll call my " perverse heart."

THE POET'S MIND.

I.

ONE eve, when Phœbus from the level west
   Lit up creation with his parting glow,
I stood alone on yonder rocky crest,
   And gazing on a crystal lake below,
Saw clearly imaged on its polished breast
   Blue sky and cloud, cliff, crag, and mountain show.
The sun went down, the moon and stars outshone,
   And these again were mirrored in the lake;
Amidst the hills the evening zephyrs moan,
   And at their breath the slumbering billows wake;
Of Nature's moods, vicissitudes were none
   But what that liquid mirror did partake.

"Oh, Mountain Tarn!" I cried, "in thee we find
　　Befitting emblem of the poet's mind."

II.

Like waters in the garish light of day,
　　It sparkles in the favour of the crowd;
Light pleasures flush it like the summer-ray,
　　Light sorrows darken like the winter-cloud;
The passions toss it in their subtle play,
　　As waves are tossed by breezes low or loud.
In life's fresh morn it mirrors all things fair,
　　For golden hopes its inmost depths illume;
Truth, justice walk the world, a gladsome pair,
　　Young beauty smiles, wide earth is clad in bloom;
Anon come disappointment, cark, and care
　　O'ershadow all, enshroud the whole in gloom;
Nor darker mountain lake in midnight blast
　　Than poet's mind by all these ills o'ercast.

ATOMS IN THE MORNING SUNBEAMS.

THE cock hath waked me from a troublous dream,
　　To watch the advent of a summer's day;
Its golden splendours through my window gleam,
　　But most I follow one distinctive ray
Which runs across my chamber like a stream
　　Wherein a thousand thousand atoms play:
They reel, and wheel, retire and make advance,
　　Now darkling hide, now sparkle into view;
Again are lost; and yet again pursue
　　The countless windings of their airy dance.

Are ye instinct with life, like us, strange things ?
 Have ye, like us, your little day of light ?
And will ye have to mount on soaring wings,
 Or darkle down to sleep in starless night ?

A DREAM OF LOVE.

LAST night my love was with me in a dream,
 Where wildly sweet the vernal favours spring
Along the marge of ever-murmuring stream,
Where thousand birds in joyous cadence sung
Their songs of love from boughs in fragrance hung ;
We wandered, we two, as the last faint beam
Of Phœbus kissed the hills in dear good night ;
My love's soft hand returned the clasp of mine,
No words she uttered, but her eyes were bright
With volumes of sweet meaning, and their shine
Lit up my bosom with a new delight,
An ecstacy no language can define ;
But morning dawns, my blissful visions flee,
And leave the world all stern and lone to me.

TO ANNIE.

TO call thee beautiful were hackneyed praise,
 For that thou'rt daily, hourly called by all
Who meet thy dark eyes' love-inspiring gaze ;
 Far more than beauty can thy words enthrall ;
 They with a surer, more resistless call

Bid pulses bound, hearts throb, and passions blaze,
Than beauty flashing forth its primal rays.
Thy beauty first attracts the gazer's eye,
And brings him instant fluttering to thy side,
As doth the rose the roving butterfly;
Thy mind's rich treasures make him there abide,
And wish that fountain never to run dry
Whence sweets of such unequalled sweetness flow,
That he would ever sip nor cloyment know.

———

ON A RAMBLE

Taken along with a highly intellectual friend, on certain heights near
Sheffield, which are well known to have been favourite resorts of the
two distinguished poets, James Montgomery and Ebenezer Elliott.

ON eve in August, when the month was young,
    But when the week had nigh outrun its care
A common wish within our breasts upsprung
To breathe together the untainted air.
Ascending then where beetling rocks o'erhung,
And ramparted a vale surpassing fair,
Up to the breezy summit we did climb,
Where oft Montgomery smoothed his sacred song,
Or Elliott forged a thunder-bolt 'gainst wrong,
And sat conversing there, my friend and I,
All heedless of the rapid flight of time,
Until the sun had sunk beneath the sky;
And when we turned our darkling steps to town,
We felt as if from heaven to earth thrust down.

'WAS MACHST DU DA?

GOOD master manufacturer, I ask
    (Nor needst thou think my question strange or rude)
If thou, whilst thou pursu'st thy daily task,
    Producest aught to swell our sum of good?
I would not grudge that thou in age shouldst bask
    In Fortune's fairest beam, if stone, or wood,
Or growth of plant, or animal, or ore,
    Beneath thy plastic touch for men became
A wholesome comfort unpossessed before ;
    But I must deem thy trade a very shame,
Its place on earth a plague-spot and a sore,
    Should it be plied for lusts of evil name—
To frame for man a vicious luxury more,
    Or put within the hands of Hate and Strife
    Another engine against human life.

THE REIGN OF RIGHT.

ONE day I had a dream—for dreams by day
    Will come as in the silence of the night :
I dreamt that Vice and Crime were swept away,
    And selfish graspings banished from our sight.
Men, hand in hand, went on their virtuous way,
    Their constant wish to aid and do the right ;
O, what a beauteous world was this of ours !
    No weaponed armies, cannon-burdened fleets,
Peace in our lowly huts, our lordly towers,
    And smiling plenty walking all our streets.
For Pandemonium, Eden's tranquil bowers
    For ever redolent of balmy sweets !
Oh ! fellow-men, were we but truly wise,
    Might Earth not thus be changed to Paradise !

ENVY.

AWAY! thou fell destroyer of our peace!
  To Tophet's deepest, darkest dungeons hie;
In chains and fetters, hopeless of release,
  By triple adamant surrounded lie
Midst fiends whose baleful howlings never cease,
  And pangs whose tortures never, never die!
Accursed Envy, when our friend succeeds,
  Thou metest, weighest, grudgest his success;
Wouldst blur and blacken all his fairest deeds,
  Abridge his fame, and make his fortune less;
Wouldst pluck his flowers, and leave him noxious weeds,
  Rejoicing, when they stung, in his distress.
Down, down to Tophet! there with fiends remain,
Nor e'er disturb our tranquil breasts again!

FAME.

I.

AND this is fame—to stand 'neath grimy crust
  Some fleeting cycles in the market-place,
A metal statue, or a marble bust,
  With some slight semblance to the form or face.
Wherein the passions pulsed ere thou wert dust,
  But straining in ambition's weary chase;
And if a prying passer should demand—
  "Whose monument is this? and what did he
Of great and wonderful, by head or hand,
  On stable earth or ever-restless sea?"
And if a townsman, half a cycle hence,
  Should tell how thou did'st rule, or fight, or preach,

Prevail by genius or by common sense,
  Behold the ultimatum of thy reach;
For such is glory, such is earthly fame—
Go, ponder it, and find a higher aim.

II.

And yet—and yet if fame should come unsought
  To him who ever faithfully pursued
The daily duties of his mortal lot,
  Methinks such fame must be accounted good,
And love of such within us oft hath wrought
  To better purposes and milder mood;
Nor seldom those exponents of esteem—
  The sculptured bust, or voice of vulgar praise,
All mean and worthless as the wise may deem,
  Have guided genius into useful ways,
As feeble hands have led the brawling stream
  To turn the mill or fertilise the maize.
But act thy part, nor fret thee for the rest—
Fame or oblivion—God will grant the best.

MUSINGS AT BURNS' MONUMENT,

CALTON HILL, EDINBURGH.

I.

THY strains have made our Country doubly dear,
  Thou foremost genius of my native land,
  Beside whose cenotaph I, pensive, stand;
With what a charm they greet the Scottish ear,
What power is theirs, the Scottish heart to cheer,
When heard upon a far and foreign strand!

And who can think of this and not deplore
The bitter hardships of thy transient day!
Ah, Burns! we are thy debtors evermore,
For when we could we had no will to pay.
In vain we lavish honours on the dead,
And o'er thine empty tomb make idle moan;
Thou didst but ask thy kind for honest bread,
They grudged thee that to give thee here a stone.

II.

Ah, when we estimate our debts to thee,
And reckon all that genius leaves behind,
'Tis strange the race of dullards cannot see
The wondrous worth of genius to mankind!
Or are we born, or are we wilful blind,
That we pursue with unrelenting hate,
Or leave in cold neglect to pine and die,
Or only recognise when all too late,
Those radiant beings sent us from on high,
To leave their bright creations here and fly!
Theirs are the gifts that solace human woe,
And lend a keener zest to human mirth.
How dull and dreary were our homes below
If genius ne'er had deigned to brighten earth.

III.

And what is genius?—'Tis a sacred power
That works unbidden in its owner's breast,
Works only at its own elected hour,
But then with impulse not to be represt,
And with effect whose grandeur years attest,
And all detractions ever fail to mar,
While dulness dimly scans the nearest ground,
Clear-sighted genius darts his glance afar,

From earth's deep centre to the farthest star,
And, nimble-footed, passes at a bound
The goal which dulness toils long years to round,
But nature is not lavish of the gift—
Attest it history's universal pages—
She scatters dullards with a rare unthrift,
But grants a Burns—a boon to countless ages.

BEAUTY.

BEAUTY! whence hast thou the subtle power
  Which steals across the heart and stirs the frame?
  Sometimes thou peepest from a tiny flower,
Sometimes thou lingerest in a cherished name;
Sometimes thou'rt in the moon at midnight hour,
Sometimes within the sun's meridian flame.
Thou sleep'st on sunny seas and starlit skies,
Gleam'st in the rainbow's hues, the lightning's streak,
Full oft art flashed on us from sparkling eyes,
Dost 'witch from rosy lip or rounded cheek.
To number thine abodes all skill defies,
To picture thine effects all arts are weak;
Thine essence doth the whole creation fill;
Seen, heard, or felt, thou art a mystery still.

END OF SONNETS.

Your Amour.

Only trifting duties,
Paid to youthful Beauties.

Your Amour.

TO MARY.

MARY, Mary, gentle cousin,
  I have loved but just a dozen—
  Well it might have been a " score,"
  Twenty darlings—never more—
    Ere I gave my heart to thee.
  Mary, Mary, can it be,
  Thou refusest love to me?

Mary, Mary, gentle cousin,
  I've forgot the other dozen,—
  " Other twenty," be it so,—
  They were loves of long ago;
    Now my love is all for thee.
  Mary, Mary, can it be,
  Thou refusest love to me?

" I am teasing; I am chaffing;"—
  Well, perchance, you may be right.
  When I meet your blue eyes laughing,
    Brimming over with delight,
  Mary, Mary, I forgot
  Niggard Fortune, pressing debt;
  Gaze on you and feel the earth
  The home of Beauty, Love and Mirth.

TO ANNIE.

NNIE, Annie of Wood Park,
Thou hast eyes December dark,
Yet, as April morning bright,
Love's enduring flame to light,
Annie, Annie of Wood Park.

Annie, Annie of Wood Park,
Thou art merry as the lark
When he sings in Summer morn,
High above the dewy corn,
Annie, Annie of Wood Park.

Annie, Annie of Wood Park,
Ne'er may worldly care or cark
Dim the brightness of thine eyes,
Turn thy laughter into sighs,
Annie, Annie of Wood Park.

ON A HORNCASTLE BEAUTY.

N ancient sculptor vowed to make
    A paragon of beauty;
And set himself, with heart and soul,
    To execute the duty.

For years he wandered o'er the earth
    In quest of rare material;
Gazing here on rustic belles,
    And there on queens imperial.

Snatching here a grace of form,
    And there a charm of feature,

He blent the whole to represent
A perfect human creature.

But had he lived in later times,
He might have spared his travel,
And found perfection all in one,
Beyond the power of cavil.

Without a shade or lineament
E 'en Envy's self could alter ;
All charms and graces he had found
Combined in Amy Walter.

TO GWLADYS,
(AGED SEVEN YEARS).

PLEASING, teasing, rosy, romping,
Merry Gwladys Fort :
When you get among your teens,
You'll be one of Beauty's queens,
Breaking hearts for sport.

Now, 'midst Beaumont's fragrant bowers,
Chasing birds, or culling flowers,
Chasing painted butterflies
Underneath the summer skies—
All that's beautiful and sweet,
There you fly with fairy feet.

Fly till you are tired and weary,
Slumber then like sleeping Peri—
Pity childhood is so short!
Ah ! methinks it would be heaven
To be back with you at seven.

Rosy, romping Gwladys Fort,
But when you are in your teens
You'll be one of Beauty's queens,
    Breaking lovers' hearts for sport,
    Pleasing, teasing Gwladys Fort.

———

TO TWO BEAUTIFUL SISTERS AT DUNKIRK.

ROSALIE and Josephine,
    Josephine and Rosalie,
    Did I but require a queen,
        One of you that queen should be.

Ay, but which? I cannot tell;
    Rosalie and Josephine
Both attract with equal spell,
    Equally might be a queen.

One is dark, the other fair,
    Both are wondrous fair to see—
Which the fairer, how declare,
    Josephine or Rosalie?

Rosy laughter, sprightly wit,
    Hover nigh where you are seen;
Graces, cupids, round you flit,
    Rosalie and Josephine.

Were I Sultan for a day,
    You should my sultanas be,
Rule my realms with equal sway,
    Josephine and Rosalie.

Rosalie and Josephine,
   These are but insane desires ;
I must be as I have been—
   One who, from afar, admires.

MEMORIES O' LANG SYNE.

(TO ANNIE.)

COME, draw your chair afore the fire,
   An' place your hand in mine,
An' let us hae a canty crack
   O' days o' auld lang syne.
For auld lang syne, my dear,
   For auld lang syne,
We'll sit an' crack a canty hour
   O' the days o' lang syne.

Hae ye forgotten Auld Wood Park,
   Wi' a' its mem'ries dear ;
The woody howes, the fernie knowes,
   The burnie wimplin near ;
The garden where the berries grew,
   When simmer days were fine ;
The apples, sweeter to the taste
   Than ony pu'ed sin' syne ?

Hae ye forgot the blythesome nichts,
   When neighbours' bairns cam' in,
As winter roun' the chimney-taps
   Made loud an' angry din ?
The Roses, Petries, Pennycuicks,
   An' mony mair ye'll min',
The cronies dear wha shared our cheer
   I' the days o' lang syne ?

Hae ye forgotten auld Lhanbryd,
   An' that Miss Ritchie's school,
Where first ye mounted what was then
   A high piano-stool ;
Where first ye tried a pencil sketch,
   An' strove in French to shine,
Or win renown in worsted wark,
   I' the days o' lang syne ?

Hae ye forgot the Saturdays
   (A blyther day was nane)
When ye wad gang to Elgin toon
   To see your Auntie Jane ?
Wi' twa three-pennies i' our pouch—
   How rich we were an' fine !—
Our pounds, though rare, will no' compare
   Wi' pennies spent lang syne.

Had ye your schemes, your waking dreams,
   Your castles reared sublime ;
Did fancy spread you flowery paths
   Adown the slopes of time ?
Hae a' your " castles i' the air "
   Come topplin' doon like mine,
An' stern realities replaced
   The dreams o' dear lang syne ?

But draw your chair afore the fire,
   An' place your hand in mine,
An' let us speak o' former days,
   The days o' dear lang syne ;
For auld lang syne, my dear,
   For auld lang syne ;
We'll wring an hour frae wrinkled Care
   Wi' mem'ries o' lang syne.

TO ELIZA.

ON some fair isle in some lone sea,
   Embosomed in tranquility,
      Far in the slumb'rous west,
O, I would make my darling's home,
Where carking cares could never come
      To vex her gentle breast.

There we would wander at our ease,
'Midst glowing fruits and fragrant trees,
      Or sit by silver streams,
Or watch the ripples on the beach,
More joyful, blissful, each in each,
      Than all poetic dreams.

TO LIZZIE,

ON RECEIVING A BOX OF EARLY VIOLETS FROM HER.

THIS morning, love, there came to me
   A messenger from you—
 A tiny box of violets,
   So beautiful and blue !
They came to whisper in my ear
   That you were always true.

They said you loved me with a love
   As beautiful as they—
A love which was not doomed, like them,
   To wither in a day,

But last as long as life itself,
   And smooth its rugged way.

O ne'er came messengers so sweet
   To any other door ;
I took them from their tiny box
   And kissed them o'er and o'er ;
And fully, fondly credited
   The message which they bore.

I made them yet, and yet again,
   With fragrant breath repeat
The message you had sent to me
   By messengers so sweet ;
And blessed you, in my heart of hearts,
   For love so true and sweet.

TO NORA.

YOU charge me with being a rover,
   Still ready to flatter and swear,
But view ye the matter all over,
   And you'll own the charge is unfair.
I've loved pretty damsels in dozens,
   And praised them in sonnet and song,
But then they were neighbours or cousins,
   And loving them I could not be wrong.

For Scriptural precepts have told me
   To love even such as are foes,
And where is the law to withhold me
   From loving friends lovely as those.

To hate a fair girl for her beauty
   Is not in the nature of man,
And plain ones I deem it a duty
   To love all as much as I can.

" I've trifled and flirted with many "—
   That fact I most freely avow ;
" There was one I loved better than any,"
   Ah, well—I have married her now.
Then say not that I am a rover,
   Still ready to flatter and swear ;
But, viewing the matter all over,
   Confess that the charge is unfair.

END OF POUR AMOUR.

In Memorias.

I am sorry not to have been able to affix dates to all these slight Memorials—a few saved out of many such—but they were mostly composed improptu, with no thought in my mind at the time of reproducing them; possibly, however, they may meet the eye of friends, who may supply dates if another edition be required.

In Memorias.

THE BROTHER'S GRIEF.

I HAD once a cherished brother,
   My mate in work and play :
But death came to our cottage
   And summoned him away.

And he left his young companions
   With a smile upon his lips,
And the heart whose love was deepest,
   To a long and drear eclipse.

O ! the light of life forsook me,
   When he was called to go ;
All was dark within and round me,
   One cheerless waste of woe.

And I wrung my hands in anguish,
   Till the font of tears was dry,
Till I learnt to look above me,
   Through the clouds upon the sky.

Then a sunburst from the welkin
   Shed its light upon my heart,
And I ceased my bootless wailing,
   And arose to play my part.

For a voice came with the sunburst,
   Its tones were low and sweet,
Saying—"Dry your tears my brother,
   They're unmanly and unmeet.

" Play the part by heaven assigned you,
 With a dauntless heart and true,
And you'll come to me hereafter,
 Though I can't return to you."

And now I struggle forward,
 And struggle with a will ;
For that voice from out the sunburst,
 It cheers me up the hill.

LINES ON JOSEPH GRANT,

AUTHOR OF " JUVENILE LAYS," " KINCARDINESHIRE TRADITIONS,"
"TALES OF THE GLENS," &c.

JOSEPH GRANT was born at the farm of Affrusk, in the parish of Banchory-Ternan, of which his father was at that time and for many years afterwards the tenant. His education was limited to a few winters at the nearest parish and district schools ; and, with the exception of a brief period towards the close of his life, when his recognised literary abilities procured him more congenial employment, he worked as an ordinary farm hand on his father's farm. His supply of books and his opportunities for study were as limited as his school education, but yet he somehow contrived to make himself a writer of no mean merit, and became possessed of a surprising amount of miscellaneous information. Besides the works published separately, he contributed tales, sketches. poems, and songs, to *Chambers's Journal*, and various other periodicals. His writings, both in verse and prose, were well received when they first appeared, and his name is still remembered with affectionate regard in his native parish and the surrounding districts. He died of a species of rapid consumption in 1835, being then in the thirtieth year of his age.

HE might have reached a riper age
 If fewer cares had driven ;
He might have left a brighter page
 Had longer life been given.

His days were brief, his lot was hard,
 For this, his simple story—

He aimed to add another bard
To swell his country's glory.

For this he toiled—for this his strength
In early vigils wasted ;
And if success appeared at length,
He wanted life to taste it.

He died as genius often dies—
God knows the special reasons—
When fairer prospects seemed to rise,
And more auspicious seasons.

There may be minstrels who have strung
The lyre with defter fingers ;
But still the simple song he sung
Amidst his mountains lingers.

And pensive strangers at the tomb,
Beside his native river,
While pondering on his early doom,
Have felt a tear-drop quiver.

LINES.

On W. E. EWAN, of Aberdeen, a young man of great promise, who died
of consumption while pursuing his studies in Divinity
at the Free Church College.

GREAT mental treasure he received,
  But not the time to spend it,
 For ere his worth was well perceived
  His bright career was ended;
 We know not why, nor need surmise,
 But trust the Ever-just and Wise.

LINES.

On hearing of the death of the Rev. JOHN WALKER, M.A., St. Andrews,
Lhanbryd, near Elgin.

COULD kindly heart escape the grave,
 Had eloquence the power to save,
 If worth the darts of death could stay,
 I should not mourn my friend to-day.

LINES.

On hearing of the death of Mrs. Russell, sometime of Myreside,
near Elgin.

HER hospitable house I found ;
    Contagious sickness struck me down ;
Her youthful family were round,
    Yet me she nursed without a frown.

With ready smile and words of cheer,
    Whilst that malignant fever burned,
Like guardian angel ever near,
    She tended me till health returned.

I rose and went my worldly way,
    Ungrateful ?   No ! but powerless still
To utter gratitude which lay
    Far deeper than my minstrel skill.

Now she is dead, and earthly praise
    No more can stir her silent heart :
But yet her name amidst my lays
    Will ease my own of half its smart.

For kindness she could so bestow,
    That those who felt could ne'er forget,
Yet owing, could confess to owe
    With pride and pleasure in the debt.

ELIZA.

(MARRIED, 10TH AUGUST, 1861.—DIED, 26TH AUGUST, 1862.)

A YEAR ago I married her—
  My peerless angel wife;
One little year, and death hath come
  To sever life from life.

A year of love! How sweet it was!
  And ah! how swift it sped!
Was it a dream—her love—her life?
  A dream that she is dead?

Is it a dream that words of love
  Were in her latest breath?—
A dream she look'd, and smiled on me,
  Even in the grasp of death?

Is it a dream that angels came
  And bore her soul away;
And left me, for the wife I loved,
  A form of speechless clay?

Ah, no! I wander o'er my house
  In solitude and gloom,
And meet with traces of her hand
  In every silent room;

And tokens of her constant love
  Appear on every scene,
To tell me what my present is,
  And what my past hath been.

I need not stand beside the grave
　In which her ashes rest,
To know that I am lone on earth,
　And she is with the blest.

A thousand mem'ries, wants, regrets,
　Perplexities, and fears,
Remind me of my bitter loss,
　And move my frequent tears.

My tears!　They flow unheeded now.
　Alas! it was not so
With her who heightened all my joys,
　And banished every woe.

But wherefore should my heart be sad
　That she has gone before,
And wooes me to a brighter home,
　Where every grief is o'er?

Oh, rather let my prayers arise,
　Benignant Heaven, to Thee,
For wings of faith to soar to her,
　When death hath set me free!

LINES.

On hearing of the death of the Rev. Mr. WHYTE, of Canisbay, Caithness.

RESPECTED Whyte, and art thou gone
    From earthly friends for ever?
A wiser man I've seldom known,
    A warmer-hearted never;
And if a life of faith and love,
    Unmixed with selfish leaven,
Find favour in the courts above,
    Thy spirit is in Heaven.

LINES.

On hearing of the death of an intimate and a very dear friend,
(W. H.,) sometime one of the Masters at the Gymnasium, Old Aberdeen.
W. H. was a deeply thoughtful student of enlarged views and a highly
benevolent mind, but of a somewhat reserved and retiring disposition,
and I believe he revealed his aspirations to few, if to any, so fully as to
myself. He died young and suddenly, and his death was a sore grief
to many friends besides me.

I.

MUCH had he thought, but died and left no sign
    Of that inquiring soul that worked within,
And strongly sought to over-leap the line
    Where knowledge ends, and mysteries begin.
" Why am I here? What labours should be mine?
    Is Truth established? Heterodoxy sin?
Must I find out my task, or is it fixed—
    Detailed already in the Book of Life?
A life of good, or good and evil mixed;
    And how should I equip me for the strife?
How labour best for this world and the next?
    How errors shun where errors are so rife?"

I know such questions stirred his active mind,
I know he died and left no sign behind.

II.

He would have fathomed in his pensive mood—
   Which often seized him 'midst the loudest throng —
The origin of evil and of good,
   Our love of virtue, and our hate of wrong,
Our headlong passions, and the baneful brood
   Of ills which these engender and prolong ;
And far beyond the trivial things of time,
   And narrow bounds of this sublunar sphere,
His restless spirit often dared to climb
   By airy ladders which itself would rear,
And question suns and systems strewn sublime—
   How they were formed, and why they did appear,
And if there might be one, if one alone,
Where virtue reigned and vice was all unknown.

III.

The Present, Past, and the dark Future, he
   Essayed to grasp, and drag their secrets forth ;
If, peradventure, in their depths might be
   A virtue yet, whose undiscovered worth
Might prove the sovereign balm for misery,
   And Edenise anew the darkened earth ;
For he was loth to think so much of woe,
   Appointed Earth by Heaven's supernal will,
And dreamt that he himself might some day know,
   By dint of study, how the sum of ill
Might be abridged for living things below,
   And might employ for this his gathered skill.
But yet to few, save me, did he reveal
   The thoughts and schemes which exercised his mind,

Or his intense desire for human weal,
　For death came early, and my friend resigned,
　Unmoved, his life, and left no signs behind.

———

ON HEARING OF THE DEATH OF THE COUNTESS OF C———.

DEAD! and so brief is the time
　　Since I saw her in rosiest health,
　In womanhood's glory and prime,
　　Surrounded by Fashion and Wealth;
Courted by those of her sphere
　　To grace the gay fête or the board,
To parents and children most dear,
　　But dearer than all to her lord.

Dead! It appears like a dream—
　　Like a troublous dream of the night;
But many a morning shall beam
　　Ere the shadows of grief take flight
From the hearts wherein she was shrined
　　As daughter, as mother, as wife:—
A heart with another heart twined,
　　The innermost life of its life.

Nor love nor affection can save
　　From the clutches of pitiless Death;
Nor Science can baffle the grave,
　　Nor charm in its mansions the breath.
Years dwindle to days and to hours,
　　The swifter because they are sweet;
We dream we are treading on flowers,
　　While sepulchres yawn at our feet.

SWEETIE.

DIED, DECEMBER 1ST, 1878, AGED 2 YEARS AND 9 MONTHS.

THE beauty fades from other flowers;
 They sleep in Winter's gloom;
 Eternal Summer fosters ours,
  In never-dying bloom.

LINES

On hearing of the death of the Rev. EDWARD NEWMAN, Vicar of
Ecclesall, which took place at the Vicarage, June 13th, 1880.

GENTLE, patient, calm of mind,
 To the will of God resigned,
 Lo! my former friend hath gone
 Out into the " Great Unknown "—
 " Great Unknown ? " to *him* not so;
 Through his whole career below,
 He looked upward and believed—
 Nay, his final Home perceived,
 Where the ransomed with their Lord
 Ever live in blest accord.

END OF IN MEMORIAS.

Varieties.

Varieties.

HOOD.

THOMAS HOOD, Thomas Hood,
All thy poesies are so good,
Wise and witty, I declare,
Thou would'st fill me with despair
Were it not that I remember,
Tiny flowerets in December,
Smaller singers in the bushes
Than the nightingales and thrushes.

WORDSWORTH.

PURE as snow upon the mountain,
Clear as famed Blandusia's Fountain
Solemn and slow,
On you go
Piling your plenteous pages,
Priest of Nature, high and low,
Revealing her mysteries to ages,
Teaching the dullest her sweets to discover,
The coldest to gaze on her beauties and love her.

BYRON,

HAROLD, a Manfred, a Juan, a Giour,
A tempest, an earthquake, a terrible power,
As brilliant as noonday, as gloomy as night,
Awakening emotions of dread and delight.

A SNOB.

WITH nose a-cock and consequential stride,
Behold a snob, of Sheffield snobs the pride;
In mental stature higher far than he,
Beneath him placed by Fortune's stern decree,
Some scores of men obey this petty god,
Quake at his frown, or hurry at his nod.
He buys their bones and sinews, health, and strength,
For they must live, and he has work and wealth.
How sad it is such goods must needs be sold
To snob like this who values nought save gold.

LINES

On hearing that the degree of LL.D. had been conferred on
C. H. SORBY, Esq., F.R.S., Sheffield.

AND men have dubbed thee "LL.D.,"
And think they thus have honoured thee!
High Priest of Nature, it were meet
That we should worship at thy feet;
Thou giv'st us honour, we—alack!

What honour can we give thee back ?
Most surely thou art one of those
To whom mysterious Nature shows
The secrets hid from vulgar eyes,
A gifted man, a heavenly wise ;
Such men, in every age and place,
Do honour, and exalt our race.

A CHOICE.

1880.

"SWEET," cry the sages unto me,
  " The uses of Adversity."
    " Well," I say,
    " Sip away ;
    Have your fill,
    If you will ;
   But for me, I do aver,
   I very, very much prefer
  The uses of Prosperity."

A TRUE FRIEND.

1880.

DOST thou desire thy friend to try,
  Ask him to lend thee in thy need,
And if he readily comply,
  In him thou hast a friend indeed.

TO THOMAS MAHONIE, ESQ.,
SURGEON DENTIST.
June 18*th*, 1880.

IN gratitude for stumps removed,
 And dentals otherwise improved.
Old Nature thou art wearing out,
 In mortal throes beyond a doubt!
The teeth thou givest waste away,
 Dost thou repair them? Can'st thou? nay,
To great Mahonie we must go,
 He plies his magic art, and lo!
New grinders empty sockets fill
 Surpassing Nature's foremost skill.

TO I. D.

THE critics will call me a rhymester you say,
 And my title to Poet deny;
But the critics may err, or scribble for pay,
 And I know that the critics don't buy.
I know that the People my patrons must be
 Before that my books can succeed;
And but little care I, how the few may decry,
 If the many shall purchase and read.
From the People I sprang; for the People I sang,
 Ere I scribbled my earliest page,
And my patrons were they, in my youth's brightest day;
 Will they scorn and neglect me in age?

ON THE DEATH OF THE REV. DR. CORBET,
OF DRUMOAK, ABERDEENSHIRE.

Dr. Corbet was for about forty years parish minister of Drumoak, and after he was almost completely deaf and blind continued to preach with an eloquence and fervour which I, perhaps, have never heard equalled—certainly never surpassed. Dr. Corbet was the first among the learned that bestowed a word of encouragement on my muse, for which, as well as for many other kindnesses received from him and his excellent wife, I must retain a grateful recollection of them while memory lasts.

SERVANT of God, thy work on earth is done;
 The Master thou didst serve, in constant trust,
Hath called thy soul to claim the guerdon won,
 Thy mortal parts to mingle with the dust.

And not for thee, but for ourselves we grieve,
 To see a stranger fill the sacred place,
In which thy breast with holy zeal did heave
 Big with the tidings of abundant grace.

Great were the gifts bestowed by Heaven on thee,
 And ardently by thee were they applied
To teach the sinner from his sin to flee,
 His feet within the " narrow way " to guide.

When age with constant sap and mine assailed,
 And all thy frame was conscious of decay,
O'er human weakness heavenly zeal prevailed,
 Thy Master's work with thee brooked no delay.

Like some apostle of the olden time
 Who drew his inspiration straight from God,
Thou lifted'st us with eloquence sublime
 Above the transient ills of this abode.

Thou taught'st to look for strength where strength
    is found,
  To battle life and triumph o'er the grave—
To Him whose gifts of grace for all abound,
  Whose arm is stretched omnipotent to save.

The more that human frailties pressed thy frame
  In deeper strength thine eloquence did flow;
Thy lips were touched most surely with the flame
  Which doth on the Eternal Altar glow.

Throughout thy life thou taught'st us how to live
  As those should live who hope for life on high,
And in thy death didst bright example give
  How calmly they who so have lived can die.

Alas! my muse refuses to believe
  That thou hast ceased to fill thy wonted sphere,
And never more shall as of old receive
  Her trembling accents with benignant ear.

The flesh alone hath followed nature's laws;
  Thy soul hath soared, rejoicing to be free;
I cannot speak of thee as—" him that was;"
  Thou art a real existence still to me.

Faith comes to lend imagination wings;
  I see thee in thy better, brighter state,
Within the presence of the King of Kings,
  Exalted high o'er all that men call great.

Dread Father, in whose radiant presence all
  Must soon or late for final judgment stand,
O, grant to me, who now upon Thee call,
  To win like him that better, brighter land.

LOVE AND DEATH.

H. AND M.

Amiens, January, 1872.

HANDSOME, healthful, hopeful, young,
With words of valour on his tongue,
He came to us one day in June,
He left us on the next at noon ;
And from the day that he departed
Our pretty May was broken-hearted ;
And when on battle-field he fell,
She bent her head and died as well ;
Though words of love we surely knew
Had never passed between the two.

OBERMEIER THE BRAVE.

(A DIRGE.)

The Berlin medical journals record the death from cholera, on the
20th of August, 1873, of Dr. Otto Obermeier, in he 31st year of his age.
Dr. Obermeier had abroad gained a high reputation as a scientific
investigator of disease. Within the last few months he had published
important observations on the blood in typhus fevers ; and when seized
with his fatal illness he was engag d in researches on cholera. According to several accounts, he injected into his own veins blood taken from
a cholera patient, in order to test the truth of a hypothesis as to the
action of the disease, and thus became its victim. So devoted was he to
his inquiry, that after he became aware of his own condition he made
microscopic examinations of his own blood, and corrected or enriched
his former conclusions by observing how the fatal malady did its work
on his own frame. He spo' e while he could speak of the elative effects
of medicines and stimulants, and had just asked for his microscope
when the final collapse arrived.

LAY within an early grave,
Otto Obermeier the brave ;
Him who gave his life to gain
Means to lessen human pain,—

Him who bravely strove to trace
To their secret lurking-place
Primal forms of fell disease:
Him who toiled that skill might seize,
Seize and crush in very birth,
Those afflictors of the earth,
Fevers dire and direr pest—
Lay him down in honoured rest.

Mighty conqu'rors, what are ye?
Braver than your bravest he;
Ye were slow to risk your life
In the thickest of the strife;
Ye your selfish ends to gain,
Drenched with others' blood the plain.
By the tainted sufferer's bed,
Whence the dearest kin had fled,
Whence ye would have shrunk aghast,
He, undaunted to the last,
Stood with pity in his breast—
Lay him down in honoured rest.

Otto Obermeier the brave,
Striving human life to save,
Striving if he could make less
Fellow-mortals' sore distress,
Sought the plague-infected spot,
Gazed on death and shuddered not,
Searched with patient microscope,
Purpose high, and holy hope;
Strained with eyes and intellect
If he could perchance detect
Workings of the deadly pest—
Lay him down in honoured rest.

Patient, watchful, day and night,
Questioned he with soul and sight,
If it might be known to man
Where the deadly scourge began ;
How its fearful way was made,
If its progress might be stayed.
Yea, despite his mortal pains,
When the poison reached his veins,
Yea, while Death transfixed his heart,
Searched how skill might blunt the smart !
With our greatest and our best
Lay him down in honoured rest.

Lay within his early grave
Otto Obermeier the brave,
But let poet roll his story
Up the heights of lyric glory
Till his name appear sublime
'Midst the names defying time.
Ne'er was highest human duty
Sampled forth in grander beauty ;
Never since the world began,
Braver life resigned for man !
Otto Obermeier the brave,
Lay his dust in honoured grave,
Trusting that his soul hath soared
Up to glory with its Lord.

IN MEMORIAM.

C. H. N.

DIED NOVEMBER 19TH, 1873, AGED 24.

DRY your tears and chase your gloom,
Scatter flowers upon her tomb ;
She was gentle, young, and fair,
Such as friends the least could spare ;
But her Lord was pleased to say,
" Suffering maiden, come away,
Earth is not the place for thee,
Thou must dwell in bliss with Me."

OUR MOTHER.

DIED AUGUST 10TH, 1876.

SHE died in her ninetieth year,
    After her eyes had seen
Her children's, children's children here,
    She died in an old age green,
Although for a few brief months she lay,
Sad proof of body and mind's decay.

And then she wandered oft and far
    Into the days of old,
Seemingly now with want at war,
    Now dreaming of wealth untold,
Now chiding old friends and children dear,
Now calling them close and closer near.

But sweet affection curtained round
   Our aged mother's head,
And willing hands were ever found
   To soften her dying bed ;
And kindred gathered to lay her low
With all the trappings of decent woe.

Thus, like a tranquil Summer's eve,
   Our mother's life went out,
Leaving nought whereat we may grieve—
   Remembrance of pain or doubt ;
She simply sank to her rest like one
Whose long, long task was worthily done.

O, thanks to you, for ever thanks,
   Ye tender hearts and true,
Who, we being fast in Mammon's ranks,
   So valiantly battled through,
To soften our mother's dying bed,
And lay in the grave her honoured head.

O, thanks for ever, thanks to you,
   And should our thanks be all,
Our gifts for services so true,
   Your guerdon shall not be small.
For the highest of all earthly meeds
Is the memory of exalted deeds.

ON THE DEATH OF EARL RUSSELL.

A NAME, 'midst noble names, sublime
　　Ere he had borne the same,
He, dying, leaves to future time
　　With large access of fame.

His country's good he ever sought,
　　According to his light,
On Freedom's side he ever fought
　　With all his mental might

Defeats he did indeed sustain,
　　Reproaches had to bear;
But yet of Honour's ripest grain'
　　He reaped an ample share.

And few on life so long might look
　　From dawn to setting day,
And meet with less that might not brook
　　The Sun's meridian ray.

How few in nature's waning hours
　　With equal right might feel—
" I have not vainly lent my powers
　　To further human weal."

We mourn when death hath come to reap
　　The green among our peers;

Earl Russell met the Sickle's sweep,
   Mature in worth and years.

Included amongst those that shed
   A lustre on their age,
His dust is with the honoured dead,
   His name on History's page.

And worse than vain lament would be
   That he has bowed to fate—
We weep not—but rejoice that he
   Retired from earth so late.

———

END OF VARIETIES.

Odds and Ends.

Odds and Ends.

THE LEAGURED CITY.

" Heavy cannonading and beating of drums were heard in the streets of Paris on Wednesday. It cannot be ascertained who were the contending parties, the city being completely invested, and communication with the outside having ceased."—Telegrams after investment of Paris by the Germans, in the War of 1870-71.

FROM out the leagured city
    Right frequently there come
The roarings of artillery,
    The rollings of the drum ;
Nor may we tell the reason,—
    No message north nor south
May pass beyond the ramparts
    Save through the cannon's mouth.

Perchance internal treason
    Has led to mortal strife,
And Frenchmen close with Frenchmen
    Opposing life to life ;
Perchance the recent levies
    Within the *Champ de Mars,*
Engaged in mimic battle,
    Prepare for fiercer wars.

It may be that the foeman
    Has found a secret port,
And cannons, French and Prussian,
    Belch forth in red retort.
Vain, vain are all conjectures,
    No message north nor south
May leave the leagured city
    Save through the cannon's mouth.

AFTER SEDAN.

IN the silence of his chamber,
   Long before the solar ray
Streamed to lighten toilsome mortals
   To the labours of the day,
Vexed by thousand restless fancies,
   Wide awake the poet lay.

News of battle-fields had reached him
   Ere he sought his couch at night;
News of Gaul's embattled legions
   Turned to rout and hopeless flight;
News of Gaul o'ercome and helpless,
   In the grasp of German might.

Now disasters rose before him,
   Worse than e'er were wailed on lyre—
Würth, Forbach, Gravelotte, and Sedan,
   With their consequences dire;
Lurid views of Metz and Strasburg,
   Girt about with walls of fire.

Visions of an empire humbled,
   Of an Emp'ror in exile,
Loaded with a nation's curses,
   Charged with all the base and vile,
All the reckless legislation
   Which could swell misfortune's pile.

"Land of France!" exclaimed the poet,
   "Land which I have loved so well,
Surely never yet did history
   In her blackest annals tell
Of a nation, which so swiftly,
   So ingloriously, fell.

"From the highest heights of Splendour,
    From a nation's proudest place,
Thou hast sunken, crushed and smitten,
    To the depth of dire disgrace;
Sycophant, and coward, and traitress,
    Written broadly on thy face.

"Wherefore didst thou, whilst thy ruler
    Held his place in Fortune's van,
Vaunt him as the best and wisest,
    As the earth's supremest man;
Then brand him basest, foolishest,
    When his adverse fate began?

"Neither best nor worst of mortals
    Was thine Emp'ror in exile,
And 'neath his rule prosperity did,
    From Calais to Marseilles,
Alike on peers and peasantry,
    On town and country smile.

"Say this war was of his seeking;
    Swear it never was of thine;
Maintain that he desired it
    For the strengthening of his line;
Can the world forget how frantic
    Were thy shoutings—'To the Rhine!'

"'To the Rhine!' in every café,
    'To the Rhine!' in every street,
'To the Rhine!' awakes the echoes
    Wheresoever Frenchmen meet.
Thou hast reached the Rhine, and crossed,
    Not in triumph, but defeat.

"And thou turnest on thy rulor
   As if he alone had erred,
As if all this bloody business
   Had by him alone been stirred,
And no hand save his had faltered
   When it grasped the hostile sword.

"If he merits the reproaches
   Which thou heapest on him now,
Shame upon thee for a nation !
   What a sycophant art thou !
What a coward, so long and lowly,
   Underneath his sway to bow !

"If he did deserve the praises
   Once so plenteously poured,
What a traitress thou to curse him,
   And reject him for thy Lord,
All because thy common armies
   Melt before the German horde !

"Shame upon thee for a nation !
   I have said I loved thee well,
Now I loathe, contemn, despise thee,
   With a force I cannot tell ;
For a nation ne'er so swiftly,
   So ingloriously fell.

"As for him thou wouldst dishonour,
   Lo ! he sits in silent pain,
Grieved to see thy foes triumphant,
   Grieved to see thy bravest slain ;
Sorest grieved to see thy quarrels,
   In which blood is poured like rain.

"All reviled, yet unreviling,
　　Patient underneath the weight
Of the frequent grievous charges
　　Hurled by unrelenting Hate,
Ne'er through all his chequred fortune
　　Did Napoleon seem so great.

"France, who roll'st theatric thunder,
　　Hurlest bolts which cannot scathe,
Gods and men alike blaspheming,
　　In thy frantic, blatant wrath,
Ne'er didst thou appear so little
　　Since thou trod'st a nation's path."

RANDOM THOUGHTS ON WOMAN'S RIGHTS.

WE don't dispute the ladies' right
　　To treat us as they please,
To win our hearts, to break our hearts,
　　To charm, perplex, or tease.
We grant their right to hook their man,
　　And wear the creature out,
As skilful angler hooks and plays
　　His salmon, pike, or trout.

We grant them bonnets, large or small,
　　Cosmetics, paints, and dyes,
Chignons and bustles manifold,
　　And hoops of every size.
We grant them robes of every shape,
　　Possessed or void of grace,

And still admire the gems within,
    However odd the case.
We grant their right to spend the cash
    Their husbands toil to win,
Tho' they, like lilies of the field,
    Should neither toil nor spin.

Ah, yes! we recognise the rights
    The darlings now possess,
And him who would ignore their claims,
    Or wish to make them less,
Who'd laugh their little whims to scorn,
    Their pleasures dare dispute,
We call a "Monster"—not a "Man—"
    That shames the name of "Brute."

We yield the ladies all their rights,
    And not a few of ours,
But still their constant cry is "Give!
    Extend our rights and powers!"
They cry for this, they sigh for that,
    They challenge rights so many,
That when they have asserted all,
    Male mortals won't have any.

Well, bless their dear, ambitious hearts,
    Why should we say them "Nay?"
They'll leave us with a care the less
    For each they take away.
We'll let them vote and speechify,
    And make the nation's laws,
Command the Senate's listening ear,
    The fickle crowd's applause.

Not only shall they make the laws,
   They shall enforce them too;
Resign your truncheons to the Fair,
   Ye stalwart men in blue;
For Rascaldom will swifter shrink
   From Mary's orbs of light,
Than from your lantern's glimmering eye,
   Grim Guardians of the Night.

They'll guide our armies and our fleets,
   Our home and foreign trade;
They'll wield the diplomatic pen,
   The lancet's trenchant blade,
For tho' we Britons masculine
   Have made a little fuss,
And e'en have conquered powerful states,
   The girls have conquered us.
Yes, he who fought at Agincourt,
   And vanquished odds so great—
Brave Henry, in his proudest hour
   Was forced to yield to Kate.

They'll teach our colleges and schools,
   They'll write and read our books;
We'll only have to qualify
   For nurses and for cooks.
They'll execute our grandest works;
   They'll talk the biggest talks;
The kitchen and the scullery
   Must henceforth be our walks!

When *little accidents* befall
   The ladies of creation,
Maternal duties shan't abridge
   Their duties to the nation;

We'll take their bantlings off their hands
   With all domestic bother,
And with the cow and bottle's aid
   Supply the place of mother.
Then England shall have real *John Bulls*,
   As you must needs allow,
When all her sons shall thus, like calves,
   Be nourished by the cow.

Rejoice! ye playful boys at school,
   The time is drawing near
When ye may play the live-long day
   Unmoved by doubt or fear;
Enjoy your cricket, ball, or hoop,
   Your marbles, tops, and rattles,
While generous sisters whet their brains
   To fight life's thousand battles!

Big brothers, what a glorious day
   Is breaking on our view!
A day, when we may sit and sing—
   "We've got no work to do!"
Our, mothers, sisters, wives, shall fill
   Each post of care and toil,
And always bring us home the means
   To keep the pot aboil!

Long life to those high soaring souls—
   The Fawcetts, Beckers, Brights;
Long life to all the glorious band,
   Upholding "Woman's Rights!"
Henceforward, Nature, we reject
   Your antiquated plans;
Let feeble man take woman's place
   And stronger woman, man's.

AN OLD FABLE.

I ONCE read a fable, I cannot tell where,
That Jove fashioned mortals—each mortal a pair—
Fast bound to each other, by cords from the heart,
Without the desire or the option to part.
So fashioned he hundreds, two mortals in one,
And set the fresh couples to dry in the sun;
But giants at war with the Lord of the sky,
Assailed his creations before they were dry,
Tore each from the other in anger or mirth,
And strewed them at random all over the earth.
Thus scattered, they roam, as the fable relates,
All striving to find their original mates;
And whenever a half its right half discovers,
Attracted they cling as the fondest of lovers;
And married they live to the end of their lives,
The happiest models of husbands and wives.
But whenever wrong halves with wrong halves unite.
They vex one another, they wrangle and fight,
Till death, or the lawyers, come in at the last,
To free the ill-assorted by wedlock made fast.

DEATH IN THE SLUMS.

1878.

" Passing recently through a crowded, poverty-stricken quarter of one of our large manufacturing towns, I observed a hearse, of the kind usually employed at pauper's funerals, receive from a mean habitation a large plain deal coffin, and rattle off with its load unattended by a single mourner.   Prompted by a curiosity which you, reader, may call " morbid " if you will, I made a few enquiries regarding the subject of the funeral, of a woman who was standing at a neighbouring door.   She answered me as far as her knowledge went, with seeming readiness, but in a tone of despairing bitterness which haunted me till, according to my proclivity, I had recast her meagre information in something of her own spirit and words, thus : —

ONLY a life the less !
Earth is replete ;
Mortals on mortals press,
Till the grave's sweet.

Only another shroud!
Wherefore repine ;
What matters in the crowd,
This man's or mine ?

Only a life the less !
Why shed a tear;
Brothers on brothers press,
Till death is dear.

Here we have need of pluck,
Muscle and bone ;
This man was down in luck,
Vigour all gone.

Sycophant's supple knee
Bends to success ;

Drew in life's lottery, he,
  Vulgar distress.
Tears are for rank and wealth;
  This man was poor,
Bankrupt in goods and health,
  Want at his door.
He had been rich, they say,
  Riches had made,
Fell into swift decay,
  Ruined in trade ;
Fell from his wonted grade,
  Sickened and pined ;
If the rich offered aid,
  Aid was declined.
Schemes and resources fail,
  Here he is found,
Down in the social scale,
  On the last round.
Here where the evil lurk,
  Hunted by fear ;
Too good for villian's work,
  Why came he here ?
Too proud for beggar's bread,
  Too sick to slave ;
O, he is better dead !
  Best in his grave.
Best that his wearied head,
  Rest in the tomb ;

Life wants his truckle bed,
  Fights for his room.
Is there a life on high,
  Any home there,
  Whither a wretch can fly
  Meagre and bare ;
Baffled in fortune's strife,
  Broken by care,
Weary of worldly life,
  Wanted no where ?

By the horrors of the place,
  By the children stunted,
By that woman's haggard face,
  By her wild words haunted,
Turned from that wretched door,
  From the homes of sadness,
Musing on our hapless poor,
  Hungered into madness.

CATASTROPHE AT TAY BRIDGE,

DECEMBER 28TH, 1879.

A HUNDRED souls as fearless as might be,
Have reached the bridge that leads to fair Dundee;
Along the iron lines the cortége came,
A moment paused the steed with heart of flame,
A moment paused, till flashed the message "right,"
Then o'er the bridge pursued his slackened flight.
The speaking wires informed the further shore—
"They Come," but question failed to answer more;
A sudden flash! a startling crash! a long delay,
Loud howled the winds, high surged the swollen Tay;
The scattered waifs at morning landward rolled,
The broken bridge the tale of terror told.
In vain the skill of man, the toil and cost,
A hundred priceless human lives are lost;
For them the bridge stretched not to fair Dundee,
But out from time to vast eternity.

THE DEATH OF THE BEAUTIFUL CHILD.

(The following is an attempt to render into simple verse Mr. MOODIE'S touching Story of the American Gentleman who was converted, and became a Sunday School Superintendent and General Christian Worker, through the death of his little daughter, a beautiful, golden-haired child, of eight or nine years of age.)

I ONCE had a child, a beautiful girl,
 With hair of a golden hue ;
With dimpled cheeks, and a rosy mouth,
 And eyes of unclouded blue.
She danced about as with fairy feet,
 She carolled like a bird,
The fairest thing, and the sweetest thing,
 That ever was seen or heard.

And oh, how I loved my darling child !
 No words of mine can explain ;
Her presence was like a beam from Heaven,
 Her absence was darkness and pain.
I stayed from business, I stayed from church
 To be with my beautiful child ;
I waked and wept when there ailed her aught,
 I trembled with joy when she smiled.

I stayed from the houses of dearest friends ;
 I swiftly answered "no,"
Whenever a neighbour asked me out
 Where my darling could not go.
The God above was not half so dear,
 The Christ that died on the tree,
The treasures of Heaven and earth combined,
 As my beautiful child to me.

But there came a day when she sickened sore,
   And sicker and sicker grew,
'Till death spread his film on her azure eyes,
   On her brow spread his clammy dew,
Laid his icy hand on her throbbing heart ;
   Bade its pulses cease for aye ;
And nothing remained of my beautiful child
   Save a lump of unanswering clay.

And the stars went out, and the moon went down,
   And the sun was swathed in cloud,
And the fairest things of earth were wrapped
   In the fold of a sombre shroud.
And I loathed my food, my rest, and my life ;
   I had no wish save to die,
And side by side with my beautiful child,
   In the sleep of the dead to lie.

But dust to dust was at length consigned,
   And they tore me away from the tomb,
And led my back to my childless home,
   To my lonely cheerless room.
And I flung me down, but not to sleep,
   I had no wish save to die,
And side by side with my beautiful child,
   In the mouldering grave to lie.

But sleep crept over me, spite of my wish,
   And I dreamt a wonderful dream—
I wandered over an arid waste
   To the banks of a turbulent stream ;
And lo! on the farther side, I saw
   A land of celestial sheen,
With beautiful arbours, and shrubs, and flowers,
   And lawns of the deepest green.

And there rose a swell as of angel harps,
   From the depths of that beautiful land,
And sweetly there fell on my raptured ears
   The songs of an infant band.
And out of their midst crept my darling child,
   To the edge of the farther shore,
And stretched her hands to me and smiled
   As she did in the days of yore.

And cried—" O, father, come over the stream,
   I am waiting you, father dear,
To lead you about in this beautiful land,
   For it's always beautiful here ! "

But ever and on that turbulent stream,
   'Twixt me and my darling ran,
And swift for a ferry, a shallow, a skiff,
   I searched like a frantic man.
And I wrung my hands when none was found,
   And cried in my anguish wild—
" O Father, in Heaven, vouchsafe a way
   To pass to my beautiful child ! "

And out from the Heavens there pealed a voice—
   " The Way to the Father see,
I am the Way, the Truth, and the Life,
   None cometh to Him save by Me ! "
And I woke from sleep and my soul was cheered,
   I wept for my darling no more,
For she is not dead, she is beck'ning me on,
   To the joys of that beautiful shore.

THE SPEECH OF GALGACUS

AT THE GRAMPIAN MOUNTAINS.

During the last year of his residence in Britain, Agricola marched northward with great force of foot and horse to sub ue the Caledonians. A fleet of galleys and provision ships, sailing as near the land as safety permitted, rendered whatever aid was practical, and enabled h m to penetrate further north than the Romans had done befor his time. The only well orga ised resistance offered was at the Grampian mountains, where the celebrated Scottish Chief Galgacus barred the great Roman's passage for a considerable time with about 30,000 Caledonian warriors, but had at length to succum to superior numbers and discipline. Tacitus, the historian, says that, Galgacus harangued his troops before the battle which took place in a speech of which the following is a paraphrase : -

GALGACUS raised his voice, his arms extended wide—

" To conquer now is all my hope,' he cried,

" For battle, choice and glory of the brave,

Is here the safety of the coward and slave :

The pathless ocean spreads behind our hosts, -

The Roman fleet besieges all our coasts,

Before us far extend the Roman bands,

Fierce devastators of uncounted lands,

Who, when the ravaged shores no more appease,

Will scour for plunder earth's remotest seas ;

For east nor west their avarice can glut,

The monarch's palace nor the peasant's hut.

No conquest can their lust of power abate,

No misery soften and no treasure sate.

To seize, and pillage, trample down, and slay,

With them is only to extend their sway ;

They wage their wars till prosperous peoples cease,

They make a desert and proclaim a peace;

But that they slumbered, with success elate,
And fell anew the slaves of adverse fate,
Yet midst those hills a few have still their home
Who never bowed the servile neck to Rome.
We, unsubdued, undaunted, yet remain
Sons of the mist, the mountain, and the glen ;
We, with our dearest dead, this pass shall bar,
Or living, show what Caledonians are.
'Tis by our discords that the Romans thrive,
Against ourselves they make our vices strive ;
They cherish quarrels where they would destroy,
And foes to crush, and vanquished foes employ.
As kites rapacious, cunning as the fox,
Their craft misleads, their greed devours the flocks ;
Such are the arms with which they wage the fight,
Success alone their diverse hordes unite.
'Tis fear, 'tis terror, bonds of feeble mould,
That subject Gauls, and subject Germans hold;
And Britons, too, inspired by like dismay,
Abase their blood, and own a foreign sway.
Our sons they drag to serve on foreign shores,
Nor less their loves than hates our land deplores,
What Caledonian breaths could dare to name,
Nor feel his bosom burn with rage and shame—
Our wives' and daughters' wrongs and cureless woes,
Outraged, insulted, by our Roman foes ;
Or worse, betrayed by trusted Roman friends,
Who wore that guise to gain their wicked ends !

T

The Roman hordes consume our scanty food,
Exhaust the field, the river, and the wood.
For them we drain the marsh, subdue the soil;
'Neath Summer suns and freezing Winter's toil,
Nay, rear the forts in which they rest secure,
To heap on us the ills we must endure.
Yet courage, ye, who glory love or life,
Not always have they waged victorious strife;
The Trinobantes, by a woman led,
Once cumbered fields with heaps of Roman dead,
Their strongholds stormed, their firm defences broke,
And had for aye escaped their cursëd yoke.
Undaunted, fearless, with the gods on high,
Shall we not these, and more than these, defy.
These bonds once broken, all will rise elate,
And whom they fear, will straight defy and hate;
Us victory lures, us all incitements urge
The land from those marauding hordes to purge;
No wives the courage of our foes inflame,
No father's voice their dastard flight will blame;
In numbers few, they see with sad surprise,
Our barren rocks, our stormy seas and skies,
In midst of which, encompassed, lo! they stand,
By gods given up to Caledonia's hand.
March, then, to battle, dauntless as your sires,
Strike for your wives, your children, home, and fires;
Before your blows, those slaves of every lust,
Shall trembling fly or, bleeding, bite the dust."

TIME WILL ANSWER ALL.

"YES, die," said the doctor, " die she will,
    Fall with the leaves she must ;
I tell you nothing in human skill
    Can save her from the dust.
As sure as the leaves on yonder tree,
She'll wither, and droop, and die," said he.

" ' Beautiful ! ' ' beautiful ! ' yes, I know,
    Her brow's the lily white,
Her cheek is the Summer rose aglow,
    Her eyes are beams of light ;
There's beauty in every golden tress ;
There's grace in every fold of her dress."

" But, yet, she's only a Summer flower,
    Beautiful to the eye,
She cannot live in the Winter shower ;
    She's sure to droop and die ;
Yes, wither, and droop, and die," said he,
" Along with the leaves on yonder tree ! '

" Ah, mother, mother ! " cried little Jane,
    " And must my sister die ;
And will they carry her down the lane,
    In that dark spot to lie,
Where cousin Rosa was laid to sleep,
In the tomb so dark, and cold, and deep ? "

" Ah, mother ! I heard what doctor said
    About the leaves, and all ;
But I have needle, thimble, and thread ;
    The leaves shall never fall,

Nor yet shall my sister die," said she ;
" I'll sew the leaves upon yonder tree ! "

" Hush ! hush ! " said the weeping mother,
    " hush !
  The will of God be done ;
It pleaseth Him, in her youth's first flush,
    To call our beauteous one
Away to a land beyond the tomb,
Where flowers and trees are in deathless bloom."

" But why must my sister go alone ?
    And why must we remain ?
And why speak ye in so sad a tone,
    And weep as if in pain ?
And why did doctor say, with a sigh,
' Yes, she must wither, and droop, and die ? ' "

" My child, I cannot answer thee now,
    But Time will answer all—
Wherefore the beautiful head must bow,
    Wherefore the leaf must fall,
And, wherefore, the way to the Land of Light,
Is often through pain, and sorrow, and blight."

FINIS.

$ubscribers' $ames.

	No. of Copies.
Rev. C. Bruce, M.A., Manse of Glenrinens, Dufftown, N.B.	1
Mr. Samuel B. Rose, Head Master, Philadelphia Board School ..	1
D. S. Hepburn, Esq., L.D.S., Eng., Oxford Street, Nottingham ..	1
Mr. Duncan M·Dougall, Dixon Lane, Sheffield	1
Sheffield Literary and Philosophical Society, School of Art, Sheffield	1
Alfred H. Allen, Esq., F.C.S., 6, Ash Mount, Sheffield	1
Mrs. W. Campsall, Howard Villa Sheffield, ...	1
Rev. R. Waltham, M.A., Oak Villa, Clarkehouse Road	2
The Right Hon. A. J. Mundella, M.P. (Sheffield) 16, Elvaston Place, London, Vice-President of H.M. Committee of Council on Education	1
Peter Reid, Esq , Proprietor, *John O'Groat Journal*, Wick	3
Alderman Harvey, Upperthorpe, Sheffield	2
Mr. Charles Copley, Hardwicke House, Walkley, Sheffield	1
Mr. Edward Cockburn, Park Ravine, Nottingham	1
Mr. Thomas Burnie, 36, Mansfield Road, Nottingham	1
Councillor W. Flather, Springfield House, Walkley Road	1
J. Young, Esq., M.D., 63, Arundel Street, Sheffield..	2
Mr. M. Henderson 50, Mount Pleasant Road, Sheffield	1
Chas. H. Greaves, Esq., (per Mr. Hall, Norfolk Brewery), Sheffield	2
Miss Athron, Princess Street, Barnsley	1
Mrs. Slater, The Mount, Sheffield	1
Mr. H. G. Dale, 74, Shakespeare Street, Nottingham	1
,, Thos. Biggin, 101, Upperthope, Sheffield	1
,. William Gray, Oak Tower, Upperthorpe, Sheffield	1
Miss A. Jones, 217, St. Mary's Road Board School	1
Mr. E. R. S. Sinclair, Berridale Villa, Heaton Chapel, near Stockport	1
Miss M. S. Cowan, Lowfield Infant School, Sheffield	1
Mr. Thos. Elliot, Head Master, Springfield Board School, Sheffield	5
Mr. Neil McLeod Watson, 123, Upperthorpe Road, Sheffield	1
Henry Elliott, jun., Esq , Solicitor, 17, Bank Street, Sheffield ..	1
Mr. Middleton, Ellerslie House, Dore	1
,, Wm. Greaves Roper, The Hollies, Spring Vale, Sheffield ..	1
,, Joseph Hall, Belle Vue, Norfolk Park, ,, ...	1
,, Fred. J. Hall, ,, ,, ··	1
,, J. H. Parker, Bookseller, Brookhill, Sheffield	3
,, John Middleton, Upperthorpe, ,, ...	1
Mrs. Keeling, Spring Vale, ,, ...	2
Councillor J. Bromley, Kenwood Bank, Sheffield	1

	No. of Copies.
Mr. John Bednal, (J. & Co.) 44, Wostenholm Road, Sheffield ..	1
Councillor W. H. Brittain, (Ex-Master Cutler,) Storth Oaks, Sheffield	1
„ J. T. Dobb, Cliffe House, Brinclifle, „	1
„ John Wilson, Andover Street, West, „	1
„ Fred. Brittain, Tapton Ville Crescent, „	1
John Shipman, jun., Esq., Hounsfield Road, „	1
E. Knowles Binns, Esq., Solicitor, Figtree Lane, „	1
Councillor J. Nadin, 10, St. George's Terrace, „	1
Mr. G. H. Crossley, Poplar Villa, Steel Bank, „	2
Alderman Edw. Tozer, (Mayor), Lawson Road, „	1
Councillor Batty Langley, Tapton, „	1
Alderman Jos. Mountain, Abbeydale „	1
John Yeomans, Esq., Solicitor, (Town Clerk), „	1
Councillor E. H. Marples, 275, Western Bank, „	1
„ James Hall, Broomhall Place, „	1
Rev. T. H. Gill, M.A., Rectory, Whalley Range, Manchester	1
Captain A. Ross, late 64th Regt., 40, Great Western St., Alexandra Park, Manchester..	1
Miss I. E. Sharpe, Summerlands, Whalley Range, Manchester ..	1
„ M. J. Falkner, Dudley Road, „ „ ..	1
„ M. Ralph, „ „ „ ..	1
„ E. Riley, 50, Stockton Street, Moss Side, „ ..	1
Mrs. Simpson, Fernie Lee, Mayfield Road, Moss Side, „ ..	1
Mr. Clarke, Withington Road, Whalley Range, „ ..	1
H. Vannau, Esq., M.A., 7, Hampton Terrace, Withington Road, Manchester	1
Mr. W. Browne, Withington Road, Manchester	2
„ Jas. Windsor, Irwell View, Old Trafford, „	1
„ G. H. Bell, Lincroft Street, Moss Side, „	1
Miss Knott, Sloane Street, Moss Side, „	1
T. Price, Esq., Whalley Road, Whalley Range, Manchester	1
Miss F. Hunter, Elmsfield, Victoria Rd., Whalley Range, Manchester	1
Mr. J. H. Phillips, 183, Moss Lane, East, Manchester	1
„ C. F. Brierley, Clayton Street, Chorlton Road, Manchester ..	1
Mr. R. Gibson, Lansdowne Terrace, Old Trafford, Manchester ..	1
Sergt.-Major Fair, Hallamshire Rifles, Sheffield	10
Mr. Robert Hanbidge, 45, Fargate, Sheffield	1
„ Colin Peat Lenton, near Nottingham	4
„ David Edward, Mill of Hirn, Banchory, Ternan by Aberdeen..	1

	No. of Copies.
Mr. Thomas Crookes, Logan Bank, Upperthorpe, Sheffield	1
„ John McLachlan, 139, Upperthorpe, „	1
„ William Ping, Head Master, Langsett Rd. Board School, Sheffield	1
„ W. F. Ratcliffe, South Sea Hotel, Broomhill, Sheffield	1
„ J. Reid, (of Messrs. Black and Ferguson,) Aberdeen..	12
„ S. Fenton, Thorn Bank, Springhill, Sheffield	1
„ James McDowall, 7, St. George's Terrace, Sheffield	1
Joseph Nadin, Esq., M.R.C.S., St. George's Terrace, Sheffield ..	1
Mr. D. Mason, 17, Westfield Terrace, Sheffield	1
Miss Annie M. Sollar, Fairlieburne, Fairlie, Ayrshire	1
Mr. James McKenzie, 66, Harwood Street, Highfield, Sheffield ..	1
John F. Moss, Esq., Clerk to Sheffield School Board, Moor Cliffe, Ranmoor	1
Mr. M. C. Burnby, Ashburn, Broomhill	1
Councillor Reuben Clarke, Lion Hotel, Wicker, Sheffield	1
Thos. Spowart, Esq., L.R.C.P., L.R.C.S., Montgomery Terrace Road, Sheffield	2
Mr. Robert Hay, 69, Birch Terrace, Sheffield	1
„ Saml. Corrie, 114, Gell Street „	1
„ James Hastings, 56, Victoria Street, Sheffield	1
„ R. Gilmour, 79, Broomspring Lane, „	2
„ William Hastings (Keir) Wilkinson Street, Sheffield..	1
„ Richard Corrie, 198, Broomhall Street, „	12
„ Barton Wills, (per Joseph Hall, Esq.,) Bell Vue, Sheffield ..	1
„ William Brown, goldsmith, 62, High Street, „	1
„ G. Ford, 12, Common Side, Sheffield	1
„ H. Grant, Park, Aberdeen	1
„ William Eyval, 10, Margaret Street, Aberdeen	1
George Stephen, 3, King Street, „	1
„ William Leys, 39, Chapel Street, „	1
Mr. George Milne, Cluny Castle Gardens, „	1
„ James Grant, „ „	2
Mrs. Coutts, Park Village, „	1
„ Ingram, 44, Loan Head Terrace, „	1
John Davidson, Esq., M.A., Schoolhouse, Drumoak, Aberdeen ..	1
Mr. Wm. Hepburn, Brucklay Cottage, Brucklay, „	1
„ Alx. F. Masson, Redford, „	1
„ James Watt, Mains of Park, „	1
Miss Robertina Burns, 138, New City Road, Glasgow	1

	No. of. Copies.
Miss Bella Robertson, 203, Dalmarnock Road, Glasgow	1
Mr. Alex. J. K. Grant, 19, Newhall Terrace, ,,	1
,, William Macdonald, 400, Great Eastern Road ,.	1
,, William Grant, 131, Canning Street, ,,	1
,, John McGregor, 3, Ethel Place, Pollokshields, ,,	1
,, Robert Stewart, 546, Rutherglen Road, ,,	1
,, Alexander McGregor, 19, Newhall Terrace, ,,	1
,, James Bremner, 6, Garturk Street, Govanhill ,,	1
John Scott, Esq., Carberry Villa, Tollcross, ,,	1
Mr. Alexander Brown, 144, Albert Street, ,,	1
,, George Scott, 5, Norfolk Street, ,,	1
,, Donald Campbell, 144, Albert Street, ,,	1
,, Robert Reid, 5, Norfolk Street, ,,	1
,, Alexander Milne, St. Germains Gardens, New Kilpatrick, Glasgow	1
,, James Culbert, 15, Montgomerie Terrace, Crosshill, Glasgow	1
,, James Hill, Larbert by Glasgow	1
John Eyval, Esq., M.A., Clifton Bank, St. Andrews	1
Mrs. Whitfield, 50, Torrington Square, London	2
Miss Whitfield, ,, ,,	1
J. Jackson, Esq., M.A., Paymaster-General's Office, Whitehall.	1
Mr. Alexander M'Callister, 22, Havelock Street, Sheffield	1
,, Robert M'Callister, 14, Wilkinson Street, ,,	1
Mrs. Hodgson, Brunswick Street, ,,	1
Mrs. Nixon, Kenwood Road, Sharrow, ,,	1
H. Thompson, Esq., Sankey Hill, Earlestown Manchester, Lancashire	1
Thomas Mahonie, Esq., L.D.S., R C.S.,167, Devonshire St., Sheffield	2
Mr. Fretwell Hudson, Chemist, Westbar, ,,	1
,, G. Mckenzie, Engraver, h., Ecclesall Road, ,,	1
,, Wm. Townsend, (Messrs. Townsend & Son,) Surrey St. ,,	2
,, Alexander Watson, 123, Upperthorpe, ,,	1
Scottish Society of Sheffield	1
Mr. Henry Waterfall, Author of "Rivelin Rhymes," Sheffield	1
,, R. Thompson, Union Street, ,,	1
Wm. Bottom, Esq., M.R.C.P., Eton House, ,,	1
Mr. C. G. Carlisle, Palmerston Road, ,,	1
,, M. Ward, Hallamshire House, ,,	1
,, Geo. Nell, Hillsbro', ,,	1
Miss M. Meadows, Neepsend School, ,,	1

	No. of Copies.
Mr. Thos. Gledhill, Head Master, Board School, Dronfield	1
„ Littlewood, 157, Spring Vale Road, Sheffield	1
„ Samuel Hadfield, Teacher of Singing, 70, Winter Street ..	1
„ John Potter, 92, Upperthorpe, Sheffield	2
Mrs. Dockray, 87, Withington Road, Whalley Range, Manchester..	1
Charles Robertson, Esq., Woodlands, Alexandra Park „ ..	2
„ T. C. E. Osborne, 19, Moss Lane, West, „ ..	1
Councillor George Barnsley, 33, Collegiate Crescent, Sheffield ..	1
Mr. Arthur Barnsley, Upper Oxford Street, „ ..	1
„ Henry Barnsley, Summerfield, „ ..	1
„ James Parker, Montpelier Place, „ ..	1
„ W. T. Carr, 72, Brunswick Street, „ ..	1
Alderman Searle, (Chairman Board of Guardians), Birkendale Cottage, Sheffield	1
Mr. T. F. Glossop, (Professor of Music), 85, Barber Road, Sheffield	1
„ John B. Corrie, 5 Hounsfield Road, Sheffield	1
„ James Christie, 13, Gloucester Street, „	1
Charles B. Stuart Wortley, Esq., M.P., (Sheffield) Harcourt Buildings, Temple, E.C.	1
Councillor W. M. Clague, Providence Walk, Walkley, Sheffield ..	1
Mr. Henry H. Eadon, Spring House, Crookesmoor, „ ..	1
Robert Belfitt, Esq., Holly Bank „ ..	1
Councillor Pye-Smith, East Bank Road, „ ..	1
Mr. William Carnie, 27, Exchange Street, Aberdeen	1
Rev. K. L. Jones, M.A., 21, Withington Road, Whalley Range, Manchester	1
Mr. J. H. Potter, Rockingham Works, Sheffield	1
Mr. Tough, Mey, by Wick, Caithness	12
Mrs. Jas. Duncan „	1
Miss Laing, „	3
Miss B. Booth, East Murkle, Caithness	1
Mrs. Dickson, Graham Street, Ranmoor, Sheffield	1
Mr. Ed. M. Dickinson, 11, Hounsfield Road, „	1
„ W. H. Carlisle, 88, Ashdell Road, „	1
„ G. Williams, 84, Market Place, „	1
„ John Roberts, Clifton Lane, Rotherham	1
„ R. Sutton, 29, Ellerslie Road, Uxbridge Road, London	1
„ John Strathearn, Tontine House, Glasgow	1
„ Joseph McCrae, 192, Claythorn Street, Glasgow	1

	No. of Copies.
Mr. James Milne, Jun., C. A., Aberdeen	2
„ John Tough, 53, Victoria Street, Aberdeen..	1
„ C. Boothroyd, 66, Common Side, Sheffield..	1
„ Archibald Jackson, 164, South Street, Moor, Sheffield	1
„ Louis Spencer, Upperthorpe, Sheffield	1
„ John Reoch, 219, Ecclesall Road, Sheffield..	1
„ W. T. Church, Moorhead, „	1
„ J. Stringfellow, 79, Fulton Road, Walkley, Sheffield	1
Councillor Bingham, West Lea, Ranmoor Park, „	1
Alfred Russell Fox, Esq., M.P.S., G.B., 56, Snig Hill, Sheffield ..	1
Skelton Cole, Esq., (Chairman of the Sheffield School Board) ..	2
Mr. Geo. G. Walker, Manor House, Whitwell	1
„ L. S. Davis, 1, Angel Street, Sheffield	1
„ John Waite, „ „	1
„ Joshua Wortley, Kingfield Road, Sharrow, Sheffield..	1
„ Joel Oliver, „ „ „	1
„ Charles Richards, 2, Park Crescent, Broomhill, Sheffield ..	1
„ Wm. Allott	1
„ Ernest Hall, Sydney Road, Steel Bank, Sheffield	2
Master W. T. Campsall, Howard Villa, Steel Bank, Sheffield.. ..	1
„ W. F. Copley, Carr Road, Walkley, „	1
H. F. Crighton, Esq. (Artist), Glasgow	4
Mr. Alfred Brierley, 42, Hadfield Street, Sheffield	1
„ Alexander Taylor, 6 & 8, Sussex Street, Middlesbro'..	1
„ Andrew Ross, Sen. Mill of Hirn, Banchory, Kincardineshire ..	1
„ Andrew Ross, Jun., Inverury, by Aberdeen	1
„ Frank Richards, 59, Market Place, Sheffield	1
John Daniel Leader, Esq., F.S.A., Oakburn, 20, Broomhall Road, Sheffield	1
B. D. Davis, Esq., (Inspector of Board Schools), 47, Victoria Street, Sheffield	1
Mr. H. Borland, 19, Angel Street, Sheffield	1
„ Thos. Eyre, Cemetery Road, „	1
„ Farnie, 3, St. George's Terrace, „	1
„ James A. Watt, 8, Graham Street, Bridgeton, Glasgow	1
Miss Rennie, 19, Newhall Terrace, Glasgow	1
„ Amy Blanche Grant, Park, Drumoak, by Aberdeen	1
C. Nuttall, Esq., (Solicitor), Withington Road, Whalley Range, Manchester	1

SUBSCRIBERS' NAMES.

	No. of Copies.
Mr. S. Robinson, 1, Sunny Bank, Alexandra Road, Manchester ..	1
Rev. Ben. Winfield, B.A., (Head Master, Commercial Schools), Stretford Road, Manchester	1
Richard Wm. Coles, Esq., (Inspector of Factories), 22, Withington Road, Whalley Range, Manchester	1
Richard Wood Esq., J.P., Plumpton Hall, Bamford, near Rochdale, Lancashire	2
Mr Wm. McLeod, Heath Bank, Demesne Road, Alexandra Park, Manchester	1
„ Alfred Fowden, 11, Booth Street, Shaw Heath, near Stockport, Manchester	1
„ J. S. Hargreaves, 4, Ash Bank, Heaton Chapel, near Stockport, Manchester	1
Mr. James Bowden, The Villa, Cale Green, near Stockport, Manchester	1
„ W. E. Erskine, 12, Birch Lane, Longsight, near Manchester..	2
„ James Sutcliffe, 31, Cooper Street, „ ..	1
„ John Hickling, 9A, Charlotte Street, „ ..	1
Peter Spence, Esq., J.P., Erlington House, Seymour Grove, near Manchester	5
Mrs. Maccullagh, Oak Lawn, Withington Road, Whalley Range, near Manchester	1
Mr. Wm. Kerr, Stevenson Square, Manchester	1
„ R. Murray, 14, York Place, „ ..	1
„ D. W. W. Parry, Fallowfield, near „ ..	1
Dr. McHardy, Bellefield House, Banchory, Ter. Kincardineshire ..	1
W. G. Lindsay, Esq., Rose Place, „ „ ..	1
Mr. James Watt, „ „ ..	1
„ John Gibson, Duncan's Bay Head, Caithness	1
„ F. J. Harvey, Clerk, *Sheffield Daily Telegraph*	1
Walter Ibbotson, Esq. (Solicitor, and Ottoman Vice-Consul), 45, Westbourne Road, Sheffield	1
Mr. Samuel Hearnshaw, 105, Burngreave, Sheffield..	1
Mrs. Shipman, Ranmoor	1
Wm. Hardy, Esq., Parkinson Street, Nottingham (additional) ..	20
Wm. F. Favell, Esq., M.R.C.S., L.S.A., Glossop Road, Sheffield ..	1
Mr. James Brindley Steer, 54, West Bar, „ ..	1
„ John Cowan, West Bar, Sheffield	1
„ Wm. McDonald, 69, West Bar, Sheffield	1

No. of
Copies.

Mr. Malcolm McDonald, Dixon Lane, Sheffield.. 1
" Archibald McDonald, " " 1
" Neil Campbell, " " 1
" Joseph Barnsley, 30, Oxford Street " 1
" Stephen Bacon, 2, Peel Terrace, Wilkinson Street, Sheffield .. 1
" John Stobbo, 2, Ethel Terrace, Mount Florida, Glasgow 1
Joseph Pedelty, Esq., 240, Paisley Road, Glasgow 1
Councillor Thomas Firth, Pitsmoor Road, Sheffield.. 1
Mr. John S. Henderson, The Woodlands, Tapton Ville 1
Miss E. Willox, (Head Mistress, G. D. Netherthorpe Board School) 1
Mr. William Tyzack, Abbeydale House 1
James Barnes, Esq., 1, Adamson Street, Burnley, Lancashire .. 1
Archibald J. Darling, Esq., 46, Warren Street, Fitzroy Square,
        London 12
Mr. Ernest Hubie Axe, 43, Bradley Street, Steel Bank, Sheffield .. 1
" Alfred Marples, Hibernia Works, Westfield Terrace, Sheffield 1
" John Robertson, 223, Broomhall Road, " 1
" Robert Watson, Clay Hills. Culter, Aberdeen 1
" John Black, Nether Haugh, by Rotherham.. 1
" A. C. Drabble, Gerard Road, Rotherham 2
Walter Canghey Fox, Esq., Surgeon Dentist, Handsworth, near
        Sheffield 1
Robert Adam, Esq., City Chambers, Edinburgh 1
John Rhind, Esq., S.S.C. " 1
R. M. Douglas, Esq., S.S.C. " 1
W. R. Trail, Esq., 41, Charlotte square " 1
Alexander Laing, Esq., S.S.C. " 2
David Philip, Esq., S.S.C. " " 4
Mr. Roderick McRitchie, 44, King Street, Aberdeen 1
" William Taylor, 71, Wentworth Terrace, Sheffield 1
" A. F. Walker, Rock Street, Sheffield 1
" Harrison T. Willott, West Mount, Scarbro' 1
" Henry Willott, West Mount, Scarbro' 1
" Edward H Eadon, Spring House, Crookes 1
" C. A. Mays, 341, Glossop Road, Sheffield 1
" A. Law, 1, Brocco Bank, " 1
" W. H. Watson, 2, Wharncliffe Villas, Broomhall Park, Sheffield 1
G. Walter Knox, Esq., B.Sc., F.C.A., &c., 15, St. James' Row,
        Sheffield 1

	No. of Copies.
Mr. G. R. Webster, Walkley, Sheffield	1
George Rennie, Esq., writer, 38, West George Street, Glasgow	1
Charles H. Firth, Esq., M.A., lecturer on history, Firth College, Sheffield	1
S. J. Lewis, Esq., Principal, Spring Vale Academy, Sheffield	1
J. H. Mudford, Esq., 11, Townend Street, Steel Bank „	1
George T. Groves, Esq., Editorial staff, *S. and R. Independent*	1
Mr. William Walker, bookseller, 8, South Street, Sheffield	1
Rev. Wm. Finlayson, Alverton House School, Liverpool	1
Mr. Robert Shepherd, Tersets, Park, Drumoak, Aberdeen	1
„ Alex. Forbes, Tillyfoddie, Strachan, by Aberdeen	1
„ John Moir, South Back Row, Lauriston, near Falkirk	1
„ David Anderson, 631, Dalmarnock road, Glasgow	1
„ Hugh Harper, North Linn, Culter, Aberdeen	1
„ Augnston Library, Culter. by Aberdeen	1
William Furness, Esq., Whirlow Hall	1
Rev. James Russell, M.A., Vicar of St. Philip's, The Vicarage, Sheffield	1
William Poole, Esq., President of the Society of Artists; h., Oakdale Road	1
Robert Hudson, Esq., Artist, Prideau Chambers, Sheffield	1
Mr. William Smith, Builder, Russell Street, Sheffield	1
„ James Hartley, Ranmoor Inn	1
„ George Bain, Becnham Park, Becnham, Reading, Berks.	1
„ John Mc'Intire, „ „ „ „	1
Master L. B. Bates, Townend Street, Steel Bank, Sheffield	1
Mr. R. De Courcy Laffan, the Schoolhouse, Derby	1
Miss M. L. Browne, 32, Dorset Square, London, W.	1
Mr. William Carson, Fir View, Walkley	1
„ E. J. Cowlishaw, (at Messrs. Walker & Halls, Electro-platers), Sheffield	1
„ Alex. Stronach, (per Mr. Trail,) 41, Charlotte Square, Edinburgh	1
Alex. Philip, Esq., 121, W., Regent Street, Glasgow	1
James Shepherd, Esq., Rossond Castle, Burntisland, by Edinburgh	2
Mr. John Pearson, Builder Stafford Road, Sheffield	2
Mr. John Mass n, Mill of Commie, St:ac an	1
„ James Rust, Bawbuts, „	1
„ N. Gilchrist, School House, „	1
The Rev. D. Scott Ferguson, „	1

	No. of Copies.
Mr. Alex. Nevin, Durris..	1
„ David Blacklaws, Kirk Town, Strachan	1
Prof. Charles Niven, F.R.S., Aberdeen University, Aberdeen.. ..	1
Mr. Schollhammer, 43, Hanover Street, Sheffield	1
„ Herbert Crookes, Spring Hill Cottage, „	1
„ S. Bright, Sheffield	1
„ Alexander, Editor, *Free Press*, Aberdeen	1
„ Groves, Fir Street, Sheffield	1
Miss M. Barraclough, Tongley House, Tongley, near Sheffield ..	1
Mr. Cawton, 11, Travis Place, Sheffield	1
„ Frank Marrian, King Field House, Sharrow	1
„ W. I. Sparrow, Psalter House, „	1
„ Henry Wood, Grange Crescent, Cemetery Road..	1
Surgeon-General Gordon, C.B., 70, Cambridge Gardens, London ..	1
J. Keith Angus, Esq., 24, South Audley Street, London	1
W. C. Leng, Esq., Editor, *Sheffield Daily Telegraph*	1
Mr. W. E. Freir, Editor, *Ironmonger*, London	1
„ Henry Salmon, 153, Upperthorpe	1
„ William Alexander, Editor, *Daily Fress Press*, Aberdeen ..	1
„ F. J. Beal, Manufacturer, Upperthorpe	1
E. D. Dunlop, Esq., Broomhill Drive, Partick	4

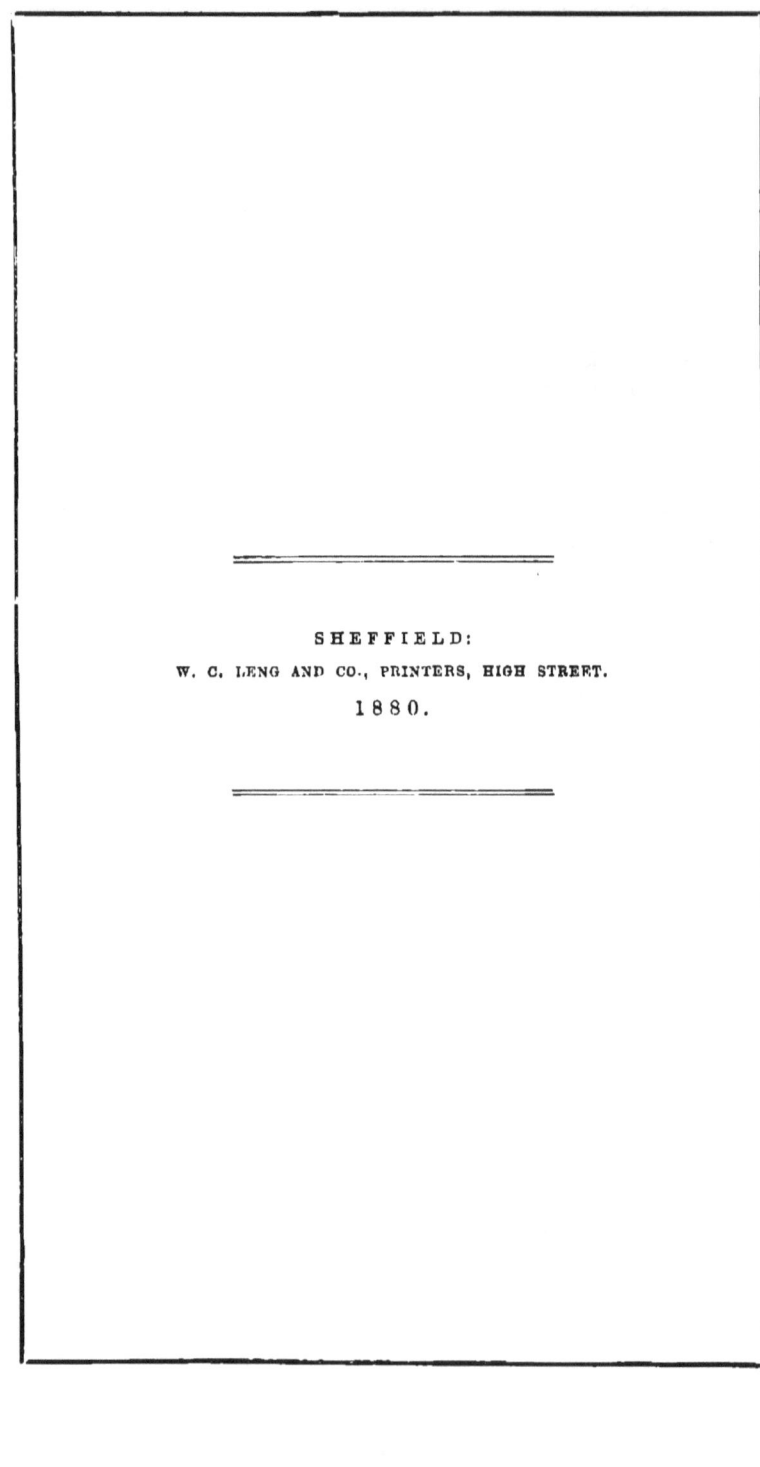

SHEFFIELD:

W. C. LENG AND CO., PRINTERS, HIGH STREET.

1880.

www.ingramcontent.com/pod-product-compliance
Lightning Source LLC
Chambersburg PA
CBHW060532030726
47498CB00004B/1160